W9-AVM-699

Kira tried to process what she had just heard. Part of her did not want to believe it. The other part recognized that it explained much of what she had been dealing with.

Kira's wounds began throbbing again, and she could feel the beginnings of a headache. "Sunim, do you mean to say that you believe the end of the world is coming?"

"I believe that the danger is real and will happen. But Master Ahn has written that there is a savior. He believed that it was written into the prophecy itself."

She frowned, unsure of what he meant. "No one knows what the prophecy means," she said.

"No one knows for sure, but there have been many interpretations, including Master Ahn's," the monk replied. "We believe that the 'one' of the prophecy refers to a royal descendant of the Dragon King—the Dragon Musado, a warrior who will unite the kingdoms and save us from the Demon Lord."

To Destiny,

PROPHECY

ELLEN OH

*Be the hero of
your own story!*

Ellen Oh

HARPER TEEN
An Imprint of HarperCollinsPublishers

"Mom, are you dedicating this book to us?"

"Of course."

"Cool! We're gonna be famous!"

To Summer, Skye, and Gracie,

my three amazing superstars who always cheered me on.

And to my husband, Sonny, who never let me give up.

HarperTeen is an imprint of HarperCollins Publishers.

Prophecy
Text copyright © 2013 by Ellen Oh
Map copyright © 2013 by Virginia Allyn

All rights reserved. Printed in the United States of America.
No part of this book may be used or reproduced in any manner whatsoever
without written permission except in the case of brief quotations embodied
in critical articles and reviews.
For information address
HarperCollins Children's Books, a division of HarperCollins Publishers,
10 East 53rd Street, New York, NY 10022.
www.epicreads.com

Library of Congress Cataloging-in-Publication Data
Oh, Ellen.
  Prophecy / Ellen Oh. — 1st ed.
    p. cm.
  Summary: "A demon slayer, the only female warrior in the King's army,
must find the lost ruby of the Dragon King's prophecy and battle demon
soldiers, an evil shaman, and the Demon Lord to save her kingdom"—
Provided by publisher.
  ISBN 978-0-06-209110-9
  [1. Adventure and adventurers—Fiction. 2. Demonology—Fiction. 3.
Prophecies—Fiction. 4. Soldiers—Fiction. 5. Kings, queens, rulers, etc.—
Fiction. 6. Fantasy—Fiction.] I. Title.
PZ7.O   2012022149
[Fic]—dc23   CIP
                                                                 AC

Typography by Carla Weise
13 14 15 16 17 LP/RRDH 10 9 8 7 6 5 4 3 2 1
❖
First paperback edition, 2014

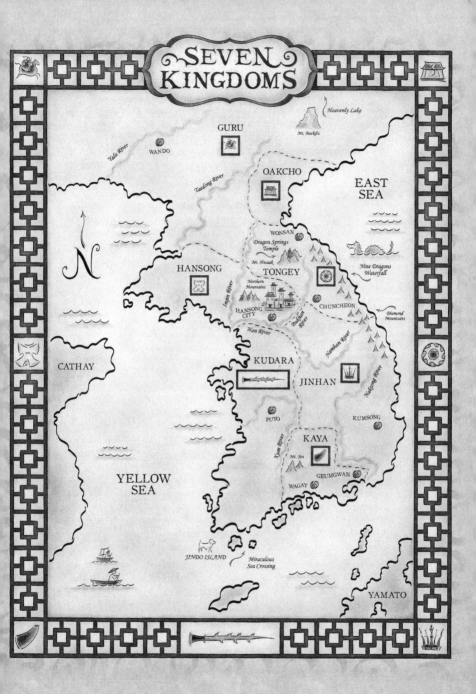

1

People feared Kira.

They called her the Demon Slayer to her face and much worse behind her back. It didn't matter that she was a first cousin to the crown prince or that she'd saved his life from a demon attack. Ten years was long enough for most to forget what really happened and instead to believe the rumors that began soon after.

Even now, standing in the congested marketplace of Hansong, she could see the averted glances and hear the urgent whispering. She wondered which rumors they were spreading this time. The one that said she'd raised a sea serpent from the underworld and planned to sacrifice the prince to it. Or the one that claimed she enchanted everyone with her yellow eyes and hunted for human prey at night.

At least they had one thing right. She was definitely on the hunt.

A ripple in the air appeared far across the square. Kira homed in on it, watching as it welled around the thick-set body of a young man in a long yellow coat walking with a smaller man down a side street. She narrowed her eyes as she took a deep breath, her sensitive nose assaulted by the pungent odor of boiled silkworm larvae, dried cuttlefish, and pickled cabbage mixed with a multitude of unwashed bodies. There, underneath it all, was the familiar waft of demon stink.

Upon her advance, a human wave surged away from her in a panicked frenzy. The good thing about being a pariah was that she didn't have an issue with crowd control. But for the sneaky little thief who had recognized her, she would have slid through the marketplace, unseen as usual. Instead, he'd shouted out her name and stolen her money purse, sidling through the legs of frightened spectators before she could catch him. The dirty rat.

Kira kept her face impassive, giving no hint of the hurt she'd become so used to hiding. All seventeen years of her life it had been this way. She adjusted the *nambawi* on her head, pulling it lower over her brows, shading her eyes. The nambawi was black with a short, sloping brim and fur lining that covered her forehead, ears, and the back of her neck—making her feel inconspicuous.

Usually.

Today she clamped it hard to her head—a shield of protection, along with the sheathed sword and bow and arrows strapped to her back. She had a job to do.

She sprinted across the marketplace and jerked around a corner, stopping in surprise. She was among the *suchae*—the untouchables, to whom the servants and slaves of the wealthy brought animals for slaughter and butchering. Her lips tightened. Theirs was a difficult life. They were despised by all for the very work they did. How could she not feel for them? Kira had more in common with these untouchables than with any of the nobles of her own class.

At the end of the dark, filthy street, Kira could see the lingering ripple of magic in the air.

She ignored the bows of the suchae and rushed into an alleyway, only to find it empty. Closing her eyes, Kira took a deep breath. Underneath the stench of garbage and sewage, she focused on the undercurrent, her nose targeting the rotten funk of dead things long forgotten. This was what she hunted.

Opening her eyes, she followed the scent to a hidden stairwell and down to a dimly lit cellar filled with barrels of roots and vegetables and the overpowering smell of fermenting bean pastes in ceramic pots. It led her to a dark corner where a large opening was hidden in the wall, behind several rows of barrels.

Kira crawled through and stepped into a narrow passageway. She was within the fetid underground tunnels of the city. She knew the tunnel, but not this particular entrance. It worried her that her quarry knew of it, too.

Hansong was one of the largest walled cities on the entire peninsula. Heavily armed soldiers patrolled the perimeter of the city, while shamans protected its walls and gates with demon-repelling magic spells. Kira held a wary respect for shamans. They were keepers of the dead and practitioners of the dark arts. But sometimes the wards weakened, and demons would enter the city.

It was Kira's job to find them and dispose of them.

The dark tunnels were lit sporadically by the sunlight streaming in from the drainage ditches above. But with her unusual yellow eyes, Kira could see just as well in the dark as in the light. Channeling her senses, she caught the odor trail again and sped off.

Before long, she heard raised voices.

Someone chuckled slyly. "When we reach the palace, the first thing I need is a little snack."

"We don't have time for that! Our mission is to kill the king as quickly as possible." The other voice was deep and menacing.

Assassins heading for the palace—this was what her father had feared.

Kira pulled out the horn bow strapped to her back and nocked the arrow. There was only one way to kill a human possessed by a demon: sever its head.

But she had to be absolutely sure first.

"What a spoilsport," the sly voice said. "One maiden isn't going to slow us down."

"Be silent!" the menacing voice said. "I have no intention of being the only one who fails my mission. If that happens, I'll cut you up into a million pieces and hide them so you'll never fully re-form again!"

Kira targeted the menacing voice, the one who was in charge, wearing the yellow coat she'd seen earlier. She watched as he grabbed his smaller companion by the neck, shaking him like a rag doll. She saw the shimmering distortion in the air and glimpsed the grotesque, leathery gray scales of a demon rolling under the skin—fangs grimacing against the flesh, as if it were still adjusting to the fit.

"There you are," Kira whispered.

With a steady hand, she pulled the bow taut and aimed carefully. The shot had to be perfect in order to release the demon inside the hollowed-out human shell. Her eyes locked onto her target.

In the split second before impact, the demon straightened. Kira's arrow missed, lodging in the eye of his comrade instead. Cursing, the demon flung his injured partner away and whirled around. His true face flickered with rage as he caught sight of Kira. He turned and fled down the tunnel.

Kira bit back a curse and raced forward. How could she have missed?

She reached the sly-voiced demon just as he pulled the arrow out of his eye. Demons could not be killed, only sent back to the underworld. Kira unsheathed her sword and decapitated him before he could rise. Thick black fluid oozed from his neck, releasing the monster caught within the human form. She ran after her prey, not even sparing a moment to clean the foul gunk off her sword.

The demon's putrid odor left a trail for her to follow. Kira quickly found the remnants of a knobby pine door scattered all over the ground. She raced through the doorway and into another passage, which opened up into the city streets at the edge of the marketplace.

Kira cursed. Her job was to keep the demon away from the people, not chase it through a crowded market.

The demon shoved past shoppers and crashed into a fruit stand, scattering reddish-orange persimmons helter-skelter. Kira cut through the crowds, ignoring the people screaming at the sight of her drawn sword. She took a giant running leap over a vendor's stall, landing at the feet of the fallen demon.

Her eyes swept through the crowd. Unease pinched at her.

Damn it! What am I going to do now?

2

Kira held the sword high and angled at his neck, trying not to show her uncertainty. She'd never had to deal with a demon in public before.

After the first attack on the prince, her uncle, the king, had decided that the citizens of Hansong should be kept ignorant of the demon threat. A pointless and stupid mandate, as far as Kira was concerned. The only thing it did was increase the rumors that surrounded her.

People thought she was the monster behind the mysterious disappearances.

They were right.

But it wasn't what they thought. The people she

"killed" were already dead.

"I arrest you in the king's name," Kira said, thinking quickly. She had to get him away from the crowd.

The demon threw a wooden plank at her and began crawling backward.

"Help! She's trying to kill me! Someone stop her! Please help!" He hurled persimmons at her.

Kira's sword slashed through the air, slicing all the fruit open. She heard gasps in the crowd.

Underneath the man-skin, Kira saw the demon grin as several grim-faced men planted themselves before her, their arms crossed. An angry muttering rose.

"She's a demon! No human can be that fast. And look at how high she jumped," a merchant shouted out. "It's unnatural!"

"No, she's a *kumiho*! Don't look into her ugly eyes! That's how she enslaves you, and then she'll eat your liver!" someone nearby warned.

Kira never moved, her eyes steady on the shifting face of the demon as he mocked her. So now they thought she was a kumiho, a nine-tailed fox demon. This was a new one. She'd be amused by the insult if their ignorance weren't so galling. She knew they couldn't see the demon's true form. They didn't know that the demon had feasted on the internal organs of its prey before donning its skin. They only saw a large unarmed man, dressed in the long yellow coat of a scholar, facing off against the most feared person in all of Hansong. Kira had no friends here.

"What's going on?" An old man parted the crowd by smacking the legs of the spectators with a red cane. Unlike the common folk, he wore a blue vest and a gold medallion over his white clothes, indicating his status as a clan leader. He approached on her right side and bowed.

"Young mistress Kang, I am Master Lee of the Hansong Lee clan. It seems people have forgotten that not only are you the king's niece, but you are a *saulabi* and the prince's bodyguard!" Master Lee glared at everyone.

Kira didn't think anyone cared that she was a saulabi, a soldier of the king's elite army. Contemplating all the unfriendly faces, Kira wondered what was the greater sin: having yellow eyes or being the sole female warrior? Would she be less of an aberration if she'd been a man?

Master Lee turned to her again. "However, I must ask you to put away your weapon. We cannot allow you to harm an unarmed man," he said. He gave her an apologetic bow.

Kira kept her eyes trained on the demon as she responded to the old man.

"I'm arresting this man for violations of the king's law and I'm taking him to the palace prison," she said.

"On what grounds? It's all a lie! She just wants to kill me," the demon protested. "Ask her!"

Master Lee peered at Kira questioningly, but she didn't respond. She was not a good liar and the truth was that she would behead him the minute they were alone.

Kira shifted her sword to attack position.

The demon rose to his feet. "Ha! See?" He faced the crowd. "Who's the villain here? I'm no criminal. I am Master Song's eldest son. Quick, someone run and fetch my father so he can put an end to this."

The crowd pressed forward restlessly.

Kira leaned closer to the old clan leader. "Master Lee," she whispered. "This man is not who you think he is. Don't trust him."

"She's a kumiho!" the demon said in a loud, abrasive tone. "She's brainwashed the royal family into accepting her, but don't be fooled. Just look at her eyes and you'll know the truth. People have been disappearing because she's killed them all, like she wants to kill me now! If you let her take me, who will she come for later? You?" He yanked on the sleeve of a nearby spectator. "Or your son?" The demon pointed at a mother holding her child. "She'll kill us. Kill us all."

"Monster!" a vendor yelled from behind his stall. "Go away! We don't want you here!"

"Murderer! Murderer!" the crowd shouted.

Kira frowned, disgusted at how well the demon played up the crowd's prejudice.

"My apologies again, young mistress," Master Lee said, looking uneasy. "Please put away your weapon. We will ask our local magistrate to sort this out."

Kira cursed her uncle for allowing the citizens to be oblivious to the dangers they faced. If she attacked, the crowd would turn on her. If she dropped her weapon, the demon would attack. Not that she was afraid. A normal human could not take on a demon in hand-to-hand combat. But she'd never been normal.

"Fine," she said, addressing the demon with a loud sigh. "Make me do this the hard way."

She slowly lowered her weapon. "You're just not that bright, are you? I mean, how are you going to escape? Do you really think these people can stop me?" Kira raised an eyebrow. "They're more scared of me than of you."

She sheathed her sword and unbuckled her weapons with slow and deliberate care, her eyes never leaving the demon's ever-shifting face.

"Why don't we show them just what kind of foul piece of excrement you truly are," she said. She smiled as she tossed her weapons over to Master Lee.

At that moment, the demon charged, powerful fists swinging at her. She dodged, rolled, and blocked blow after blow, then somersaulted backward away from his brutal attack.

He pursued her with punishing punches and kicks. His body seemed to swell in size. Hard-pressed, Kira fought with knee blocks and flying leaps, but he was stronger than she'd expected.

With a rapid-fire twirling jump, the demon planted a vicious mule kick on her chest, sending Kira hurtling into the crowd behind her. Her nambawi flew off her head, leaving her face exposed.

Rough hands pulled her up and shoved her toward

the demon. Kira leaped forward, unleashing a series of breakneck kicks so fast that her leg whirled with the speed of a spinning top. The demon grabbed her leg and slammed her to the ground. Before she could catch her breath, he seized her by the neck and lifted her off her feet. He drove his other hand like an eagle's claw into her diaphragm, seeking to rip out her liver.

Kira slammed her forehead into his face, then jabbed her thumbs into the demon's eyes. With a howl of pain, he loosened his grip. Kira dropped onto her hands and whipped her leg up and over, smashing her heel onto the top of his head and bringing him to his knees.

She heard Master Lee call her name. He unsheathed her sword and tossed it to her. She snatched it out of the air and swung down in a high arc, decapitating the demon. Black ooze seeped out of the deflating corpse.

"There's no blood!" a man gasped.

Kira heaved a painful breath. The king would be furious at the public demon slaying.

Master Lee approached her as she cleaned her sword.

"Thank you for giving me my sword," she said.

The old man snorted. "That boy was never any good at *taekkyon*. The demon gave himself away as soon as he began to fight." He sighed deeply. "How are we going to explain it to his father?"

"Tell him that this was not his son," she said.

A young boy pushed his way forward and shoved her nambawi into her hands before running off. Kira pulled on her hat, noting the confusion in the faces of the crowd. There was a palpable difference in the air—a lessening of anger and hate.

Master Lee bowed.

"Thank you, young mistress, for saving us," he said. Behind him, a sea of heads lowered in unison, shocking her.

She scowled at their hypocrisy. All it took was one demon slaying for their beliefs to be shaken.

But now, for having opened their eyes, Kira would have to face someone she feared more than any demon.

3

Kira grimaced in pain as she adjusted the collar of her clean jacket before heading to her father's office. She pressed lightly against the bandage she'd wrapped around her middle and hoped the ginseng salve she'd slathered on would provide some relief soon. Her unusual strength made her a fast healer, but she still needed a full night's rest to recover.

One of the queen's guards ran up to her, his black scale armor clanking in his haste.

"Young mistress Kang, Her Majesty requests your presence at the Fragrant Pavilion immediately," he panted.

Kira hid her exasperation. "I need to report to the general," she said.

"Your pardon, young mistress," the guard said, avoiding her eyes. "The queen says it's urgent."

She nodded and followed the young guard. His nervousness was not unusual. She had an uneasy relationship with most of the soldiers of the Hansong army. The only reason they respected her was because of her father, the supreme commander.

Fragrant Pavilion was the queen's retreat. The two-storied hexagonal building sat on an island in the middle of a lotus pond teeming with brightly colored carp. It got its name from its position at the north end of the palace compound in the shadow of the mountain, where the northeasterly breezes would sweep the fragrances of the seasonal foliage through the building.

Leaving the soldier behind, Kira crossed the elegant wooden bridge that curved over the water to the pavilion. Inside, Kira faltered as she caught the mocking glances and sneers of the queen's court ladies. It was as if she'd stumbled into a beautiful flower garden filled with poisonous snakes. Kira was good at ignoring them, but still their contempt burned her. At her approach, one by one they flicked open their fans before their faces—a wall as fragile as butterfly wings and yet completely insurmountable.

How she hated them.

Upstairs, she walked into a large, spacious room

containing only one oversized lacquered cabinet and a few low-sitting tables. The floor was padded with a thick rush mat and covered with satin floor cushions of vivid purples, pinks, and yellows.

Queen Ja-young's sumptuous silk red-and-gold *hanbok* pooled around her on the heated floor. Her ebony hair, which reached nearly to her heels, was tied up in an elaborate hairstyle. Kira's mother, Lady Kang Yuwa, sat next to the queen, a lovely vision in a gold-patterned blue hanbok.

The queen eyed Kira and frowned.

"Kira, when are you going to wear that beautiful pink hanbok I gave you?" the queen asked.

Kira knelt on the floor and bowed deeply, hiding her irritation. She'd just killed two demon-possessed humans seeking to assassinate the king. Clothes were the last thing in the world she should have to worry about.

Queen Ja-young sighed as Lady Kang took Kira's hand tightly between her own. Kira felt a rush of affection for her gentle mother. Even though Lady Kang was the queen's older sister, her calm, generous personality and her lack of jealousy made her the queen's number-one confidant. Politics and ambition kept the queen from trusting anyone. And Kira knew from experience just how shallow and mean-spirited the court ladies could be. Queen Ja-young depended on her older sister for counsel and companionship.

"I'm sure Kira had no chance to change; after all, you

did request that she come immediately," Lady Kang said.

The queen snorted. "Well, at least she is obedient. I asked Taejo to join us, and he refused my request, to return to his sword training," she said. "He is growing so quickly. How I wish I'd had a daughter."

Queen Ja-young picked up a roll of red silk and unfolded an intricate scene of embroidered gold-and-silver cranes flying over a mountain lake.

Kira patted her mother's hand, noticing how frail she looked. "Mother, are you well?" she asked.

"Don't worry, child, I am fine," her mother reassured her.

"Your mother has not been well since your birth," the queen said. "You were such a big baby!"

"Such a beautiful baby," Lady Kang said.

"I remember when the shaman said your mother's tiger dream meant that she was carrying the greatest warrior of all of the Seven Kingdoms. And then when you were born, your father laughed so hard I thought he'd have a seizure!" The queen giggled. "How can a girl be a warrior? But look at you now. The first female warrior of the saulabi."

Kira suppressed a sigh. The queen loved to tell this story. But her version didn't quite match up with Kira's own recollections. Her aunt conveniently ignored how much the king despised Kira for being different.

"I take full responsibility for your warrior status, since it was at my urging that your father trained you to be the prince's bodyguard," the queen said. "That's why it is up to me to see to your future."

Kira glanced uneasily at her mother.

"It is time to consider a betrothal for you," the queen said.

There was a moment of shocked silence.

"I'm not sure that's a good idea, my queen," Kira replied.

"Kira needs time to consider the idea of marriage first," Lady Kang said.

"She doesn't want to get married, that's the problem," the queen retorted. "She runs around the entire kingdom, fighting like a man!"

"Isn't that what you wanted of me?" Kira burst out. "To protect my cousin from harm?"

"Yes, but Hansong has been safe for so many years. There's been no demon presence since that terrible incident ten years ago."

Kira pressed her lips tight, swallowing the words of denial. This was what happened when you hid the truth—a false sense of security. She wanted to show her aunt the wounds on her body.

"Until now," her aunt continued in a gentler voice, "all of us have believed it would be impossible to find you a husband, especially given your . . . differences."

"Until now?" Kira asked sharply.

Her mother released Kira's hand and turned to face her. "Lord Shin Bo Hyun has asked for your hand in marriage."

Kira couldn't believe her ears. Shin Bo Hyun was a young noble, an officer of the Hansong army, and a nephew to the highest-ranking cabinet member. She pictured him in her mind. Handsome, but not in the soft and pasty court way. His rugged face was sun-browned, and his hooded eyes always looked as if he was laughing at a private joke. He was a particular favorite of the court ladies, who loved to moon over him and try to catch his attention in the most ridiculous ways. But not Kira.

As children, Shin Bo Hyun had made it his mission to tease Kira. He would play nasty little tricks on her, like pushing her into the carp pond, sneaking pepper into her sweet rice punch, or putting honey in her shoes. As they got older, the tricks stopped but his attention remained the same; he was always teasing her about her strange-colored eyes or unnatural behavior.

A hot surge of anger pulsed through her veins. Was this another one of his jests? Since that first fateful encounter with the demon, she'd been trained like her brothers as a saulabi. Her life was so different from that of the other court women. They were raised to expect marriage and children as their due. Kira was an outcast. How could a warrior become a bride?

"Forgive me, Your Majesty, but I will never marry."

"Kira, this is not a request," the queen said. Her voice was cold and quiet.

"How can I marry anyone?"

"You'll do it because it is your duty."

Kira shook her head. "No! Ask me for anything else but this!"

"Please, Kira! You must calm down," Lady Kang interjected. "My dear sister, let my daughter get used to this idea. After all, you said so yourself. She's thought of herself as more boy than girl for all these years. Give her time to consider what it means to become a woman."

Lady Kang threw Kira a pleading glance.

"Your mother is right," the queen said. "Kira, you are my only niece and I wanted to see your future settled. But I forgot how shocking this must be to you. Once you've given it some thought, you'll realize that this is a great honor."

Silence followed. Kira knew they were both waiting for her to apologize, but it was as if a demon had a hold of her tongue. She knew arranged marriages were a way of life for all citizens of Hansong. An unmarried woman was a burden to her family, an outcast. But Kira was already an outcast.

Several tense minutes later, the queen dismissed her, a look of disappointment shadowing her lovely face.

Kira bowed deeply to both her aunt and mother, suppressing the urge to bolt out of the pavilion. She resented having to think of marriage when demons were overrunning her city. Once again she cursed the king for insisting on complete secrecy. If her aunt knew of the constant threat to her husband and son, would she bother with this betrothal?

Keeping her head high, Kira walked past the gossiping court ladies, when she heard a loud, complaining voice.

"How can they marry her off to Lord Shin Bo Hyun? She fights like a man, she's strong like a bear," the voice said. "Why, she's liable to kill him in his sleep!"

"She's not that bad," someone said. "I think she's kind of pretty."

"Pretty like a kumiho," another voice cut in. "Just look at those creepy eyes!"

"Don't be stupid," the first speaker snapped. "Kumihos are supposed to be so beautiful to look at that they can seduce any man in the world. She would just frighten him to death!"

Laughter erupted as the ladies whipped their fans into a frenzy. Kira couldn't tell if it was the throbbing pain of her wounds or the achy tightness of her chest that made her eyes water. But as she left the pavilion, she vowed to break the betrothal, at any cost.

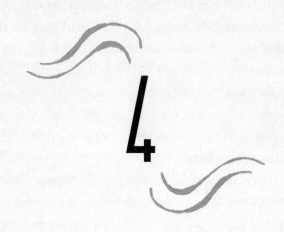

4

Kira's stomach dropped when she arrived at her father's office. The king's guards were lined up outside the doors. She'd hoped to see her father first before facing the king.

To say Kira didn't have a good relationship with her uncle was an understatement. He never hid his disapproval or dislike of her and barely tolerated her position as the prince's bodyguard. To King Yuri, Kira would always be the demon child, a freak of nature, and a terrible embarrassment to the royal family.

Better to get it over with, she thought.

The supreme commander's office was spacious and drafty. In the center, a long desk was piled with scrolls and heavy parchment; behind it, a padded stool. There were no other seats in the room. The king was dressed in full armor at the front of the desk, next to her father, General Kang, and her two brothers, Kyoung and Kwan. On the other side of the desk stood Brother Woojin, a small bald man wearing the typical gray robes of a monk. He came from the famous Dragon Springs Temple of the Tongey Kingdom and had been the prince's tutor for seven years.

At her approach, the general stopped talking. Kira bowed to the king and her father and then clasped her hands behind her back.

"Daughter, I would take umbrage at your lateness in reporting to us, but I understand that the queen demanded your presence first," the general said.

"Yes, sir," she replied. She kept her head bowed, unwilling to meet the king's eyes.

"Furthermore, we have received word that there was a public demon slaying in the marketplace today," he said. "Is this true?"

"Yes, sir," she said.

"You deliberately violated the king's decree?" he asked.

Sweat dripped down her neck as she stole a quick peek at her uncle. The king's face was as impassive as her father's.

"I'm sorry," she replied. "He persuaded the people to protect him. I had no choice. He was heading for the palace to attack the king."

Looking up, she saw her father and the king exchange glances.

"Your Majesty, this is the third attempt on your life in one month," her father said. "And there is trouble in the other kingdoms as well. We've received word that the Yamatos have invaded Kaya. But of greater concern is the news that King Asin of Tongey, King Mun of Jinhan, and all three of Mun's sons were murdered. Most likely by demons."

He faced the king. "This is no coincidence."

Troubled, Kira stared at the back wall, which was covered with an intricately painted map of the Seven Kingdoms that made up their peninsula. Hansong was located in the middle, bordering the Yellow Sea to the west, Kudara to the south, Jinhan to the east, and Guru, the largest of the kingdoms, to the north. The small kingdoms of Tongey and Oakcho lay between Guru and Jinhan.

For years the southern kingdom of Kudara had coveted Hansong's prime location. The two kingdoms were separated by the Han River and kept an uneasy peace. Fortunately, blood ties with Guru and Jinhan kept them on friendlier terms. King Yuri's maternal clan hailed from Jinhan, and Queen Ja-young's older brother was the king of Guru.

Kira examined Kaya's location at the southernmost tip of the peninsula, close in proximity to the island nation of Yamato, and bordered on both sides by Jinhan and Kudara. If there was a connection between the invasion and the murders, then trouble was not far from Hansong.

"It is as I suspected. They are killing off the descendants of the Dragon King," Brother Woojin said. He pressed his hands together. "You are in grave danger, Your Majesty."

"What do you mean, *Sunim*?" Kira asked, calling the monk by his honorific. "What's going on?"

The king ignored her and waved off the monk's words. "It's Kira's job to sniff them out."

Kira was surprised to see the anger on both of her brothers' faces. They were tall and imposing men. Both had dark-skinned complexions and deep-set eyes. Kyoung, the eldest, was wide and broad-shouldered, while Kwan was lean and wiry. They were two of the deadliest saulabi fighters in all of Hansong. Kira had always looked up to them and they looked after her. She was shocked when Kyoung, the more even-tempered of the two, exploded.

"Your Majesty, you ask too much of her!" Kyoung said. "There's only one of her and thousands of them."

"Calm yourself," the general said. "While we can definitely expect more attacks, the palace is too large to cover completely. Which is why all royal guards will continue to stay with their patrol at all times once they have been cleared by Kira."

Kira nodded. A few months ago, a demon had possessed a guard and made it through the palace gates.

Fortunately, Kira had been close by and eliminated the threat before he could reach the inner sanctums of the palace. Ever since then, the palace servants were not allowed off the premises, and her father had put her in charge of sweeping through the ranks of all the military units every morning to check for demon possession. While she appreciated her brother's concern for her, she wondered at its excessiveness. What was she missing?

The king gave a loud oath and threw down the silk scroll he'd been holding.

"These attempts on my life are a ruse. The real danger is still to my son," the king said.

"Your Majesty, I'm afraid that the danger is to you both," Brother Woojin said.

"Sunim," the king said sharply. "How many times do I have to remind you that what happens to me is not as important as what happens to Taejo? He must be protected and kept alive at all costs. He is the last of my line."

He gazed at Kira with barely concealed contempt.

"Kira, you have broken my decree and failed in your duty to keep the public safe from knowledge of the demon threat," he said. "How can I trust you to protect my son?"

She burned at his words, in anger and shame. Kira knew that to the king, her only value was as the prince's bodyguard. But for her cursed talent, she would have been killed or banished long ago.

"I swear on my life. I will protect the prince," she said,

her voice thick with the tears she refused to release.

His eyes bore into hers for a long, uncomfortable moment before he dismissed her with a careless flick of his hand. "I will not punish you this time."

Kira bowed. "Thank you, Your Majesty."

"I must go. Your father will brief you on the situation," the king said. "Lieutenant Colonel Kang and Lieutenant Kang will attend to me now."

Without a backward glance, he left the room, her brothers following close behind.

As the metallic clinking of armor faded into the distance, she tried to tamp down the anger that always overcame her when dealing with her uncle, but to no avail.

Kira cried out in frustration. "Why must he hate me so much?"

5

Brother Woojin placed a comforting hand on Kira's shoulder. "Perhaps *hate* is too strong a word," he said.

"You're right; *loathe* is more appropriate. That's why he always looks at me like I'm a disgusting dung fly he wants to squash," she said.

"Kira, don't say such ridiculous things," her father replied. "You are the prince's bodyguard. His Majesty doesn't hate you."

Kira snorted. "Just because he finds me useful doesn't mean he likes me. I know he keeps hoping that one day I won't return and he'll finally be rid of the monster in the family."

"Ya! Kira!" her father yelled. "Watch what you say!"

Aggravated, she began to pace. Her father could be so blinded by loyalty that he missed the obvious and erased away past slights. But Kira could never forget so easily.

She'd been seven years old when she had her first vision and killed her first demon-possessed human. Lord Noh, the ambassador to Cathay and an old friend of the king's, had returned to court after ten years away, no longer human. But only Kira could sense the change. The nightmares that she'd been having, about the prince being attacked by a demon, suddenly made sense. When she tried to tell the king and queen, no one believed her. All she got were ten lashes across her back and the sure knowledge that the king wished her dead.

She'd never forgotten what he said to her that day. "Children die all the time. Why not you?"

Kira had known it was up to her to stop the demon in Lord Noh's body. She began to follow him everywhere and saw him kidnap the prince and kill all his guards and nursemaids. She was the only one who saw him raise a monstrous *imoogi*, half dragon, half snake, from the depths of Green Heaven Lake. Kira still had nightmares about the imoogi. It was taller than the highest trees and as black as the darkest ink, spiraling over the water with undulating coils. When it roared, its huge fangs gleamed in the sunlight. While Noh's attention was focused on the imoogi, Kira grabbed her cousin and ran away. Even then she was faster and stronger than any normal child.

But she couldn't escape Lord Noh. Unable to outrun him, Kira pulled out her dagger and stabbed him in the throat, releasing the demon and sending the imoogi back to the underworld.

But Kira's most vivid recollection of the events was the sight of her uncle's disappointed face when he saw that she was still alive.

Now her father patted her shoulder and turned her around. "Regardless of your feelings for the king, you must respect him. He is our sovereign leader."

Kira shrugged and gave a little smile. "Do you think he would hate me less if I'd been a boy?"

Her father hesitated and then nodded. "It would have made it easier for him to accept you."

Not surprised by his answer, Kira sighed before changing the subject. "What's going on? What about the murders and the Yamatos?"

"The Yamato nation is now led by *Daimyo* Tomodoshi, a ruthless man who started out as a mere captain of the Kudara army. Sent as part of a diplomatic mission to the Yamato court, he apparently rose to commanding-general status by ambushing and killing off important tribal leaders. He has proclaimed himself daimyo and is now more powerful than the Yamato king, who is a mere figurehead."

Kira was surprised. "But I haven't heard any of this before."

Her father waved at the numerous scrolls covering

his desk. "News doesn't move quickly from the islands to the mainland. This is information we have received from our spy network. I'm still not sure of what is happening. But it is troubling. The danger is the daimyo and his surprising rise to power."

"Surprising?" Kira asked. "Do you think it's unnatural?"

Brother Woojin spoke up.

"Young mistress, in your studies, you learned of the great battle for civilization between the gods and the demons," Brother Woojin said. "The Heavenly Father battled with the Demon Lord for seven years before defeating him. Had the outcome been different, then the world as we know it would have ceased to exist, and humans would have been enslaved by the demons. It was the Heavenly Father who banished all the fiends to the underworld. Only the lesser demons, imps, and hobgoblins can enter our world, for like insects, they were too numerous to banish."

Kira was puzzled. Why was the monk talking history?

"After the great battle, we were a united country called Gojosun under our founder, King Dang, son of a she-bear, grandson of the Heavenly Father, who ruled for nearly two thousand years." The monk pressed his palms together and raised them to the sky. "It was King Dang who became the great Dragon King. He had the power of prophecy, longevity of life, wisdom of the ages, and mystical power over nature. He could summon the winds, raise the seas, and even bring forth a rumble from the bowels of the earth. He foretold a time when the world would be faced with an evil unlike anything seen before. It would sweep through our peninsula, into Cathay and the lands beyond, and wipe out the civilization of man," he said.

"The Dragon King's prophecy," Kira breathed. "He said that the Demon Lord would one day return to destroy mankind." Dread coursed up her spine.

Brother Woojin nodded, looking pleased with her quick understanding.

"When King Dang died, his sons bickered and fought for the throne until Gojosun was broken apart, leaving it vulnerable to invaders. Eventually, King Dang's heirs formed the Seven Kingdoms, and the prophecy was nearly forgotten."

He pulled a bundle of bamboo sticks from the folds of his robe. Unrolling the bamboo scroll, he revealed the beautiful pictorial characters of *hanja* flowing down each strip. The monk stroked the bamboo reverently. "This is a copy of Master Ahn's scriptures, the first head monk of Dragon Springs Temple, who recorded the Dragon King's prophecy. 'Seven will become three. Three will become one. One will save us all.' Ever since then, my brothers have made it our mission to study the scriptures and discover how to protect the world from the coming danger."

Brother Woojin addressed the general. "With the rise

in the number of demon possessions, it is clear that a greater force is at work."

"But how?" Kira asked.

"Through a human medium," Brother Woojin said. "We understand the daimyo of Yamato is skilled in the demon arts. The Demon Lord has sought out a human subject to bond with. We believe that through the daimyo, he has begun his campaign for domination."

Kira tried to process what she had just heard. Part of her did not want to believe it. The other part recognized that it explained much of what she had been dealing with.

Kira's wounds began throbbing again, and she could feel the beginnings of a headache. "Sunim, do you mean to say that you believe the end of the world is coming?"

"I believe that the danger is real and will happen. But Master Ahn has written that there is a savior. He believed that it was written into the prophecy itself."

She frowned, unsure of what he meant. "No one knows what the prophecy means," she said.

"No one knows for sure, but there have been many interpretations, including Master Ahn's," the monk replied. "We believe that the 'one' of the prophecy refers to a royal descendant of the Dragon King—the Dragon Musado, a warrior who will unite the kingdoms and save us from the Demon Lord."

"A royal descendant of the Dragon King? That would explain why they're assassinating the royals," Kira said. She laughed derisively. "And why is it always 'the one' that saves the world, like some fairy tale? One man against the Demon Lord and his legions of evil soldiers? Unbelievable! Good luck finding that poor guy. If he's smart, he'll either kill himself or run far, far away."

Brother Woojin tut-tutted as he frowned at her. "Young mistress, this is no laughing matter."

"I'm sorry, Sunim. But it's just too ridiculous," she said. "Father, you don't believe this, do you?"

The general stepped away from the map he'd been studying, a troubled look on his face.

"Who's to say if any of this is true? No one has ever been able to clearly decipher the prophecy," he said. "What knowledge we have is shrouded with myths and legends, to the extent that we can't know what is truth and what is fiction. I've been trying to study the prophecy myself. But ultimately it is all conjecture and interpretation."

"It's more than theory, General Kang," the monk said. "These myths are real; the prophecy is true."

General Kang sighed. "Perhaps. But one thing I do know is that we are weaker divided. If the Seven Kingdoms were united, as we once were under the Dragon King, the Demon Lord would find it harder to attack us. Instead, we must rely on some myth about a royal savior—"

"Dragon Musado," Brother Woojin interrupted.

"—who will save the world." General Kang rubbed a hand over his eyes and turned back to the large wall map. "Whether or not we believe that there is a savior is irrelevant. What is important is that the daimyo believes it and is not taking any chances. And neither will we."

Kira absently gnawed on a fingernail, her eyes fixed on the map. Hansong appeared so vulnerable, hemmed in by danger from all sides. "Then the prince is in danger also," she said.

"As are you and your brothers," the general said. "All three of you are possible heirs to the throne."

"Yes, but the greatest danger is to the prince, for he is descended from the Dragon King through both his mother's and father's lines," Brother Woojin said. "His blood will run purest. It is why the demons have targeted him from birth."

The general waved his hand, irritated. "He is but a mere child of twelve years!"

Kira started in surprise. "What? Do you believe Taejo is our savior?" Taejo was just a boy. What could the monk be thinking?

Brother Woojin clucked his tongue in reproof. He spread out his book on the table again, his fingers flicking through the bamboo strips until he reached the middle. He motioned Kira closer to read the inscription.

"The last time the Demon Lord entered our world, it was all the gods could do to keep a few of us safe." He pushed the book away and faced the general. "This is only the beginning. We must protect the prince, or all is lost."

With one last bow, Brother Woojin left the room.

"Has the world gone so crazy that even a rational being like Sunim would believe utter nonsense?" Kira pulled at

35

her hair. "Or am I the mad one for not believing?"

General Kang dropped down onto the padded stool. Buried in the piles of scrolls and books were several jade figurines and his heavy gold seal. He picked up the small statue of a *haetae*, a mythical fire-eating dog. With its round head, long hair, and massive body, it didn't look much like a dog. Kira liked it because the haetae was the guardian of justice and protector from disasters.

She could see the deep grooves that worry had etched into her father's forehead and around his eyes. Even as she knew she should not add to his already heavy burden, the words slipped from her mouth.

"Father, did you know about my aunt's plan to betroth me to Shin Bo Hyun?"

He gazed at her, no expression on his brown, weathered face.

"Yes, I knew."

Kira's stomach lurched with a deep sense of betrayal.

"Father! I can't marry. I will never marry! I'm not wife material!"

"Don't belittle yourself," her father said. "You will make a wonderful wife and mother one day."

Kira's hands curled into tight fists as she glared at him. "I'm a warrior, not a court lady. My duty is to protect the prince."

"Your mother keeps reminding me that you're also a woman," her father said. He put down the statue, still gazing at it fondly. "But I've treated you no different than your brothers. My soldier girl."

He sighed and then faced her. "Just like your brothers, you have a duty to marry well and have your own family. But not with Shin Bo Hyun."

The sudden relief unknotted her stomach.

"Thank you, Father!"

"Don't thank me yet. It's nearly impossible to say no to the queen. It was Lord Shin who broached the idea of betrothing his nephew to you to Their Majesties. And you know how protective the king is of his friendship with Lord Shin. He never lets us forget that he's the king's oldest and closest friend." The general grimaced.

Kira was well aware of her father's opinion of Lord Shin. The senior adviser had tried to disgrace her father ten years ago, and they hadn't gotten along ever since. Lord Shin Mulchin was once a contender for the throne of Hansong. The previous king had no children and no siblings. Shin was the king's heir from his paternal line and related to the Kudara royal family. Lord Kim Yuri descended from the prior king's Jinhan maternal line and married Guru royalty, Kira's aunt. When Shin's line fell out of favor, the last king chose Yuri as his heir.

Kira always wondered why Shin would remain in Hansong after such a disappointment or why he and her uncle were such close friends. She had, however, heard a rumor that Shin had saved Yuri's life when they were boys.

"But I don't understand why Lord Shin would wish

for this betrothal. He's the one person who hates you more than he hates me."

"He doesn't like anyone. To be honest, I'm not sure he is even that fond of his nephew, other than for whatever political gain he can provide," her father replied. "But you are the king's closest eligible female relation; it only makes sense to push for such an alliance. And as Lord Shin's nephew, Bo Hyun has ties to the Kudara royal family that the king may be interested in promoting."

Kira snorted. "I'm far from eligible!"

Her father stood up and came to stand before her. "Kira, you are my only daughter and my pride and joy. I have seen you grow into a strong, intelligent, and brave young woman. Be proud of who you are, my child."

She dropped her eyes and spoke in a whisper. "I'm so different. I terrify people."

"Your differences are what make you unique. They're what make you special. You have nothing in common with these ignorant wretches who thrive on superstition and fear. You were meant for greatness. Why, I would be less surprised if you were the Dragon Musado instead of the prince."

Kira could feel her cheeks flushing in pride.

"That's impossible. I'm not a leader—"

"You're a warrior. And nothing is impossible unless you believe it is so," he replied.

"Why are we even talking about this?" she asked. "There's no such thing as a Dragon Musado. It's just a fairy tale that the monks are making up!"

With an abrupt turn, her father marched toward the large map of the Seven Kingdoms.

"But what if it's true? I can't discount it. I've seen too many unusual things in my lifetime to ignore this prophecy. The most unusual and wondrous thing I've ever seen is my very own daughter." He paced back and forth for a moment as he spoke. "When your mother was carrying you, we all believed that her tiger dream was an omen—a sign that you would be a great warrior. And we were right. But over the years, as I have watched you grow and seen your remarkable talents, I've come to realize that the dream was in fact not an omen but a visitation."

"A visitation?" Kira asked. "What do you mean?"

"In your mother's dream, a large tiger leaped out of the bushes and placed its head gently on her lap. Its golden eyes were the same color as your own. I believe that tiger was the embodiment of your tiger spirit. Your gifts come from it—your great strength and speed, your keen senses, and your ability to hunt demons. There is no one else in the world like you. It is your tiger spirit that makes you who you are."

Kira blinked in surprise at her father's words.

"Kira, I've never shared this story with anyone else, not even your mother. But when you were a very small child, I took you and your brothers on a pilgrimage to Stone Temple. On our way, we stopped for lunch and you wandered off. When I found you, you were lying between the paws of a sleeping tiger, fast asleep. At my approach, the tiger growled at me and I froze. It rose to its feet and stalked away. I should have been frightened, but I wasn't. I knew that the tiger would not harm you."

Her father's words brought to mind a long-ago memory. She had an impression of being lost and then comforted by the warmth of a large but gentle animal. She also knew that when she was very injured or sick, she would dream of a tiger and she would always feel better.

"If I can believe that the heavens have blessed me with a tiger-spirit daughter, then how can I doubt the existence of a Dragon Musado?" he asked.

Kira didn't know how to react to her father's words.

"I believe that one person can change the world. Whether he is the Musado or a girl with a tiger spirit. The monks teach that we mere mortals cannot question fate. But I say that we control destiny by our every action. Our power lies in the choices we make." Her father placed his warm hand on her cheek. "In the choices you make. Remember, stay true to yourself and do what your heart tells you is right, and not what is easy."

She pondered her father's words, profoundly affected by his confidence in her.

"Father," she replied, "I will not disappoint you."

6

She stood in the dark recesses of an archway on the palace's southern walls. The walls were built over a high-ridged cliff that led to a straight drop over the widest part of the Han River, serving as a natural defense for the city.

From the depths of the river, there rose an unnatural mist, dense and thick. She watched as a lone figure came out onto the walkway. The gold braid that edged his black jacket was a clear mark of his senior officer status. He wore a vest of scale armor with a long sword tied to his waist. His face was obscured by his helmet.

Kira breathed in the chilly air. It coursed through her lungs, heightening her sense of dread as she watched the officer move through the mist. He stopped to speak to a sentry.

Suddenly, the officer stabbed his fingers into the sentry's neck. Other than a small gasp, no sound could be heard as the officer moved on, leaving the guard frozen in place, his face a comical grimace of shock.

Moments later, five guards met the same fate. The traitor moved to the center turret and waved a lantern high above his head three times.

Ten assassins, dressed all in black, skimmed over the top of the river. They scaled the wall with their hands and feet, as if they weighed no more than air.

A cry from within a high sentry tower was cut short by a shower of arrows. Out of the thick, rolling mist of the river, hundreds of lights began to flash. They were from the lanterns of a huge fleet of enemy ships.

Kira ran and found herself face-to-face with an assassin. Lashless solid black eyes stared at her, unblinking above a dark leathery mask. She flinched as the mask shimmered and peeled away, revealing razor-sharp fangs. A snarling demon launched itself at her face.

The sickening rip of flesh brought her flailing out of her dream.

She rolled off her futon and stumbled from her room. She could smell the stench of the demon.

Heedless of the pain of the stone pavement on her bare feet, she shoved past guards on duty as she flew up the fortress-wall staircase and onto the bricked walkway.

Five sentries gaped at her, first in shock and then in amusement. She realized how bizarre she looked, dressed in her white nightclothes, her thick hair billowing around her shoulders.

Ignoring the guards, she peered over the ledge of the southern wall. The waters below were dark and calm. No fog—just the moonlight shimmering across the softly lapping water. Kira gazed long over the expanse of the river, noting the quiet wooded landscape of Kudara across the way.

She closed her eyes in relief. Her vision hadn't occurred yet, but she knew that it would happen, like all her past ones.

Ever since her first vision warned her of the demon attack on the prince, Kira had learned to remember and analyze her dreams. The handful of visions she'd had over the years had always come true. Her stomach churned: a traitor was in the senior ranks, and a demon attack was forthcoming. She had to warn her father at once.

Without a word to the curious guards, Kira rushed down the stairs and collided with the person she least wanted to see, Lord Shin Bo Hyun. The young lord wrapped his strong arms around her, drawing her close to him.

"Kira, what an unexpected but welcome surprise," he said as he released her slowly. "What brings you out in such delightful disarray?"

Kira's shock was soon replaced by anger. He was the

only person, outside of her family, to speak to her with such familiarity. Stepping away, she tied her hair with a piece of cord she always kept on her wrist and shoved it all under her shirt.

"Your pardon, my lord," she said between gritted teeth. "Please excuse me as I am unfit to be seen."

"I beg to differ," he said. Kira could hear the laughter in his voice. "The vision of your beauty will keep me awake tonight."

Ignoring him, she tried to pass, desperate to talk to her father.

"Don't leave," Shin Bo Hyun said as he blocked her path. "Come walk with me for a little while. After all, we are to be married." He reached over to pull at her hair.

Kira whipped her hair away and walked backward, stopping only when she felt the cool stone wall behind her. "We are not betrothed yet. My father has not agreed to it," she said, trying to compose herself.

He closed the distance between them, forcing her to look up into his face even as she put up a hand to keep him at bay.

"I doubt even your father can refuse the king and queen on this." He bent down to whisper into her ear. "I must say I was quite surprised by my uncle's request that we marry. You know that he's not your family's biggest supporter. And while I didn't think I'd have to marry this young, I am very pleased with this betrothal."

"That makes one of us, my lord," Kira said.

"We are slaves to our family obligations," he said. "Duty binds us. But I think this duty will not be so onerous. And it will be far less dangerous than chasing demons."

She narrowed her eyes at him, surprised at his words. Kira pushed him away. "I disagree. I think it will be far more dangerous." She paused. "For you."

He laughed; his teeth flashed in the dim light. "I've always really liked you."

"Huh, you had a funny way of showing it," she said.

Shin Bo Hyun shrugged and stepped closer. "I did enjoy torturing you when you were little. You were always so serious and self-righteous."

"And you are an egotistical show-off, who always thinks he's right," she retorted.

"See, that's why I like you," he said. "You've never been a fawning toady like all the other court ladies with their pretty words and empty heads. All they do is simper and giggle and say 'yes, my lord,' 'of course, my lord,' 'whatever you say, my lord.' The thought of being wed to one of them makes me want to cut my ears off. At least you I can tolerate."

This stopped Kira short. She didn't understand him at all. He was unlike any of the other nobles of the court, who usually pretended she didn't exist. That was the problem—he'd never ignored her.

She studied his face. His dark-brown eyes were deep-set and creased with laugh lines, at odds with the severity of his prominent nose and hard jaw. In repose, his face was cruel, like a hawk, making him seem older and more mature than his nineteen years. But tonight, in the dim light of the lanterns, his eyes crinkled in good humor and he looked young and approachable. No, she didn't understand him at all.

"Why?" she asked. "I'm the dreaded Demon Slayer. People think I'm a kumiho. Why would you want to have anything to do with me?"

"Because you'll never bore me," he said.

"So if I'm boring, you'll object to the betrothal?" she said hopefully.

He observed her with a curious gaze. "My uncle is the head of the family. I owe him my duty. To do otherwise would dishonor my entire clan. I would marry a bald, cross-eyed idiot if that is what he asked of me."

"Oh, that makes me feel so much better!" Kira sneered at him. "There goes my plan to shave off my hair."

"That would be a crime," he said. "I'm afraid I wouldn't allow that."

"You have no right to tell me what to do," she said. "And don't tell me you will when we're married, because that's not going to happen!"

"I don't understand you," he said with a puzzled expression. "You are bound by your duties even more rigidly than I am. You can't disobey the queen."

Kira grew flustered. Her entire life had been geared toward serving the royal family. She didn't want to disobey the queen. But this was the one thing in her life that she wanted to control.

"I don't want to marry! Especially not you," she said. The images of her nightmare flitted through her mind again. "I don't have time for it."

"Perhaps I can change your mind," he said.

"No," Kira bit off the word, wishing she could bite his head off.

"I'll take that as a maybe," he said.

Kira struggled to breathe normally, hoping he couldn't hear the erratic beat of her heart. There was something so mesmerizing about him—the sleek lines of his masculine body, the broadness of his shoulders. Disgust at herself triggered a fresh wave of anger.

"Leave me alone!" She shoved him hard.

Shin Bo Hyun put his hands up in a conciliatory gesture.

"There's that legendary temper." He grinned. "I was wondering when it would show up. I've always loved making you mad. Your eyes turn a deep golden color."

Crushing the urge to punch him, Kira shouldered past him and stomped away. As she rounded the castle wall, she glanced back to see if he was following her. Shin Bo Hyun remained where he was, staring after her with a thoughtful expression.

Wiping him from her mind, Kira ran to her family quarters. She knew one thing with absolute certainty.

Trouble was coming.

7

Several days later, the palace was bustling with news. A diplomatic envoy had arrived during the night from Jinhan, demanding an immediate audience with the king. Since then, the hallways had been filled with senior advisers, military generals, and diplomats, as messengers raced all about the palace grounds.

Kira watched her young cousin pace the entire length of the courtyard. His large white dog came bounding over.

"Hey, Jindo," she said. She bent down slowly to caress the dog's thick, soft fur.

Jindo lapped at her face and butted her shoulder

playfully. His fluffy tail curled up to nearly touch his back, at odds with the proud tilt and carriage of his large, triangular head. Her cousin was lucky to have such a loyal companion.

It would be another hour before the sun rose. But everyone was ready, and the hunting dogs strained eagerly against their leashes.

There was no sign of the king.

"Where could he be?" Taejo asked.

Kira shook her head in commiseration and leaned against a column. She knew her cousin was anxious about his first real boar hunt. But the truth was that this trip was merely a ruse to take the prince to safety. When she'd told her father of her dream, he'd consulted with the king and they'd agreed to this course of action.

Just then, a loud salute heralded the arrival of the king, General Kang, and several court advisers. The king was dressed in an armored tunic instead of his hunting outfit.

"Father, are you not coming?" Taejo asked in alarm.

"Forgive me, my son, but troubling news has reached us from Jinhan and the south. It appears that the Yamatos have captured Kaya and are now pressing on Jinhan's southern borders. We have sent troops to them, but we must prepare for war to reach Hansong."

"Then we should cancel the hunt and I should stay home with you," Taejo said. "What if something happens while I'm gone?"

The king laughed as he cuffed his son on the cheek. "Do not fear! Our walls are unbreachable."

Kira shivered at her uncle's words, her nightmare flashing before her eyes.

"You will have your first boar hunt and stay at Stone Temple until I can join you," the king said.

"But Father—"

"That is an order," the king said with mock sternness.

Someone tapped Kira on the shoulder. Turning around, she saw her brother Kwan motioning her over to where the general stood waiting for them. She followed Kwan into a large garden pavilion, out of earshot of the hunting party. Kira and Kwan were dressed alike, both in their saulabi uniforms underneath black leather hunting armor. Kira's dark hair was tied neatly in a long plait and covered with her nambawi, as usual. She carried her bow and arrows and her sword strapped onto her back.

There was a frown on General Kang's rugged face.

"Kyoung left yesterday for Jinhan," he said. "Today, I send my two youngest off with the prince. My heart is heavy."

He rubbed his forehead. "I admit to having misgivings about this trip, but Kira's dreams have never been wrong, and the king wants to keep Taejo safe from harm. The boar hunt is a perfect diversion for sending Taejo away. The traitor will not know we are suspicious, and we can find him while the prince is hidden."

General Kang turned to Kira. The flickering flames of

the lanterns surrounding them lent shadows to his face.

"What is it, Father?" Kira asked.

He shook his head as if to ward off his worries. "The king insists that Lord Shin escort your group. He will send a message to Lord Shin when it is safe for the prince to return."

Kira swallowed a curse. Not only was Lord Shin her father's greatest political enemy, he was the most detestable person Kira had ever met. The joke in the palace was that if the Heavenly Father himself were to grant Shin immortality, Shin would complain that he'd be cheated of a fancy state funeral. Good moods never lasted long around him. If he weren't such an influential member of the court, no one would tolerate him.

General Kang paced before them. "I would feel better if Kyoung or I were going with you. But there is nothing I can do. The world is off-balance, and I find myself unsure of what is to come." He stopped pacing and gazed first at Kira and then Kwan. "You must stay safe, my children. Be wise."

General Kang gripped his son's shoulders. "Even though the king has placed Lord Shin in charge of this mission, you are its true leader. I know I could leave the prince in no better hands! Now, go on and prepare to depart while I speak with your sister."

Kwan bowed and marched off.

General Kang's countenance was still troubled.

"Kira, you have vowed to the king to protect the

prince with your life," he said. "Now I ask you for something more. You are closest to the prince. He looks up to you. You are more than his bodyguard; you are also his big sister. Promise me that you will always care for him, as if he were truly your brother, and not just your prince. Advise him, guide him. Help him grow into a great king."

The heaviness of his words and bearing struck Kira with foreboding. "But you will be there for him, too," she said.

"Of course," her father said, a rare smile on his face. "But he likes you better."

Kira bowed. "Father, you have my word."

"That is all I need," he responded. He pulled a pouch from underneath his armor.

"I have something for you," he said. Opening the tiny bag, he took out the jade haetae figurine that always sat on his desk. "Keep him with you. He has always been good luck for me, helping me make the right decisions at the right times. Now I think you may need his guidance more than I."

He placed the haetae and the pouch in her hand. He leaned over to touch his forehead to hers and then cupped her cheek. "I'm proud of you, little tiger."

She smiled to hear his nickname for her, something he hadn't used since she'd grown so tall. The smooth jade was cool to her touch. She traced the fangs and bulging eyes of the haetae. After placing it in its bag, she hung it over her neck and tucked it away within the folds of her jacket underneath her armor.

In the courtyard, the king called over Lord Shin, who was dressed in a gaudy red-and-silver hunting outfit with leather padded armor. Kira couldn't help comparing the senior adviser to his nephew. Where Shin Bo Hyun was tall, muscular, and handsome, Lord Shin was wraith thin and sharp-featured. And although he was the same age as the king, he looked a decade older.

Kira noted Taejo's unhappy expression and sighed. It was going to be a long trip.

"My old friend," King Yuri said. "Take good care of my son for me. Treat him as if he were your own."

Lord Shin bowed deeply. "Of course, Your Majesty. I will endeavor to do the best I can, to insure the safety of your son at all costs, even if it is at my own expense and were to cause my demise. Regardless of the incompetence of your guards, rest assured that I, Lord Shin Mulchin, will not fail you."

Kira saw a look of satisfaction replace Lord Shin's normally morose expression. How like Shin to insult everyone else in his eagerness to kowtow to the king.

Only then did she notice the tall figure standing by Lord Shin's side. Shin Bo Hyun wore a broad, toothy smile as he made his way over to Kira. He had a way of walking that reminded her of a wolf readying for a kill, deliberate and predatory.

"Kira, I was hoping to join you today for the prince's

boar hunt, but my uncle informs me that I am needed here," Shin Bo Hyun said.

Kira scowled and looked around, hoping that someone would rescue her.

He shrugged. "Ah well, I would have been happy to relieve him of his duty. But as you know, no one can refuse the king's request." He nudged her with his elbow.

Kira ignored Shin Bo Hyun and lowered her gaze. To anyone watching, her response would appear proper.

"Pity about this trip. I've been looking forward to spending time with you," he said. "Perhaps one day, we can have our own hunting excursion."

Shin Bo Hyun stepped a little closer, causing Kira to step back with a quick angry glare. She stared at the tips of his black leather boots.

"I'll eagerly count the days till your return."

"I'm so glad you have something to keep you occupied," she replied in a low, biting voice. "But don't let it overburden you."

His eyes flickered with a flash of humor. "She speaks."

"She also kills," she said.

He let out a low laugh. "You have no idea how much I look forward to our marriage."

With a short bow, he sauntered away. Fuming, she placed her trembling hands over her hot cheeks and willed them to cool.

"Gah, I can't stand that man!" She took a deep breath and rejoined the hunting party, catching the end of the king's talk with her cousin.

"Son, you must listen to Lord Shin, for he acts in my stead," King Yuri said. Then with one last wave, he went inside.

Taejo gazed after him, his face as wilted as a poppy flower in a drought.

"It was not his choice to abandon you today," Kira said, nudging him on the shoulder. "One day you'll be king, and you'll find yourself making difficult choices, too."

The smaller boy shrugged and nodded before mounting his horse. Jindo kept close to his master's side.

Kira looked for one more glimpse of her father. Instead, she caught Shin Bo Hyun's amused gaze, causing her mood to grow dark once again.

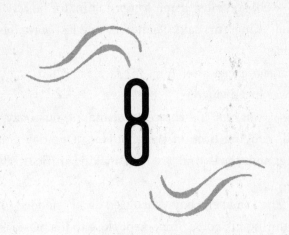

8

A contingent of thirty soldiers escorted the hunting party along with a pack of ten dogs, including Jindo. Twenty-five were the prince's personal guards. Each wore a knee-length silver tunic of scale armor and carried twin swords in iron sheaths. The other five soldiers were Lord Shin's private bodyguards.

Taejo's chief of guards, Captain Pak, and Brother Woojin rounded out the party. The monk was dressed in his usual gray robes, his only weapon a long black staff tied to his saddle. Around his neck, he wore his one valuable possession, a 108-beaded prayer necklace of green jade.

"Captain, tell your soldiers not to ride so close to me;

I'd rather not choke on their dirt for the entire trip," Lord Shin complained.

Kira and Taejo exchanged amused glances. "I wish he would choke on it," Taejo said. Kira rolled her eyes heavenward.

Several days in the mountains with Lord Shin would sorely test all of their patience. For Kira, this trip was difficult in so many ways. While Captain Pak had always been respectful to her and kept his men in check, Lord Shin's soldiers didn't bother to hide their contempt. They muttered insults under their breath and spit on the ground whenever she drew near. It was all Kira could do to keep her temper in check.

The dirt road they followed narrowed and widened with the passing terrain. It was the beginning of the tenth month, and the trees were vivid with their autumn plumage.

The sun had begun its descent when the tired group came to the outskirts of a bustling village. Farmers drove ox-drawn carts through the dirt streets, while groups of peasant women ambled, carrying hefty bundles on their heads.

Soon they arrived at a large and prosperous inn. A portly man hurried out to meet them, followed by several white-clothed servants.

"Welcome to my humble establishment," the man said with a deep bow. All the servants bowed in unison behind him.

"Is it possible to find a clean room in this establishment?" Shin asked in a languid voice.

The innkeeper nearly touched his forehead to his knees in his effort to kowtow to the senior official.

"Of course *Daegam*, Your Eminence, we live to serve you! And I will have a fine dinner sent to your room." The innkeeper fawned over Lord Shin.

"My young nephew is with me," Shin said, waving a hand over at Taejo. "Make sure to take good care of him."

They'd agreed earlier that the prince's true identity should be kept secret, although Kira was too well known to disguise.

The innkeeper began to direct his servants, who rushed over to assist Taejo and Brother Woojin. Taejo parted reluctantly from Jindo, who was sent away with the other hunting dogs. The innkeeper was just about to lead them inside, when he caught sight of Kira. His face contorted. "Daegam, must that one be allowed into my establishment? She will scare off my patrons."

Kira pulled her nambawi down lower, wishing she could smash the man's face.

Lord Shin smirked. "Ah, the famous Demon Slayer. Yes, she is a fearsome sight, isn't she? The king was kind enough to lend her services to me as a personal guard for my nephew. Now take me to my room and make sure you don't serve me the same slop you serve your . . . other guests," Shin said.

The innkeeper bowed again and led Shin away.

"My wife is a wonderful cook," he bragged. "Best in the village! You won't be disappointed."

"I can only hope your food tastes better than the way your establishment looks."

Kira shook her head in disgust.

At the entranceway to the public room, she hesitated, made uneasy by the crowd. Bracing herself for the worst, she stepped inside.

9

Bamboo walls partitioned the public rooms into three sections: a crowded main room that stank of vomit and feet, and two smaller dining rooms that sat empty. Kira scanned the area, noting that several of Captain Pak's soldiers had already positioned themselves in the main room, while Captain Pak and Kwan canvassed the area outside. It was Kira's duty to keep close to the prince.

She breathed deeply through her nose. Nothing unusual.

Taejo walked restlessly around the main room, Kira and his guards close behind. At their entry, the crowd didn't quiet down, but Kira noticed their keen attention.

Several groups of men sat together, drinking from sma
brown ceramic bowls as loud discussions arose in merry
disagreement. Kira picked out the merchants from the
farmers, and the mercenaries from the builders. Even
knowing that no one outside the palace had ever set eyes
on the prince, she was on edge.

"Perhaps we should follow Lord Shin's lead and retire
for the night," Kira said to Brother Woojin and Taejo.

Taejo's face fell.

The monk shook his head. "Don't worry, young
mistress. I believe our charge will be safe here." He waved
at the soldiers who had filled the room.

"And besides, *Noona*," Taejo whispered, "no one will
bother us while you are nearby." He grinned, his eyes
twinkling with mischief. He only called her noona, "big
sister," in private, or when he wanted to get his way.

Kira smiled reluctantly, glad that he could joke about
her role in his life. It couldn't be easy for him. Taejo still
had nightmares about the demon that had attacked him
when he was a toddler.

She saw the innkeeper whispering to his customers.
Within the next few minutes, everyone in the room
would know who she was. That was fine. The good thing
about her reputation was that most people stayed well
away from her.

The men reeked of body odor and the sweet and
pungent smell of *makkoli*, the milky rice wine. Kira felt
a slight headache coming on. It was part of her curse,

this extraordinary ability to pick up scents. As with anything, there was good and bad. She could smell a demon in hiding or wild honey in the forest. Scents could not escape her. Nor could she escape them. Privies were torturous for her, and public rooms filled with malodors sometimes made her ill.

Trying her best to ignore the scents, she swept her gaze around the room. In a far corner, another group crowded around an incongruous pair pondering a *baduk* game covered with strategically placed black and white stones. Taejo nudged her and motioned over to the game. They moved closer to watch the play.

A middle-aged merchant, dressed in rich robes befitting his prosperity, sat glaring at his junior opponent. While both players had an even number of captured stones, the older player looked frustrated.

"Excellent strategy!" Brother Woojin whispered into Kira's ear. "I see the young one has set up a truly devious trap. He is surely a master player."

Kira nodded in admiration. Baduk was a very simple game to learn but an incredibly difficult one to master. The object of the game was to take control of as much of the board as possible by capturing or surrounding the opponent's stones. It took most people a lifetime to get as good as the player before her.

He looked to be about Kwan's age—nineteen or twenty years at most—with long, dark-brown hair tied loosely at the nape of his neck. Kira studied his narrow face.

He had handsome features that bordered on prettiness, with large, deep-set eyes that stared unwaveringly at his opponent. In fact, Kira thought he was better looking than half the court ladies of Hansong. She grinned at the idea of how incensed the noblewomen would be at such a comparison.

Suddenly, she realized that the baduk player was gazing at her. Embarrassed, she looked away and relaxed only when he returned his concentration to the game.

Kira couldn't help but be curious about this young man. He was dressed in a dark-gray silk jacket and pants of high quality, which proclaimed his noble status, but his clothes had seen better days. Yet the collar of his white shirt under his jacket was clean and crisp and showed careful attention to his appearance. By his side sat a heavyset youth with a chubby face who watched the game with an intense, nervous focus.

The merchant cursed as he moved one of his pieces, only to have it captured. Scowling, he conceded the game and threw a small leather bag at the young player, who caught it and surveyed the contents before nodding. He and his companion rose from the table and left the common rooms just as her brother entered, heading straight for her side.

"Kira, I'll escort Taejo to his room," he said. "The captain wants you to do a thorough perimeter check before you take your post tonight."

Kira nodded and headed for the courtyard. She was

most concerned about imps, the small demon spies that wandered out usually at nighttime. Although they were not as dangerous as demons, if they latched on to an unwary human, they could manipulate them, wreaking death and violence.

Satisfied that the external area was safe, Kira proceeded to the stables. Inside, she was surprised to see the young baduk player sitting beside Jindo. At her arrival, Jindo raced over and licked her hands in greeting.

"I hope you don't mind that I've been playing with your dog," the baduk player said. "He's very friendly."

Kira raised her eyebrows. "Friendly?" she asked. "That's a first! Jindo only likes a few people; everyone else he frightens to death."

Jindo returned to the baduk player's side, rolling onto his back and exposing his belly. The young man laughed and rubbed Jindo, causing the dog to pant in satisfaction.

"Well, I guess he likes me! And I like him too," he said. "You're really lucky."

Before she could reply, someone dashed into the stable.

"Young master!" the new arrival said. "I brought us some dinner. It's not much, but it smells good. Are you sure we can't stay here for the night? It looks like it's going to rain. We should at least sleep in the stable."

He passed over a bowl of rice gruel topped with slivers of dried seaweed garnish and sat down to eat from his own bowl, when he noticed her. Jumping to his feet, he bowed low.

"I'm so sorry," he said. "I didn't expect anyone else to be here."

He looked up and gaped in sudden alarm, pointing a finger at Kira's face.

"Y-y-you. Y-y-you're. You," he stuttered, then cleared his voice. "You're the Demon Slayer of Hansong!"

Kira withdrew, ready to leave.

"I heard you were here, but I didn't think I'd get to see you! Wa!" He stood entranced by the mere sight of her. "I heard you killed a demon in Hansong market a few days ago. A live demon! They say he was as big as a bear with red eyes that could burn you from the inside. Is that true? Is that why you left the city? Are you on the hunt?" he asked.

Kira gazed at him blankly.

"Aish, Seung! I'm dying of thirst and this is really salty. Did you forget my tea again?" the baduk player cut in.

Seung smacked himself in the face. "Forgive me, young master! I'll go right away!" With a quick bow to Kira, Seung dashed for the door.

"I'm sorry about that," the baduk player said. "He doesn't mean any harm."

Kira smiled. "It's all right. He didn't offend me," she said.

"I'm relieved." He smiled back. "Although I'm surprised to find that you're not as fearsome as your reputation makes you out to be."

Kira sniffed. "Your eyesight is clearly lacking. I wondered why you weren't cowering in my presence."

Jaewon laughed.

"Well, to be honest, I don't know what I was expecting! Maybe a two-headed monster that breathed fire or some other frightening creature. But all I see is a very pretty young girl—a very tall, but pretty young girl," he said.

She reddened at his words. "Eh, I knew your eyesight was bad."

He shook his head, looking down at Jindo and scratching the dog's ears. "No, just soft in the head. My grandfather used to say I had tofu for brains."

"Ah," she said. "That explains everything!"

Although she knew she should return to the inn, she didn't want to leave. She'd never felt so comfortable with another person outside of her family and Brother Woojin.

"So where do you hail from?" she asked.

"Forgive me. I am Kim Jaewon of Geumgwan clan of Kaya," he said. "But my family is from a small mountain village. I guess my ancestors preferred farming to politics."

Kira was surprised. Geumgwan was the ruling city-state of the Kaya confederacy, and a Geumgwan Kim would be descended from the nobility. Why would a noble have to worry about sleeping in a stable?

"Did you leave because of the Yamato invasion?" she asked.

He shook his head. "We left home four years ago, but

I've heard many have had to evacuate."

"So you're with your family?" she asked.

"No," Jaewon answered, his face shuttered. Kira could sense pain and sadness behind his curt response. It made her curious to know more about him.

The stable door creaked open, and Seung hurried in with a tea tray. Placing the tray on a bench, he poured two cups of tea.

"Here you go, young master," he said as he handed over the small brown teacup. He then brought over a cup of tea for Kira.

"Young mistress Kang, please let me offer you a cup of tea," Seung said.

Pleased, Kira took the cup and sipped the hot barley tea. "Thank you."

"My pleasure," he said with a broad smile. "I'm so delighted to meet you. There is so much I would like to ask. For example, is it true that you're the only person in the world who can actually see demons?" he asked.

Jaewon let out a loud hiss. "Seung! Don't bother her with your stupid questions!"

"It's not stupid! I really want to know! Everyone says she has unnatural powers and even killed a demon when she was only seven years old! They say she might even be a kum—"

"Ya!" Jaewon rose to his feet and slapped Seung lightly on the head. "Be quiet! Stop spouting nonsense and making people feel bad!"

Seung covered the top of his head with his hands and apologized. "Sorry, sorry! Please forgive me. It's just that I was so excited to meet you is all," he said.

Kira was more amused than offended at Seung's contrite expression.

"You know, some people think that I'm actually a demon. Aren't you afraid of me?" she asked.

Seung frowned, his eyebrows knitting together into a puzzled expression. "No. You don't look like a demon."

"Well, that would be the point. Demons can only exist in our world by taking possession of a human body. You wouldn't be able to tell if someone was possessed."

Seung leaned forward excitedly. "But you can, right?"

"I've always been able to sense them. Something about the way they smell and look. I don't know how to explain it." Kira shrugged. "It's a curse I have been blessed with."

Seung's eyebrows nearly disappeared into his hairline. "How can you say that? It is not a curse. It is a gift from the gods, and you mustn't disrespect it." He spoke with an earnestness that Kira found endearing. She had a feeling that he was the type of person who didn't speak ill of anyone.

"I'll let you in on a secret," she said. "You can kill an imp because it crosses over in its physical form. But you can't kill a full demon. You can only behead the body it possessed and send the demon back to the underworld. If you are ever attacked by one, aim for the neck—it's the only chance you'll have of surviving."

"If I ever get attacked by a demon, I'd much rather have you by my side," Seung said with a shudder.

Kira grinned. "It probably would be safer for you."

Seung tugged at Jaewon's sleeve. "Perhaps we should go whichever way young mistress is going."

"Just eat your dinner already." Jaewon shook him off.

"I'm frightened now."

"That's your own fault for being so nosy."

Seung frowned and scratched his head. "I don't see how it's all my fault. She's the one that's telling us about demons. So really it's her fault."

Kira bit her lip, trying not to laugh. "Why is it that you sound more like a South Seas man than Kim Jaewon?" she asked.

Seung's wistful smile transformed his plain face.

"Because I'm a country bumpkin from Kaya and he's the chief's son!" Seung said. "Oh, how I miss my home! Do you know that we are famous for our green tea, which grows wild all along our mountains? The finest in all the land, I daresay! In fact, merchants from Cathay cross the sea to purchase our teas." He let out a deep sigh. "But it has been more than four years since we've been home. I miss my mother's cold noodle soup and her steamed dumplings."

"Oh no! He's talking about food; now he'll never stop!" Jaewon said. He glanced at Kira, his eyes crinkling with good humor. "You see what I have to put up with all the time? It's a miracle I've not gone deaf yet."

He gave his friend a little shove. "Ya! All your chattering is driving me crazy. And you are boring our guest to death. Be quiet and eat your dinner already."

"I talk a lot because you hardly talk at all," Seung grumbled. "Just because you can go days without saying a word doesn't mean that's normal. Why, you're not even a monk or anything, but one would think you took a vow of silence. A person needs to have conversations once in a while in order to feel human, you know."

Jaewon looked at Kira and rolled his eyes.

For all his harsh words, Kira could see the depth of affection between the two friends as they continued to bicker back and forth. Their banter reminded her of Taejo and her obligations.

"I hate to interrupt, but I have to go," she said. "Perhaps I'll see you in the morning?"

Jaewon shook his head with regret. "We won't be here in the morning," he said. "But I hope that fate will let us cross paths again in the near future."

Kira bowed and dropped her eyes to hide her disappointment.

"I'll wish you a safe journey then," she said.

Outside, she sighed, sad that she might never see them again. For the first time in her life, she'd felt a bond with someone she might have called friend. But who would befriend a demon slayer? She shook the thought away. Her only value lay in her ability to protect the prince. What did it matter if she had no friends?

10

Early the next morning, Kira woke to an urgent knock. She jumped up and noted Taejo still asleep under his covers. Only then did she open the door to greet her brother.

"Lord Shin is gone! He left in the middle of the night with his men," he said in a low voice.

Kira's immediate reaction was relief, followed quickly by suspicion.

"What happened?" she asked.

"He left a message that the king has been badly wounded and that he had to return home immediately," Kwan said. "But if a message came from Hansong, we did not receive it."

Kira tensed up at his words. From behind she heard a thump and realized Taejo was awake.

"My father's injured?" Taejo bolted up. "We must go home!"

Kira exchanged glances with her brother. Everything about this was wrong, all wrong.

"No, sorry, only Lord Shin was to return," Kwan said.

"But why did he leave without me?" Taejo asked.

Kira wanted to know the same thing. Why did Lord Shin sneak away in the middle of the night? It was suspicious.

Taejo glared at Kwan and stormed out of the room, shouting for Captain Pak.

"*Oppa*, what does the captain think?" Kira asked. She only called him big brother in private.

Kwan shrugged. "He hasn't said anything, but he doesn't need to. It's pretty clear Shin planned this. He was the one who insisted his men be put on guard duty. We didn't know they were gone until the relief found their post empty."

"That sheep-faced, son of a leper whore!" Kira's gut churned. "He's the traitor. We have to warn our uncle, even if he doesn't believe us!"

Her brother snorted at her outburst. "The captain has already sent one of his men to Hansong. We need to leave now."

Kwan and Kira rushed downstairs. Taejo was arguing with Captain Pak and Brother Woojin.

"Why can't you take me home now?" Taejo asked.

"My orders are to deliver you safely to Stone Temple," Captain Pak said.

Taejo rushed over to Kira at her approach, his young face pale and serious.

"Lord Shin said my father is injured; we have to go home!" he insisted.

Kira shook her head. "We don't know why Lord Shin left. His actions have made him untrustworthy. Any information from him is also suspect."

"But we don't know for sure if my father is hurt or not," Taejo said. "We should go home and find out!"

"The safest course for us right now is to follow your father's orders as soon as possible." Kira gave him a sharp look when he tried to protest. "Go on up and get ready."

Taejo heaved a heavy sigh and returned to his room.

"What I don't understand is why Lord Shin would take the dogs and the packmaster with him," the captain wondered aloud.

Kira stilled at his words.

"Perhaps he felt safer traveling with the dogs," Brother Woojin responded.

No, that's not it at all, Kira thought. Something about the dogs being gone was troubling her.

"Where's Jindo?" Kira asked.

"He's in the stables," the captain said. "I doubt anyone could ever force Jindo away from his master."

A dull ache throbbed at the base of Kira's skull.

"Captain, we need to change our route," Kira said. "It may no longer be safe to go to Stone Temple."

"But the king is to send word there," the captain protested.

"Kira's right," Kwan said. "We have to assume our plan has been compromised. We need an alternate route that takes us near the temple, but far enough away to avoid it in case we spot trouble."

As Kwan and the captain charted their course, Kira went to pack her bag. The sooner they got away, the better.

They rode in two lines, with several guards riding in the front and back of the prince. Taejo sat hunched over in his saddle, looking younger than his twelve years.

It was late afternoon when they stopped at a small village in the foothills of the mountains. A steady rain had begun, drenching all of them to their skin.

In the courtyard, Kira dismounted absently, focused on getting her things out of the rain. She realized there was no one to greet them. Kira paused in midstride as she took note of her surroundings.

"Something's wrong," she said.

She scanned the area, but all she could see was a sodden landscape. Kira caught a whiff of the familiar stench of decay and death. Kira swung around to face the building, her eyes widening in horror.

At that moment, Jindo began to bark.

"Captain!" Kira shouted. "Don't enter!"

The captain retreated, calling his men to him. Suddenly, a shower of arrows thudded all around them, taking out four of their men. An animal-like roaring filled the air as the dark forms of Yamato soldiers surged from the inn and surrounding buildings.

Kira grabbed her bow and arrows and shot every one of her thirty arrows, downing any who came near the prince. Exchanging her bow for her sword, she charged forward. Jindo was snarling and attacking any that came near, while the prince's guards formed a close but protective circle around Taejo, each armed with twin swords.

The Hansong royal bodyguards were all masters of *sang gum hyung*, the double-sword form, and none were more skilled at wielding the twin swords than the captain. Kira admired the brutal efficiency of the two-handed attack. It was not something easily mastered, and yet it wrought triple the damage against a single sword.

Before she could reach the prince, the foul stench of demon rot smothered her senses. Instinct caused her to dive to the left, barely missing the deathblow of a Yamato soldier. Rolling on the muddy ground, she leaped to her feet and looked up into a nightmare. He looked human, until she caught sight of his eyes. They were completely black—no pupils, no irises—with lids that retracted, frog-like. It was an abomination—something that should not exist in her world.

"What are you?" she asked.

The demon creature smiled, exposing sharp, glittering teeth. "I am the first of my kind, but I will not be the last. Half demon and half human. We will be the end of your world."

"You're nothing but a monster," Kira said.

"I am the future."

"Not my future, you hideous half-breed!"

She swung her sword at its head. The creature blocked and parried, forcing Kira away from Taejo and the guards. It was immensely strong, fending off Kira's blows as if they were puffs of air. The creature crashed its sword with harder and harder strikes against Kira's, sending her staggering back, slipping in the wet grass. It gave her no respite, its sword seeking an opening. Within minutes, Kira was breathing hard as her sword arm trembled against the punishing blows.

"You won't find it easy to kill me, Demon Slayer," the half-breed said with a harsh cackle.

"Personally, I think it's harder to look at you," she said, and grinned.

The half-breed snarled as their swords clashed and beat upon each other in a frenzy. It feinted to the right and then spun around and attacked viciously from the other side. This time Kira did not back down, meeting each blow with an extra burst of strength. She swung her sword in a high arc, forcing the creature to meet it. Pivoting under its arms, Kira kicked the half-breed in the abdomen. The creature somersaulted in midair and landed on its feet.

At that moment, Kira heard Taejo screaming. She could see the Yamato soldiers escaping with the prince. With a harsh yell, she attacked, slashing and thrusting as hard as she could, frantic to save Taejo. She stumbled over a muddy rock, and the creature sliced at her neck, knocking her sword away.

"Foolish girl, did you think you could defeat me? You're nothing but a pathetic mortal, while I'm the best of both worlds! I exist in yours and yet I'm stronger than any of you. Stronger than any demon!"

It raised its sword and lunged down at her with a killing blow. Kira reached into her jacket for her hidden dagger. Whipping around in a full circle, she thrust her dagger up into its chin. The half-breed's sword dropped to the ground as it clawed at her arm, trying to reach her face. Its arms flailed uncontrollably, and then it fell back.

"Too bad you die like a human," Kira said.

She staggered away, unable to contain the shuddering that racked her body. How could such a thing possibly exist? And were there more of them? The very thought of it chilled her. As if demon possessions weren't bad enough, now they had to worry about a new race of creatures out to destroy them. Heavenly Father help them!

She left the dagger impaled where it was and picked up her sword. A quiver full of arrows lay spilled on the muddy ground. Seizing her bow, she raced over to where the others were still fighting. She killed twenty enemy soldiers in a row, uncaring that she was shooting them in the back. When she ran out of arrows, she grabbed her sword again and charged into the fray. She needed to end this now and go after her cousin. Slicing and stabbing with inelegant speed, she slid in by Brother Woojin's side as he fought off three soldiers with his long staff. In less than a minute, she killed all three of them and moved on, never resting, letting her instincts and her training take over until finally there were no more enemy soldiers left.

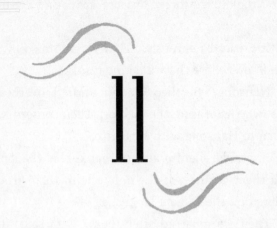

11

Kira stood breathing hard, covered in mud, blood, and other parts of the human anatomy that she didn't care to think too hard about.

"Kira!" Kwan shouted as he and Brother Woojin came running up to her. The monk looked exhausted, while Kwan dripped blood both from his sword and a deep wound across his cheek. "They took the prince!"

"I know," she said. "I've got to go after him now!"

She scanned the area. "Where's my horse?"

Not too far away, she saw Captain Pak speaking to his remaining men. Catching Kira's eye, he headed over to her.

"We've lost more than half of our force, and the horses took to the forest. My men are rounding them up," he said.

Kira paced nervously. "They've got Taejo! We don't even know where they're taking him!"

"Hansong," Brother Woojin said. "I overheard the ones who captured the prince. Their orders were to return to Hansong with him alive."

Kira said a silent prayer of thanks that the monk was with them, for he was the only one in their group who understood the Yamato language.

"Then we must go after them," Kira said. "If we're lucky, we'll catch them before they enter the city. If not, then we'll have to go in through the sewers."

Captain Pak nodded and took off, yelling out to his men.

Kira kept her emotions clamped down as tight as possible, worried that she wouldn't be able to control her anger. The rain had dulled her senses and she'd been less vigilant than she should have been. She'd failed her father and Taejo. But mostly, she'd failed herself.

Darkness fell, and they lit torches as they buried their fallen comrades. Kwan reported that everyone inside the inn was dead and the small village was deserted. Kira cursed the Yamatos and the demons even as she knew this was a sign that worse was to come.

Unable to keep her thoughts in check, she paced about the bloody courtyard, when a keen whine caught her attention.

"Jindo?" She followed the sound and found the white dog bleeding from its chest, a broken arrow caught under its top leg. "Oh no, please no."

As she worked to remove the arrow, Brother Woojin arrived with cloth and water to help bind the wound.

"He won't be able to travel," Brother Woojin said.

"If we don't take him with us, he'll follow behind, even if it kills him," she replied. "I can't let that happen. I'll take care of him."

"Our sole concern is saving the prince," the monk said.

Kira's lips tightened. "I know."

A loud shout heralded the return of the captain's men with several horses. Kira was relieved to see that they'd found her horse as well as Taejo's, their packs still attached to the saddles. Mounting, she calmed the animal as Kwan carefully lifted the injured dog in front of her.

They set out at a furious pace to Hansong. A soft mist rolled off the muddy roads, lending a feeling of unease to Kira's heightened nerves. The sky had cleared and the stars gleamed in their indigo canvas. The Yamatos had a good head start—at least two hours.

Kira vacillated between anger and guilt, berating herself for not noticing the demon presence earlier, for not paying attention to her initial unease. Reaching into her satchel, she found the little haetae her father had given her. Its ugly face with its fanged grin and bulging eyes comforted her. Looking at it strengthened her resolve. They would find Taejo and they would save him.

The captain's bruising pace brought them to the mountain trail at the outskirts of Hansong City by early morning. As the moon sank lower into the west, she knew the hour of the hare had just begun.

They rode carefully up the steep trail. By the time they reached a clear opening with an aerial view of the city, the sun was rising over the horizon and painting the land a shimmering red-gold. The high ridge provided a view of the southeastern wall of the city and the mountain-cliff pagoda, overlooking the Han River. Here the river curved into a horseshoe.

Kira slid off her horse and stumbled to the top of the ridge. Black clouds of billowing smoke rose high above the inner city. Reds, yellows, pinks, and blues fluttered in the wind as hundreds of court ladies fell from the cliff onto the jagged rocks of the river below.

"I don't understand! Why are they doing this?" She collapsed to her knees.

"They are jumping because they fear the enemy more than they fear death," Brother Woojin said. He took off his prayer necklace, wrapping it around his hand. He began to pray.

Clouds of colorful silk floated in the river, like broken flowers twirling in the current. Was it only a few days ago that she'd walked past the court ladies and their fluttering fans? When she'd seen the queen and her mother?

Kwan came up behind her. "We have to go."

"Mother," Kira whispered. Kwan's hand tightened on her shoulder before he walked away.

She followed him in a daze, unable to accept what she'd just seen.

"She wouldn't jump," she said to herself. "She wouldn't jump."

As they mounted their horses, Kira took one last look. There was nothing but black clouds.

12

It wasn't until the hour of the snake was well advanced that they reached the Hansong fortress wall. The midmorning sun brightened the main road, forcing them deep into the recesses of the forest to avoid detection. Here they would rest and care for their spent horses.

Captain Pak's scouts spotted unfamiliar armed soldiers patrolling the top of the fortress walls and Kudara ships lining the banks of the Han River. But the city was quiet; there was no movement on the roads leading to the locked gates.

Kira cursed under her breath. Her father had been right. Kudara was in league with the Yamatos. The daimyo, who must have orchestrated the murders of the kings, had been from Kudara. And Brother Woojin believed that Taejo was the link to the prophecy. She had to rescue Taejo.

"The only way in is through the sewer tunnel," she said, addressing Captain Pak, Kwan, and Brother Woojin. "I know these tunnels better than anyone in Hansong."

She knelt on the ground, sketching a rough map in the dirt. "There's no way you and your men are going to pass through the marketplace unseen. It would be better for me to go alone, find out where they took the prince, and then report to you."

Kwan shook his head. "No, not by yourself."

The captain agreed. "You'll need at least one backup with you."

"I'll do it," Kwan said.

"OK, but we need disguises," Kira said.

"Leave that to me," the captain said. He walked away, calling for his scouts.

As Kira stood up, Jindo lurched to his feet, trying to follow. Kira pushed him gently down with a firm no.

"Don't worry, boy," she said. "We'll find him for you. We'll bring him out safely. I promise."

Not much later, the soldiers returned with two battered conical straw hats worn normally by farmers and monks, and two long coats so covered in dirt and mud that it was hard to tell that they'd once been white.

As she put on the coat, Kira noted the bloodstained

tears on the interior and the stench of rotted flesh. Saying a quick prayer for the souls of the departed, she gritted her teeth and handed Brother Woojin her bow and arrows but kept her sword. Taking off her nambawi, she shoved it inside her uniform and put on the straw hat.

As she and her brother prepared to leave, the captain handed Kira a small dagger to replace the one she'd left in the half-breed monster.

"You must find the prince," Captain Pak said. "We cannot leave without him. If you are not back within the hour, we're coming in after you."

Kira nodded. They headed down the riverbank on foot, keeping to the woods, away from the road.

Soon after, she smelled the entrance to the sewage tunnel, a recess built below the city wall and hidden by the forest that spread out from the riverbank. Kira held her breath as she pushed her way through the opening and down a short set of stairs, Kwan right behind her. Hansong was the only city in the entire peninsula that had sewage tunnels whose real function was a secret escape route for the royals.

It was dark except for the sunlight filtering through the drainage grates above them. They rushed through the tunnel and exited into an alley behind a public bathhouse. On the main thoroughfare, Kira noticed the shops were closed and very few people walked the city streets. Those who were kept their heads down, carefully avoiding eye contact. It was such a change from how life had been just a few days ago.

At the marketplace, the normally crowded stalls were only half full with vendors, and few customers. Enemy soldiers patrolled the perimeter. The red uniforms of Kudara soldiers were mixed in with Yamato soldiers, who wore coarse white uniforms under simple black armor vests.

"Where is the tunnel?" Kwan asked.

Kira pointed down an alleyway on the left side of the marketplace, across the main promenade. Suddenly, a crowd began to form at the other end of the street. People came running out of buildings, pointing in horror, while others wept and wailed. Angry shouts forced the crowd to the sides as a dozen enemy soldiers beat back those who didn't move quickly enough. Her nose confirmed what her eyes could also see: these soldiers were possessed. Their skins undulated with the movements of the demons within.

She hunched down, her hat obscuring her face, to avoid the restless eyes of the demon soldiers. She heard Kwan curse under his breath.

Kira looked up and froze, horrified. It was King Yuri, in heavy chains that wrapped around his neck, hands, and feet—his robes filthy and torn as he faltered under the weight of his shackles. Behind him walked Taejo, holding up his exhausted mother.

But it was the sight of her father, tied up like a

common criminal, that sent Kira into a mindless fury. Reaching for her sword, she started to shove past the spectators when a hard jolt on the head sent her crashing to the ground.

13

Kwan pulled her up and shook her. "What are you doing? Get ahold of yourself and don't do anything stupid!"

Mortified, Kira bit her lip so hard she could taste blood. She willed her body to remain still even as her mind screamed in outrage and fear. Taejo looked tired, his face carefully blank. But her father's face showed signs of a recent beating.

The general walked with his head held high, giving no hint of any strain or emotion.

Kira gazed at her father, wishing he'd look at her and know that she and her brother were there. The general marched past, ignoring the soldiers that prodded him with their swords. One lone horseman rode behind the procession, his red-and-gold robes gleaming in contrast to those of his prisoners. Anger coursed through her at the sight of Lord Shin's arrogant face.

"They've got to be heading for the palace steps," Kwan said.

Kira agreed. Royal pronouncements were always made on the tiered steps for the citizens to see. And Shin was out to make a spectacle of the royal family.

Kira and Kwan pushed through the crowd and ran into an alley. At the end of the alleyway, Kira found a tunnel entrance covered by a shed.

Kwan began pulling the shed away from the wall. "Come on, Kira, help me already!"

Rage and fear warred within her as his words rang in her ears. Something cracked inside of her. With sudden violence she twisted and kicked the side of the shed, causing it to collapse.

"Have you lost your mind?" Kwan said. Grabbing her by the arm, he yanked her against the wall. "Are you trying to get us caught?"

Her brother shook her hard again.

"Calm yourself," he hissed. "Which way do we go?"

Kira pulled open the door that had been hidden behind the shed. She went down a dim stairway, into a hallway that forked off into a series of dark tunnels.

"Oppa, stay close," she said. "You can't see in the dark like I can."

At the end of the hall, she entered a very narrow passageway. It was only wide enough for one person to pass through at a time, and it was pitch-black. The only sound she could hear was Kwan's breathing behind her and the slight echo of their footsteps. She stepped out into a tunnel that ran parallel with the city's underground sewage system. The foul stench was overpowering.

The tunnels forked, but Kira didn't hesitate, veering left. At the end of the tunnel, steep stairs led up to another drainage ditch, which opened to a side alleyway near the palace compound.

A large crowd of people stood outside the palace walls. There was no sign of the royals or of the traitor. Kira and her brother walked into the crowd, but no one paid any attention to them. Everyone was watching the raised platform before the grand entrance to Hansong palace as military leaders and senior advisers to the king were dragged forward in chains. Yamato archers marched before them, readying themselves for the public execution.

One of the prisoners cried, "For Hansong! For King Yuri!" The crowd took up the refrain, their mighty shouts silencing the deadly thud of the arrows.

Kira could hear Kwan cursing as servants carried away the bodies.

The sudden pounding of drums heralded Lord Shin's arrival. He strode up the stairs and seated himself in the king's sedan chair. Behind him came the exhausted royals and the greatest general of Hansong.

"People of Hansong!" Lord Shin cried as he rose. "Here is your famous king before you now!"

He grabbed Yuri by the neck and threw him onto the ground in front of the crowd.

"My old friend!" King Yuri sneered as he fought against the chains that bound him.

Shin laughed as Yamato soldiers hauled the king to his knees. "My good friend," he taunted. "How many years has it been, Yuri?"

"Traitor!" Yuri roared.

"It took you thirty years to discover this? How foolish you must feel."

"I trusted you! You were like a brother to me!"

Shin stroked his beard as he contemplated the king. "Then you're a fool. I've been planning this ever since the old king turned his back on me and my rightful claim," he said. "Instead of returning to Kudara, I stayed, biding my time. And now, Kudara and Yamato have united under the daimyo to conquer the Seven Kingdoms. My patience has been rewarded. Hansong is mine."

"May the gods curse you and your entire clan! May your name live only in infamy!" The king raged against his chains like a madman.

"Yes, yes, but first I will get to see you die."

A Yamato soldier drew his sword and approached the king.

The crowd's protests grew louder. Kira started forward, only to be hauled back by her collar.

"No, Kira," Kwan said. "There's nothing we can do."

She jerked convulsively at the high-pitched whistle of the sword, the sound of Queen Ja-young's agonized scream, and Taejo's sobs echoing in her head.

Lord Shin made to pull the fainting queen into his arms.

"Don't touch her!" Taejo yelled. He leaped at the older man, punching and kicking like a crazed animal. Shin flung Taejo away and cursed at him.

Kira bit her lips, trying to control herself. Taejo was now a horse length away from her.

"We have to do something now or they will kill him," Kira said to Kwan.

"We need a distraction," Kwan said.

Kira edged closer to the prince. Pushing her hat up, she gazed across the platform and caught the general's shocked gaze.

"Father."

The crowds faded away, and all she could see was her father's face. He nodded at her. In his eyes she saw all his love and pride and she knew at that moment what he would do and what she must do.

The general let out a war cry, knocking down his captors with his chains. Grabbing a sword with his bound hands, he sliced and stabbed his way toward Lord Shin. As the traitor hid behind his guards, Kira saw her chance. Leaping onto the platform, she grabbed Taejo and tossed him down the stairs toward her brother.

"Go now!" Kira shouted.

Kwan caught the prince as if he were a sack of rice and ran toward the alleyway. Kira held out her hand to her father.

"Father!" she cried.

"No, Kira! You have to leave me!"

The general threw down his weapon.

Kira started. "No, Father!"

Suddenly, a sword impaled him from behind.

A scream ripped from her throat as she watched her father's eyes glaze over.

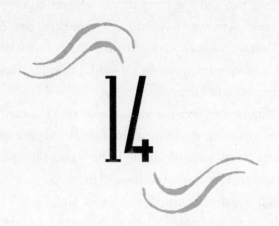

14

Kira barely noticed the Yamato soldier lunging at her. Twirling, she flung her straw hat in his face and swiped his sword. She then reverse side-kicked him so hard, he flew into the air and landed in a heap in front of the other guards.

"Stop them!" Shin yelled.

Kira took one last look at her father's body and jumped into the crowd, forcing a pathway through the spectators. Behind her, she could hear the guards giving chase. Kira ran for the tunnels, when a huge roar of a thousand voices filled the air.

"Save the prince!" It was a rallying cry that erupted from the masses.

Glancing back, Kira was shocked to see the citizens of Hansong fighting the Yamato soldiers, blocking their progress. Arrows flew into the crowd as the Yamatos cut down those who tried to stop them. But with every death, more citizens came forward, impeding the enemy so they couldn't follow her.

Kira turned into the alley, leaped into the tunnel, and closed the stone covering above her. The memories of her father's death kept replaying in her head. She swallowed her tears. This wasn't the time to mourn.

Up ahead, she could see Kwan and Taejo running. With a burst of speed, she caught up with them just as Taejo began to stumble. She held Taejo's arm and dragged him along. She knew they had a good chance to escape if they didn't slow down. Only the royal family knew about the underground tunnels. Shin would not know where they were or where they would come out.

The tunnels seemed endless, causing her alarm to grow. She kept hearing the echo of military boots chasing them. She didn't know if they came from behind, in front, or above. Finally Kira could see the exit. They ran up the staircase and into the marketplace alley, heading straight for the sewage tunnel.

Once out of the tunnel and on the other side of the city walls, they moved swiftly through the woods. Not far away, Captain Pak and his men waited with their horses.

"They're after us! We've gotta go now!" Kira shouted.

Jindo whined as a soldier lifted him quickly onto a horse.

"Jindo!" Taejo climbed behind his wounded dog, burying his face in Jindo's fur.

Kira and Kwan threw off their disguises, rearmed themselves, and clambered onto their horses. They rode furiously toward the main road.

Behind them, Kira heard the loud creaking of the city gates. A small contingent of mounted Yamato soldiers charged after them.

As she rode, Kira grabbed her bow and unlatched her arrow case, attached to the front left side of her saddle. She nocked her arrow and twisted back. She zeroed in on the lead rider and let it fly. Nearby, she saw Kwan and two other soldiers twist and loose their arrows.

They took out half the Yamato contingent by shooting backward. Kira was grimly amused to see how bad the Yamato shots were.

A sudden commotion up ahead caught her attention. It was another contingent of Yamatos, surging from the northern woods in a surprise attack. They were a mix of mounted men and infantry, fifty in all.

"Ambush!" she shouted.

Kira's senses were assaulted. Nearly all the foot soldiers were demon possessed.

"Make for cover!" Captain Pak ordered. He whipped out his twin swords as the enemy rushed forward.

"Captain!" Kira yelled. "Aim for the neck!"

Pak crossed his double swords like scissor blades, slicing off the heads of the demons with remarkable ease. With deadly accuracy, Kira shot off her bow in rapid succession, dispatching several attackers in a row.

"Get out of here now!" Pak yelled.

Kwan slapped Taejo's horse, guiding him away from the attack and toward an open break in the eastern edge of the forest. Brother Woojin rode close behind them. Half the enemy soldiers broke away from the main fighting, trying to cut them off.

Dusk had descended, making it hard to see for everyone except Kira and the demon soldiers. Kira raced after the others, twisting in her seat and choosing her targets carefully, knocking a pair of them off their horses and impeding the progress of the others. But still the Yamatos pursued them.

Urging her horse ever faster, Kira maneuvered through the forest, dodging low-hanging branches that threatened to knock her off. She came to an abrupt halt in front of a large riverbank.

The others had already plunged their horses into the fast-flowing river. Kwan was in the lead as arrows rained down upon them.

"Jindo!" Taejo shouted.

The dog had jumped off Taejo's horse and began swimming for shore. As Kira urged her horse into the water, she saw Jindo had made it across and was limping into the forest, barking loudly.

Sudden anguished yells of surprise signaled a change in the situation. Arrows flew across the river, killing their pursuers. Kira reached the sandy shore close behind the others, when Jindo reappeared, limping over to Taejo's side.

Kira gasped in shock as a man stepped out of the shadows.

"What are you doing here?" she asked bluntly.

15

Kim Jaewon, the baduk player, bowed in greeting.

"Helping, I think," Jaewon said with a quizzical look. She could hear the laughter in his voice. It flustered her.

"Kira, do you know him?" Kwan asked.

Before she could respond, Jaewon cut in. "Why don't we move into cover first?" he said.

Jaewon waved them over to a clearing into the woods, where Seung stood next to two grazing horses.

"Young mistress! It's so good to see you again!" Seung said.

Kira had to smile at his happy face. She quickly

introduced the pair and explained how she'd met them at the inn.

"Thank you for saving us!" Taejo said to their rescuers.

"Thank your dog," Jaewon replied. "We would not have known of your troubles if he hadn't chased us down. He's a smart one." He reached over to stroke Jindo's head. "Your dog led us here."

"But what are you doing out here?" Kira repeated.

Jaewon cocked an eyebrow, causing Kira to mutter an apology.

"No need to apologize," he said, his eyes steady on hers. "We were traveling to Hansong when we spotted a scary-looking army riding toward the city. We decided that our fortunes would be better served going the opposite direction."

"That would probably be the same army that's after us. We've lost all our men," Kwan interjected. "We must leave now."

"Where are you headed?" Jaewon asked.

"To Mount Hwaak, up north, in Tongey," Kwan said.

Seung nudged Jaewon and made dramatic eye rolls at Kira.

Jaewon sighed and said, "We'd be happy to ride with you."

Kwan hesitated for a moment before nodding. "Another bowman would be greatly appreciated."

Relief flooded through Kira. She and Kwan were good fighters, but there were so many of the enemy. They would need all the help they could get to keep Taejo safe. She could not bear the idea of losing him again.

Seung came over to her side. "I feel much safer traveling with you now," he said. He scampered away before Kira could correct him. Safer was the last thing he'd be.

They traveled old forest trails, avoiding the main road and only breaking for water. It wasn't until the middle of the night, the hour of the rat, that the group could finally rest.

They set up camp near a narrow stream. Kira did a quick but thorough check of the perimeter while Jaewon and Seung rubbed down the horses. There would be no fire tonight.

Kira's boots and trousers were still wet and uncomfortable. She slid down onto the ground and rested her head on her arms. Taejo leaned against her, Jindo at his feet. She could feel Taejo's body, shuddering in uncontrollable spurts.

"It's so different when it's real," he said.

Kira nodded. She knew what he was talking about. This was his first experience in battle. It was easy to kill, but hard to forget. For Kira, it was the sounds of death that always stayed with her. The tearing of flesh and bone, the screams of agony, the death rattle. Even after ten years of fighting demons, the sound still unnerved her.

"I'm never going to be a warrior like my father," he

said. "How do you do it? Act like nothing happened?"

Kira wrapped her arm tight around his shoulders. "It isn't easy, but you get numb after a while. You have to or you'll start to lose your soul a little each time."

"My father's dead." Taejo's body shook with racking sobs.

Kira held him close, letting his fingers dig into her arms.

"I knew you would come for me," he said.

"Always," she replied.

When he finally stopped shaking, she rose to her feet and pulled him up.

"Go and change into dry pants and shoes. You need to stay warm."

He nodded and stumbled away.

Kira walked over to where Kwan was brushing the dried mud off the flank of his horse.

"Oppa, we must avenge Father's death." Her voice seemed overly harsh to her ears.

Kwan's hands stilled. "Now is not the time."

"Then when? What about our mother and aunt? How will we save them?"

Kwan frowned at her. "Our mission is to protect the prince," he replied. "We made an oath. Everything else must wait."

"I can't wait!"

"You must!" He rubbed a hand over his eyes, but Kira could see his tears. "It is what Father would have wanted us to do. Would have expected us to do."

He opened the supply bag and passed out small rice balls to everyone.

"We'll rest here for a few hours, but then we need to continue," Kwan said. Sitting down, he eyed Jaewon curiously.

"Thanks for your help today," Kwan said. "It was very fortunate for us that you were there."

Jaewon glanced at Taejo and then at Kwan. "Who are you in trouble with?"

Kwan hesitated before answering.

"Let me introduce you to the crown prince of Hansong, Prince Kim Taejo," Kwan said. "The Yamatos have invaded Hansong, and he is no longer safe."

"Your Highness." Jaewon and Seung stood and bowed to Taejo.

"Please don't," Taejo said. "I am prince of nothing right now. I am just Kim Taejo. My kingdom has been invaded, and my father has been assassinated." Taejo dropped his head into his hands.

"You are still the crown prince, heir to the throne of Hansong. And when you are coronated, you will be king," Kwan said. "While it would be wise to keep this information to ourselves until you are safe, you should not forget who you are."

"We've lost the captain and all my guards. Demons are after us. How can we escape?" Taejo asked.

"Don't lose faith," Kira said. She put an arm around

him and hugged him. "I'll always be here for you."

Kira pulled out some blankets and made up a bed for the prince. Taejo lay down without a word and turned away. She rolled up next to him, watching as the others made their beds, while Kwan paced the perimeter. She chewed on her nail and then spit in disgust. Her hand was grimy.

Reaching into her jacket, Kira pulled her father's gift out of the small pouch that hung low around her neck. "Father," she whispered. She gripped the haetae hard in her fist, trying to shut out the image of her father's death, desperately wondering what was happening to her mother and praying that she was still safe.

No matter how long it takes and if it costs me my life, I will have revenge. I swear to you, Father. You will be avenged.

16

They reached the Tongey border the next day and rode steadily north, bypassing the villages they came across, and passing several more nights in the forest. Kira's demon-sensing abilities were strained from lack of sleep and constant vigilance by the time they reached Mount Hwaak. She'd killed several imp spies before they could return and report back their location. But she knew she wouldn't be able to rest until Taejo was safe within the temple grounds.

"We need to get up the mountain before the sun sets, or we will never be able to find the entrance," Brother Woojin said.

They rode single file up the narrow mountain trail embedded with tall spires jutting up like rocky daggers. Their horses wove in and out between the spires until they reached a sheer granite face. Brother Woojin dismounted and put his hand under a ledge and pulled on a hidden lever. A stone door swung open to reveal a long, wide corridor that led to a large courtyard, where a fountain sprayed crystal-clear water.

Kira was captivated. They were within the secret valley of the Dragon Springs Temple. Golden-red rays glinted over the shiny granite walls surrounding the valley. The temple building was built directly into the stone side of the mountain. Below it were orchards and gardens and softly sloping hills stretching into a vast sea of green.

Several monks came forward to meet their party and greet Brother Woojin.

"Welcome to Dragon Springs Temple," Brother Woojin said with a tired smile.

Kira was surprised to see how simple the temple was. Unlike Stone Temple of Hansong, with its gold-gilded columns, multicolored eaves, tiled walls, and three-storied pagoda, the ancient temple before them was an elegant one-story wooden structure.

Jaewon whistled as he gazed across the entire valley.

"This is a wonderful place," he said. "I wonder how long it's been here?"

"The temple is over five hundred years old," Kira said.

Taejo looked at her in surprise. "How did you know that, Noona?"

She shrugged. "Unlike you, I was listening to Sunim's history lessons." She nudged him as he gave her a reproachful frown.

"It's dedicated to the Mountain Spirit, believed to be the spirit of the Dragon King," Kira continued. "And it wasn't always hidden. The temple was built into the mountain. But as the world around the temple changed, the monks began to fear for their simple way of life. Legend has it that the mountains grew around the temple to keep them safe. The monks only leave the valley to trade with nearby villages, look for new disciples, or go on a pilgrimage. That is how Brother Woojin came to us."

"I feel fortunate to have seen it," Jaewon said. "The prince will be safe here. We can continue on our journey once again."

"You're leaving?" Taejo asked in alarm.

"Yes," he said. "The sooner the better."

"But why?" Taejo asked. "Where are you going?"

Jaewon shrugged. "I'm not sure. Haven't decided yet."

"Then stay with us," Taejo said.

Jaewon didn't answer.

"Noona, don't let them go!" Taejo said. "We need them."

Kira hid her disappointment.

"They've already been such a great help to us. We

can't ask for any more," she said.

"But we need them," Taejo persisted. "You think so too, don't you?"

Kira sighed. "It would be great, but it's too much of an imposition."

Jaewon snapped to attention; a small smile played on his lips.

"If you were to ask me, I might change my mind," he said.

Kira blinked in surprise. "What?"

Taejo poked her in the arm, grinning. "You heard him! Just ask him," he said.

"You mean you would stay with us?" she asked Jaewon.

He nodded.

"So why'd you say you'd leave then?" Kira was annoyed.

Jaewon shrugged his shoulder. "It's nice to be wanted."

He nudged Taejo, who began to giggle.

Suddenly, the stress and lack of sleep from the nights on the road hit Kira hard. Too cranky to handle their teasing, she glared at them both before stomping away.

Out in the hallway, she found a young novice who led her to her room. It was so small that once she unrolled the futon and made her bed, it took up the entire space.

Sliding under the covers, she drifted off.

A moment later, she heard a loud purring and opened her eyes to see the ghostly form of a tiger circling her. It settled down, pressing its warm body against hers.

"My tiger spirit." A sense of well-being filled her as her body absorbed the tiger's healing energy. Kira caressed the soft fur and fell into a deep, dreamless sleep.

17

The next morning when Kira and the others walked into the monastery's prayer room, Brother Woojin and another monk were already seated on the raised floor. The windowless interior chamber was lit with hanging lanterns shaped like lotuses. A small gilt-bronze statue of Gwaneum, the goddess of mercy and compassion, stood on an altar. Painted on the wall behind it was a large mural of Gwaneum riding on the back of a magnificent golden dragon.

Brother Woojin waited solemnly as Kira and the others stood before him. He was dressed in a formal black robe with a red silk shawl over his left shoulder and tied under the right arm. Beside him sat the head monk, a very old man with small, narrow eyes and a long, pointed white beard, whose intricately designed shawl indicated his high rank. He beamed as Kira, Taejo, Kwan, Jaewon, and Seung stood before them.

"Greetings and felicitations!" The frail monk had a deep, melodious voice. He raised his arms expansively. "I am Master Roshi."

The visitors sat cross-legged before the two monks.

"Master Roshi has been expecting you for a long time," Brother Woojin said.

Kira caught her brother's eye in surprise.

"Do not look so baffled, young ones. I knew this day would come in fulfillment of the Dragon King's prophecy," Master Roshi said.

"What do we have to do with the prophecy?" Taejo asked.

As Master Roshi began to relate the history of King Dang, the Dragon King, Kira detected the telltale signs of boredom on Taejo's, Kwan's, and Jaewon's faces—twitchy lips, glazed eyes, the slight hunching of their shoulders. They'd all learned these stories as children. But Seung was enraptured.

Listening to Master Roshi's melodious voice, Kira's attention began to drift. The lanterns that illuminated the room seemed to dim, casting the room into shadows. As she contemplated the painted mural, she heard the others talking, but their voices sounded muffled. The scales of the golden dragon shimmered. A rushing sound filled her ears. The dragon reared up on its hind legs and flew off into the painted blue sky, the goddess still seated on its back.

In its place, a battle began to rage between humans and demons. The demons cavorted on a battlefield, dragging humans into the depths of an underground inferno. Kira sensed an evil presence waiting deep underground. She couldn't see it, but it terrified her. A chasm broke through the field, pulsing like a living thing, sending blasts of hellfire everywhere. Kira couldn't stand to watch anymore. She closed her eyes, but the scene played vividly in her mind. She glared at the painted skies. Where were the dragon and Gwaneum? Why weren't they helping? Why had the heavens forsaken their people?

She felt a sharp poke from Kwan. The room was silent. Both monks were staring at her—Master Roshi with an expectant expression.

"What is it you see, young mistress?" he asked.

She blinked. The golden dragon and the goddess Gwaneum were looking down at her once again. Feeling dazed and peculiar, she shook her head. She'd never had a vision while she was awake before.

"I saw a nightmare," she said with a shudder. "The end of the world."

Master Roshi's expression sobered immediately. "Yes, that is what awaits us if the daimyo is successful."

Kira wished her father were there. She missed his

wisdom and his strength. Her fingers dug into her thighs. She just couldn't bear to believe he was gone.

Master Roshi took a sip from a small teacup. He gestured to Brother Woojin, who then continued the story.

"In order to prepare for this time, King Dang hid away his three most prized possessions: the tidal stone that controls the seas, the jeweled dagger that controls the earth, and the jade dragon belt. When reunited with the dagger and the stone, the belt will allow the wearer to control the fourteen dragons of the heavens and the powers of wind, rain, lightning, and all the other physical elements. The Dragon King's treasures have not been seen for over a thousand years. We have made it our life's work to study the prophecies and the possible location of the treasures."

"I've never heard of them," Kira said. "How do you know this is all true?"

Brother Woojin picked up the bundle of bamboo sticks Kira had seen in her father's office. He untied and unrolled the scroll.

"It's all written here in Master Ahn's scriptures. While the original is kept safe in the temple, every monk is given a copy of the scriptures to study."

"So you know exactly where the treasures are?" Kira asked.

Brother Woojin shook his head. "We only have theories."

Taejo heaved a loud sigh. "I don't understand," he

said. "Who is supposed to find the treasures and save the world?"

"Master Ahn believed it would be the Dragon Musado—our savior," Roshi said.

Brother Woojin said, "The prophecy states, 'Seven will become three. Three will become one. One will save us all.' Master Ahn added the following: 'But only in the hands of the Dragon Musado will the Dragon King's treasures destroy the Demon Lord, wreaking the vengeance of the heavens on earth.'"

He passed the bamboo scroll to Kwan, who began to study it.

"The monks have long believed that the 'one' refers to a person, he who will unite all the kingdoms again. He will be the heir to King Dang's throne—the Dragon Musado," Brother Woojin said.

"Yes, but who is he?" Taejo asked.

"We do not know for sure," Master Roshi said. "But we believe that he is a direct descendant of King Dang, for only a direct descendant would be able to wield the power of the three treasures."

"I am a direct descendant," Taejo said. "And so are Kira and Kwan."

"Yes, and so are the kings of Guru, Oakcho, Tongey, and the Jinhan Kingdom," Master Roshi cut in with a wave of his hand.

"So any of us could be the 'one' of the prophecy?" Taejo asked.

"It is possible," Master Roshi agreed.

"I believe it is you, Your Highness," Brother Woojin said.

Roshi looked sharply at him. "We do not know for certain who it is."

"Your pardon, Master," Brother Woojin said with an apologetic bow. "Let me explain my reasoning. Centuries ago, Master Ahn had a dream that he was to send his monks out to all the kingdoms and educate the royalty in the hope that one day, one of our monks would return with a prince who would be the savior of our lands. It was foreseen that a direct descendant of the Dragon King would arrive at the temple. He would be the one to defeat the Demon Lord. And now you are here. Master Roshi thinks that it is too early to know who the Dragon Musado is. But I have no doubts. And I believe that it is dangerous not to warn you of what is to come."

Taejo's mouth gaped at the pronouncement.

Kira could hear her father's voice in her head: Why, I would be less surprised if you were the Dragon Musado instead of the prince. She wondered what her father would say if he were there. She felt a sharp pang of loss.

"Excuse me," Jaewon said. "Why are Seung and I here? We are not part of this prophecy."

Master Roshi and Brother Woojin seemed amused.

"My son," Master Roshi said. "Your fate has led you here. Your destiny is now intertwined with that of your friends."

Suddenly, Kwan leaped to his feet, startling Kira.

"Why would you assume that Taejo is the one? My brother, Kira, and I are also descendants!" Kwan said.

"None of you are royalty. The One will unite the kingdoms. He will be the future king. Prince Taejo is a direct descendant from both his maternal and paternal lines. King Dang's blood runs deep in his veins," Brother Woojin said. "He is the reason I went to Hansong."

"Wait," Kira interrupted. "Please forgive me, Sunim, but Prince Taejo is just a child! How can he be the Dragon Musado? *Musado* means 'great warrior.' It would make more sense if the Musado was our uncle, the king of Guru."

"Kira's right," Taejo said, sinking down into his seat. "I'm not a warrior. I'm only twelve."

"There is a chance that I am wrong. That is why, before the start of the last month, I will lead you to the Dragon King's birth cave in the Diamond Mountains to seek out the first of the treasures. If I'm correct, then I believe the treasure will reveal itself to you as the true Dragon Musado," Brother Woojin said. "Until then, you will stay here at the temple, where it is safe. The Demon Lord is also seeking the Musado. We must not let him find you."

Kira caught sight of her cousin's face. *Look at him, just a scared kid. How could they think he's the Musado? He can barely take care of himself.*

She gave his arm a comforting squeeze. "Never fear, little cousin," she said. "I will always protect you."

As she rose to her feet, she caught Master Roshi's intense gaze.

"Remember," he called out to her, "unlike Brother Woojin, I am not convinced that the prince is the Dragon Musado."

18

The next day they held a *jesa*, the ritual memorial feast for King Yuri and General Kang. The three cousins dressed in white hemp funeral robes. They unbound their hair to signify their grief. The itchy fabric of the robe chafed at Kira's neck and wrists, an added reminder of the pain of loss that always ached inside her.

The monks chanted in rhythmic harmony as disciples rang bells. Master Roshi raised his arms to the air and made an invocation to the heavens. He then invited Kwan to step forward as chief mourner.

Kira's throat tightened. A new wave of grief washed over her as she watched her brother step into the role that her father had always played in memorial services for their ancestors.

The jesa rituals had never meant anything to Kira until now. Today, her father would not be there to help her light the incense. She would not hear his rich voice chanting the ancestral prayer and inviting the spirits to dine with them. Her mother would not help serve the meal afterward.

She missed her mother and worried about what was happening to her. Was she all right? Was she hurt? Was she still alive? It was the not knowing that agonized her.

When the temple bell began to toll, the monks led them through the doors and into the shrine.

Two altars stood side by side, piled high with five rows of food and a large bowl of rice wine at the end.

"Kira, Taejo," Kwan called to them. "It's time."

From the small pouch she always wore close to her heart, Kira pulled out her little haetae. Kwan had inscribed the names of their father and uncle on paper mounted onto wooden tablets and positioned at the heads of the altars. She set the figurine in front of her father's tablet while Taejo left a beautiful ivory-hilted dagger, an eleventh-birthday present from the king, in front of his father's. Before each altar stood a large copper incense urn filled with sand.

They each lit a stick of incense and placed it in the urn. Long, smoky tendrils wafted up into the air in serpentine spirals. Kwan and Taejo poured cups of rice wine and placed them in front of the personal mementos. Kwan uncovered a rice bowl and stuck a pair of silver chopsticks into the rice, letting them stand like a pair of incense sticks. Taejo repeated the same movements on his father's altar.

All of them stood and bowed twice before each altar, genuflecting completely, their foreheads touching the floor.

Suddenly, Kira heard a voice calling to her. Raising her head, she peered at her little haetae. It seemed to shimmer in the candlelight. Her father's smiling face flashed before her.

"Father?" she whispered. "Father, are you here?"

The haetae continued to shine before her, as if in answer to her question. As if to tell her that everything would be all right.

My little tiger.

Kira pressed her face against the cool wood of the shrine floor, and cried for her father.

Kwan left the next day to search for Captain Pak. He was sure the captain and his men had survived the attack and would be seeking the temple. Since Kira needed to stay with the prince, Jaewon and Seung agreed to go with Kwan.

Kira found the valley quiet and peaceful and deadly boring. To keep herself busy, she trained with the monks. Their warrior-like drills were as rigorous as anything her father would put her and her brothers through. They didn't use swords, and archery was only for target practice, but the monks were still dangerous foes.

As the only female, the monks had given her a small room at the very end of the dormitory building. She was a solitary person by nature, more inclined to listen rather than speak. It was not unusual for her to feel alone even in the most crowded of places. Her differences had always kept her apart. But a new kind of loneliness had crept into her soul. She missed the familiar normalcy of her life— the noisy training of the saulabi, the chattering gossip of the servants, the ebb and flow of the palace routine.

After seven days of forced confinement, Kira couldn't stand it anymore. She had to get out. She went to find Brother Woojin.

The monk was in the garden, meditating under the shade of her favorite gingko tree. She sat cross-legged in front of him and waited for him to acknowledge her presence.

"Young mistress, how may I serve you?" he asked.

"Sunim, when will we be ready to seek the first treasure?"

He folded his hands in his lap. "The time is not yet right. We must wait until the end of the eleventh month of this year."

Kira's body sagged in disappointment. It was only the sixteenth day of the tenth month.

"I know it is hard for someone as used to action as

you are to sit and wait, but the time will go quickly. You must be patient."

She bowed in agreement, hiding her dismay. Cooped up like a prisoner within the temple walls, she felt sucked dry of energy and happiness. Desperate, she reached for any excuse she could think of to attain some freedom.

"Sunim, would it be all right to take the prince on a local hunt? It has been a while since we've had any meat, and I'd like to catch some game for us," she said.

"Yes, it must be difficult for you meat eaters," he said. "Although none of our monks can help you with your hunt, I will make sure you have a guide."

Kira bowed in thanks and left, anxious to share the plans with Taejo and prepare for the hunt.

Taejo appeared at Kira's door, dressed in his leather hunting armor and boots. His sword was slung on his back along with a bow and arrows borrowed from the monks. In his hands, he carried his father's hunting spear.

"I'm going to catch me a big boar today!" he shouted.

"No," Kira said. "We're not attempting a boar. It's too dangerous, besides being a terrible waste since we can't bring it to the temple. We catch only what we can eat."

Taejo looked disappointed, but just for a moment. "Can I bring it anyway?" he asked.

Kira nodded and filled their water pouches and packed rice balls wrapped in dried seaweed. She'd toyed with the idea of leaving Taejo behind, but the monks said the hunt would be safe as long as they stayed within the shadow of the mountain. Besides, with all that he'd been through, a simple hunt would raise his spirits.

"Your Highness and young mistress," Brother Insu said as he approached them. "The light within me shines to meet the light within the both of you."

Kira was delighted to see the gentle monk from Kaya. He was one of Kira's favorite temple companions. Whatever she needed, Brother Insu always tried to provide.

Today, he was to be their guide. As soon as Kira entered the stable, Jindo bounded around their feet. It was hard to believe the dog had suffered a recent injury.

Leading their horses, they passed through the long passageway to the stone door. Several monks lifted up the heavy latch and pulled the door open. Kira, Taejo, and Brother Insu followed the narrow trail that snaked down the mountainside to the edge of the forest.

The morning sun was bright, but the woods remained fairly dark. A chilly wind blew hard along the floor of the forest, stirring up the fallen leaves and sending them into a frantic whirlwind of crackling colors. Protected within the confines of the temple valley, Kira had forgotten how cold it got in the mountains. Autumn was changing into winter. She wished she'd brought a heavy coat.

They reached a small clearing alongside a rushing stream. Brother Insu dismounted and tied his horse to a low-hanging branch.

"I will set up camp here," he said. "This area should

be sufficient for your needs. As long as you stay close to the stream, you will have no problems finding me again. But remember, stay within the shadow of the mountain and be very quiet. Sound carries a great distance in these woods."

"Thank you, Sunim," Kira said.

Brother Insu bowed. "May you return as you leave, in peace and harmony."

Kira and Taejo left their horses with Brother Insu and began trekking upstream. They took with them their water pouches and weapons. Kira also carried a small satchel with food and supplies.

They hiked silently for a short distance. Taking a deep breath, she caught the musky odor of wild ginseng. Following her nose to a shaded section, she spotted large, leafy plants with small red berries sprouting on top.

She knelt before the plant and gently dug it up, pulling out a long, knobby root with tendrils. Cutting off the leafy stems, she placed the ginseng carefully in her bag and rose to her feet.

"Who's that for?" Taejo asked.

"I thought we could give it to Brother Insu as a thank-you."

They moved deeper into the forest, Jindo padding ahead of them, his ears alert as he sniffed the air. The big dog froze, one paw raised in midstep as he scrutinized a thick bush. Kira readied her bow and signaled for Taejo to keep quiet. Jindo rushed into the shrubs, flushing out a small white hare. Taejo shot his arrow, missing his target as it zigzagged back into the thick underbrush.

Taejo yelled and charged after the hare. Cursing under her breath, Kira chased after him when she noted the strong odor of a wild animal. A group of boars and piglets fled past her, shrieking in outrage. She hurried forward only to stop short.

Taejo stood petrified before the largest boar Kira had ever seen.

19

The boar charged at Taejo. Snarling and barking, Jindo came rushing up from behind Kira and launched himself at the animal's throat, trying to wrestle the fierce creature to the ground. It bucked high, flinging Jindo over its back. Taejo pulled out his hunting spear and tried to stab the boar.

"No, Taejo!"

The boar slammed into Taejo, who fell backward and landed with a heavy thud. Quickly, he jumped to his feet and ran toward Kira, the boar close behind him.

Dropping her bow and satchel, Kira raced to meet him. "Throw me the spear!"

Catching it out of the air, she raised the spear high past

her ear and stepped right into the path of the maddened animal. It made a deep, ugly grunt before attacking. At the last possible moment, she leaped aside, slashing down with her right arm, aiming for the left flank. The blade pierced through the heavy hide. The boar's high-pitched shrieking turned into a scream as it vaulted away, ripping the spear from Kira's hands.

Grabbing Taejo by his collar, she dragged him all the way over to a large maple tree and rapidly pushed him onto the overhanging branches. "Climb up and stay there! That's an order!"

"Look out!" Taejo screamed.

The boar was rushing toward them. Holding the hilt of her sword with two hands, she stabbed at an angle, deep into its neck. Leaving her sword where it was, Kira then grabbed hold of the spear still protruding from the boar's left side. Using all her might, she launched her body onto the spear and she shoved it deep into the animal. Its front legs buckled under her weight, until finally it fell.

She looked up at Taejo.

"You all right?" she asked.

He started and looked around for Jindo. Not far away, the great white dog lay against the trunk of a cypress tree. Taejo jumped down and scrambled over to him.

Kira retrieved her bloody sword and spear. Glancing around to make sure there were no other boars or predators in the area, she ran to grab her belongings. They'd made a lot of noise. Even Brother Insu back at the camp had to have heard the battle with the boar. She hurried over to Taejo, who was checking Jindo for injuries. Jindo yawned and rose to his feet. Kira knelt before him and patted his head, receiving a lick from his raspy tongue.

Kira rummaged through her bag for a clean cloth and camellia oil to clean her blade.

"You did it!" Taejo said with pride. "Can you believe the size of that thing?"

Kira put her sword in its sheath and leaned against the trunk of the cypress tree.

"I think that boar was harder to kill than a demon," she said.

"Thank you, Noona, for saving me." He paused. "Again." His eyes were teary. Kira knew he was thinking of all they had lost.

"Come on," she said. "Let's carve a portion for us."

She rose to her feet and was immediately overwhelmed by the odor of approaching demons. She yanked Taejo up and pushed him behind her, freeing her sword in one fluid movement.

Jindo growled.

From the depths of the darkened forest, a small contingent of mounted soldiers appeared, surrounding them.

"Shin Bo Hyun?" Kira said in disbelief.

Her fiancé gazed back at them, a slight smile playing on his lips.

20

"Your Highness," Shin Bo Hyun said. He dismounted and bowed. His men fanned out behind him, filling the clearing before them.

"Thank the heavens we've found you both!" he said. "We've been searching these woods for days to no avail. How fortunate we were to hear the ruckus that led us here."

Kira took a close look at the thirty-odd men in Shin Bo Hyun's company. They were Yamato soldiers disguised in Hansong uniforms, with at least four demons in their ranks. She spied the slight shimmer in the air above them, the telltale sign of an otherworldly being in the human world. Jindo was by her side, barking and snarling. With no horses and the soldiers closing in around them, she could see no possible escape. She wondered if the young lord knew of the demons among his men. They held no loyalty to humans, unless called by one, and even then, it was an uneasy truce. Shin Bo Hyun was no shaman—he would find it hard to control them. Perhaps she could use this to her advantage.

Her eyes darted about, taking note of her bow and arrow case a short distance away. Taejo stepped forward to stand by her side.

"What do you want?" he asked, his voice filled with hostility.

"I'm to take you to the queen," Shin Bo Hyun replied. "She's been so worried about you."

In the background, loud noises indicated approaching horsemen. Shin Bo Hyun signaled to his men, and several moved off to investigate. Not long after, Brother Woojin and a group of temple monks appeared. Brother Insu rode behind them, leading Kira and Taejo's horses.

Catching sight of Shin Bo Hyun and his men, the group stopped. Brother Woojin looked unsurprised.

"Greetings, Sunim!" Shin Bo Hyun said. "I'm relieved to see you again. It was my understanding that your party was to head to Stone Temple, but I was unable to find any trace of you there."

"Good day, my lord," Brother Woojin replied. "I'm sure you can understand our state of panic and distress at the time. We feared Stone Temple was too close in proximity to the enemy, and it was our mission to keep the prince as safe as possible."

He gazed at Shin Bo Hyun and then at Kira. "But how fortuitous to find you here," the monk continued. "What news do you have of our kingdom?"

Shin Bo Hyun frowned. "It is sad news. Our king is dead, as is Lady Kira's brave father."

He hesitated before turning somber eyes to Kira. "Kira, I'm afraid to tell you that your mother perished in the attack."

Kira stilled her body even as her mind reeled at his words. She didn't believe him. Couldn't believe him. *But,* a small voice inside of her said, *the court ladies were jumping off the cliff.* She shook her head. No, she didn't believe him.

"The kingdom is in disarray. But we were able to evacuate Her Majesty to safety. I have been tasked with finding the prince and my betrothed, and bringing them to her."

Taejo started forward at the incredible news, but Kira held him back.

"Tasked by who? Your uncle? The traitor?" Kira demanded to know.

"No, by the queen," Shin Bo Hyun answered.

"Where is the queen? Who is with her?" Brother Woojin asked.

"My men are keeping her safe. They are pushing north to Guru, but it has been slow going due to the queen's health."

"What do you mean? Is she sick? What's the matter with my mother?" Taejo shouted.

"She is not physically sick, Your Highness. It is more of an emotional malady she suffers from. One that I'm sure will be cured with your safe return," Shin Bo Hyun said.

"I must go to her." Taejo tried to break free of Kira's hold.

"No. He's lying. Don't believe anything he says," Kira said in a low voice.

Shin Bo Hyun stared at her, a shadow of regret passing over his face. "The truth is that I must deliver the prince to his mother."

"My apologies, but I can't allow that," Brother Woojin said.

The young lord faced the monk. "I'm afraid there's nothing you can do to stop me. You've been completely surrounded since the moment you arrived."

Shin Bo Hyun's soldiers had circled behind the monks. Brother Woojin was not fazed. His penetrating glance brought Kira to the balls of her feet, ready and waiting.

"And so have you," Brother Woojin replied.

And with that, a swarm of monks attacked the soldiers, flying down from the trees and seemingly out of the air. Armed only with their long staffs, the monks knocked soldiers off their horses and circled Kira and the prince.

Shin Bo Hyun cursed and drew his sword as he wheeled around to face them. Right before him stood the little monk, who'd moved with lightning speed.

"Sunim! There are several demons within the enemy's ranks. They'll be impossible to stop without a sword," Kira called.

"Then you must take the prince to safety!" Brother Woojin said, standing firm in a defensive posture.

Kira grabbed her bow and arrow case as they ran away, her sword still at the ready. They did not get far when a Yamato soldier attacked them. Kira parried his blows as Jindo rushed his feet, knocking him to the ground. Enraged, the soldier jumped up and drew a dagger. Brother Woojin smashed the soldier in the head with his long staff.

"Hurry! You must make for the temple!"

Kira nodded and kept Taejo close by her side. She scanned the area, searching for the horses. She heard Shin Bo Hyun shouting as he fought off two monks.

"Young mistress! Over here!" Brother Insu waved them over.

They raced toward Brother Insu when a demon soldier captured a young monk right before them, sending the horses into panic.

Taejo was screaming. The demon soldier gorged upon the monk's liver as the monk begged the gods for mercy. She shot an arrow through the monk's head to end his suffering. The monster roared at them, still holding the limp body in its hands. Kira drew her sword and flashed forward, severing its neck.

Another demon soldier appeared before her. Kira could see right away that it was an older possession that had inhabited the human host for too long. Scaly gray hide shone through the flesh. It reached for the prince with a hand that was more claw than human. Kira slashed down with her sword, slicing the arm off at the elbow. With a reverse swing, she decapitated the creature.

Her senses finely attuned to the sickening stench of the unholy ones, she knocked Taejo to the ground with her foot as the momentum of her swing whirled her around to slice off the head of another demon that tried to sneak up on them.

Pulling her cousin up, she half dragged him toward the waiting horses. Up ahead, several soldiers appeared and raised their bows, preparing to shoot. Kira shoved Taejo to the ground and felt the whirring of an arrow whip past her ear. She deflected an arrow with her sword even as she felt the sharp burn in her left arm where another scored a hit.

Before they could shoot again, Shin Bo Hyun appeared, shouting at them.

"No, don't shoot!" He was too late. The arrow had already been released. Distracted by the young lord's actions, Kira didn't notice the danger until someone shoved her from behind. In slow motion, she saw Brother Woojin pierced with the arrow meant for her.

Kira dropped her sword and pulled out her bow, shooting off a rapid succession of arrows and felling several soldiers. She saw Shin Bo Hyun dash for cover behind a line of trees. She heard a choked sob. Taejo was holding the injured monk in his arms.

Around them, the others fought on, but the bodies of the temple monks littered the ground. Long staffs were no match for swords and demons.

"Young mistress, you must get the prince away from here!" Brother Woojin said as he tried to push the prince away. The arrow had punctured his left shoulder; bright red blood flowed from the injury, staining the fallen leaves below him. "Leave me!"

"I won't leave you!" Taejo shouted.

Before Kira could respond, a disfigured demon soldier lurched into view, heading straight for them.

"My master will be so pleased with me," it hissed. "Not only will I kill the missing prince, but I will dispose of the Demon Slayer also."

Kira stepped forward and blocked its path.

"You can try," she said. "But I don't think so."

Her words were quickly put to the test by the powerful double-sword attack the creature let loose on her. It took all her strength to defend herself. She was tired from the previous boar hunt, and her left arm was on fire from her injury. The blood had coursed down her arm, making her hands slick. Barely deflecting a killing blow, Kira staggered back.

Just when she thought she couldn't hold out much longer, a sword slashed through the demon's neck, decapitating it.

Shin Bo Hyun spit at the widening pool of black sludge pouring from the corpse. He kicked the deflating body of the demon before stepping over it. He grinned at her surprise. "You looked like you needed some help," he said.

"Why? He was one of yours!"

Shin Bo Hyun's face darkened. "No. I had no idea there were demons among my soldiers. I would never have allowed it."

"I don't believe you," Kira said. She picked up her sword and held it before her two-handed, praying that more help was on its way. Behind her, Taejo seemed oblivious to everything but the wounded monk.

Shin Bo Hyun stepped closer. "It doesn't matter. I'll forgive you." He stopped to take in the tableau before him. "Are you ready to return with us, Your Highness?" he asked.

"I will never go anywhere with you!" Taejo shouted. "I'll kill you first!"

"How many more lives must be lost before you recognize the futility of your actions?" Shin Bo Hyun asked.

"Yours will be the next," Kira responded, raising her sword high.

Shin Bo Hyun held up his hand. "Kira, you are my

betrothed. Please put down your sword and join me at my side. It is, after all, where you belong."

"I am not your betrothed and I will never join you!"

"I beg to differ. The king and queen agreed to our betrothal. We are, in fact, engaged—and it is binding, unless you plan to dishonor your family," he said.

"Shin Bo Hyun! You're nothing but a traitor!"

"No, I'm not," Shin Bo Hyun replied in all seriousness. "I am completely loyal to my family, as are you. It is my uncle who is the traitor. I merely do his bidding."

"And by what perverted logic does that make you not a traitor?"

"We cannot choose our families, no more than we can choose what we look like. I may not like my uncle, or what he is doing. But I have no choice but to follow his orders." He pointed at her. "Like you. I know you. Loyalty to clan over loyalty to king, isn't that right?"

"My king is my clan!" she shouted at him.

Shin Bo Hyun sighed. "Let's not be obtuse."

Kira fought to keep her composure. "Your hypocrisy disgusts me. And frankly, I don't understand why in the world you would want to marry a woman who plans on killing you."

"Ah, but it is so much more exciting that way!"

Kira rushed forward, aiming for his neck. Their swords met with a loud clash of steel. Shin Bo Hyun blocked and pushed her sword to the side. She instantly backed off, aware that she was fighting in anger. She'd forgotten how good a swordsman he was—as good as her brothers.

He smiled. "Your eyes glow like the brightest gold when you are angry. I can't wait to see how they will look in our marriage bed."

Disgust rose like bile in her throat. She charged, striking blow after blow as the young lord blocked and pushed back, but he did not take the offensive. Why wasn't he attacking? Why was he playing with her?

Rage made her sloppy. She twisted her sword sideways and thrust at his rib cage. He parried her strike to the side and grabbed her sword hilt with his left hand.

"Don't you realize that you are mine?" he asked. He quickly disarmed her and held her tight in his embrace. "Now, Kira, let's go home."

21

Kira stared up at him in shock, noting how his eyes seemed both fierce and tender. She slammed her forehead into his chin. He yelped in surprise and loosened his grip.

A sudden shout erupted from Taejo as he hurled himself at Shin Bo Hyun, his short sword slashing the young lord across his arm. Cursing, Shin Bo Hyun blocked Taejo's wild blows and then knocked away his sword.

Kira kicked at Shin Bo Hyun's legs just as Jindo attacked his left arm. The lord fell backward and then flipped himself over, away from Kira and the dog.

From the woods came the sound of an approaching army. Kira was relieved to see Kwan and Captain Pak, leading a force of fifty genuine Hansong soldiers.

Captain Pak flung himself from his horse and with his twin blades drawn, challenged Shin Bo Hyun.

"Ah, the good captain arrives in time to save the day!" Shin Bo Hyun said.

The combatants circled each other and struck, their swords scraping and clanging in a discordant din. Even wounded, Shin Bo Hyun was a formidable adversary.

All around them, the tide of the battle turned as Shin Bo Hyun's men were overcome by the new soldiers.

"Noona! Help me!" Taejo cried out.

Brother Woojin's face was gray and his eyes remained closed. Gathering up the loose fabric of his robe, she pressed it around the arrow shaft.

Kira looked up to see that Pak had disarmed Shin Bo Hyun, but the other man got hold of a fallen staff and bashed Pak in the face before retreating.

Shin Bo Hyun whistled for his horse and in seconds he was mounted. He gazed one last time at Kira before riding away. She was stunned by his look of deep unhappiness. Even more troubling was the recognition that a small part of her was glad he was escaping.

The captain threw a frustrated glance at Shin Bo Hyun before rushing to their side.

"I thought you were dead!" Taejo said.

"Here, let me help, Your Highness," the captain said, taking off his leather gloves as he pressed his hands over the monk's wound.

All color had leached away from Brother Woojin's face. His eyes fluttered to gaze up at them.

"Sunim! You saved us," Kira said.

"But now, this is your job alone," he replied. "You must protect Taejo always."

"Don't talk, Sunim. Save your strength," Captain Pak said.

"No, listen to me, there is no time. The temple is no longer safe for the young prince. You cannot return there. He must be kept safe." Brother Woojin gasped, visibly weakened. "Take him to the last of his family, King Eojin of Guru. Ask for my fellow monk, Brother Boyuk. He will help you."

"Sunim!" Taejo cried. "Please don't die!"

Brother Woojin called Kira's name. She leaned over so he could see her.

"Young mistress," he whispered. "Protect him with your life, or all will be lost."

"On my honor," she said.

A soldier approached the captain and spoke quietly to him. Captain Pak nodded and rose to his feet.

"Your Highness, the enemy has been routed. But we must leave soon. These woods are not safe for you."

Taejo didn't move. He held on tight to his tutor's hand.

"I won't leave Sunim!"

"You must," Brother Woojin said. He winced in pain.

"The monks will take him back to the temple," Captain

Pak said kindly. He signaled to his men. They helped the prince to his feet and guided him away.

Kira was overcome with pain and guilt. They should have stayed in the temple. She should never have taken the prince on a hunt. She gazed at the carnage. The smooth heads and gray robes of the temple monks littered the forest floor. Survivors were praying over their lost brethren.

Some of the dead were monks she had sparred with, eaten meals with. They had laughed, sung, and prayed together. But now they were gone. Tears seeped through her tightly shut eyes. She'd made a grave miscalculation, and many people had died because of it.

"Kang Kira, you're wounded! Let me help you." Jaewon put out a hand to help her, but she ignored it.

"It's all my fault," she said. Unable to bear his sympathy, she walked away.

She stopped short when she came upon a still figure propped up against an ancient tree stump. It was Brother Insu, his open eyes fixed in death. A sharp pain shot through her chest.

She knelt at his side. "I'm so sorry," she whispered. She placed a trembling hand over his eyes, closing them forever.

22

The savory smell of roasting meat filled the air. They had ridden for hours before making camp by the banks of an unfamiliar river. Kira sat under heavy furs, trying to warm up. Her left arm had been tightly bandaged but still throbbed in pain. Taejo was rolled up in his blankets, Jindo panting softly by his side. Kwan and Jaewon were also nearby, enjoying the fire. Kira sensed Jaewon gazing at her, but she avoided him.

Taejo sat up. "Where are we?"

"We are some one hundred and fifty *li* east of the temple, still in Tongey territory," Jaewon replied. "You were fast asleep, easy to transport. In fact, easier than the enormous boar you hunted."

"How did you carry it?" Taejo asked.

"Ah, the efficiency of the Hansong soldier!" Captain Pak said, coming up from behind to pat his shoulder. "We don't leave meat behind, if we can help it. We butchered the carcass, then wrapped the meat in maple leaves and cloth. We kept the skin intact for you. Perhaps when we get to the northern kingdom, we'll find a tanner."

Taejo shrugged at the captain's words. He squeezed between Kira and Kwan in front of the fire as Seung passed wooden bowls of food to everyone. The meat was rich, the juices soaking into the rice and barley below it, but it could have been bark for all the pleasure it gave Kira. She ate to fill her stomach, uncaring of what she placed in her mouth.

When she was done, she looked at her companions. Her brother sat hunched over, staring into the fire, while Jaewon and Seung ate quietly nearby. The captain sat across from her, eating ravenously.

"Thank you for coming to our aid today. How did you escape from the Yamatos?" she asked.

"These soldiers here were part of the Hansong garrison deployed to the Jinhan Kingdom," Pak said. "When Jinhan fell, their commanding officer charged them to return home and protect our capital. But it was too late—Hansong had already fallen. Fortunately for me, they came to my rescue during the Yamato attack where we parted."

"My oldest brother, Kyoung," Kira said. "He was deployed to Jinhan. Have you seen him?"

Pak shook his head. "I haven't seen him, but don't worry, young mistress. Word is that he made it safe out of Jinhan and is traveling north."

Kira was relieved to hear Kyoung was alive.

"We were very fortunate today," she said. "How were you able to find us?"

"You must thank your brother, for he is the one who led us to you," the captain said.

Kwan was studying his bowl, his face grim. It was unusual for him to be so quiet. He'd not spoken a word to Kira since his return. Something was wrong, but Kira was afraid to find out what it could be.

Jaewon cleared his throat and spoke up. "The gods are definitely watching over you both," he said. "We met up with the captain and all his new men not too far from the river crossing."

"Fortunate indeed! We had no way of finding the temple without you!" Captain Pak interjected.

Jaewon nodded and continued his tale. "When we reached the mountains, the monks were already on a search mission because of a troubling vision Master Roshi had. He sent us after the others. That's how we found you."

"Do you have any news about Hansong? About my mother?" Taejo cut in.

Jaewon hesitated and glanced at the captain.

Captain Pak leaned forward, resting his elbows on

his knees. "We were able to gather some news from locals and fleeing refugees. Your mother, the queen, is a prisoner of Lord Shin, who has proclaimed himself the king of Hansong. She is being kept in the dungeons until she agrees to marry him."

"She will never marry that murderous traitor!" Taejo shouted.

"She may not have a choice," Captain Pak said. "They have threatened to kill you if she does not. The only reason she hasn't agreed is because she knows they haven't captured you yet."

Taejo jumped to his feet and began to pace. "We have to rescue her," he said. "We must go back!"

"You know that's impossible," Kira said.

"No, it's not! I command you to take me!" Taejo raised his voice. "My father's dead; I won't let them kill my mother, too!"

Kira and the captain both rose, trying to calm him down, but Taejo was hysterical.

"If you will not take me, I'll go myself! I don't need any of you!"

"*No!*" Kwan shouted. He slammed his bowl down on the ground, the remaining food splattering everywhere. "Don't be stupid! If you went home and were captured, the queen would wed Lord Shin just to save you. He would become rightful king of Hansong. And then he would kill you anyway, just as he has killed everyone else."

His anguish made Kira freeze in place, remembering

what Shin Bo Hyun had said. She had not believed him.

"No. Not Mother," she whispered. She approached her brother. "Where's Mother? What happened?"

"She's dead," he said. Kira could see her brother blinking back his tears. "They killed her, and I wasn't there to help her."

It was so much worse to know the truth. Something was pressing on her chest, making it hard to breathe.

She gripped her brother's arm. "Oppa, it's not true," she said. "Please tell me it's not true."

Kwan lifted his eyes, revealing his grief. "It's all my fault, Kira. I should have left the prince with you and gone back for Mother. But I didn't. And now she's dead. It's all my fault."

He pushed her away and bolted from camp.

"Oppa!" Kira ran after him, but he disappeared into the woods. She wandered along the perimeter of camp until she reached the river and sat on a log half buried in the bank, wishing all of this were just a nightmare she would wake from. Her mother was not a soldier. She should have been safe. Kira saw again the procession of colorful hanboks falling from the cliffs into the Han River.

When the tears came, she shook with anger and grief. She stuffed a fist into her mouth to smother her sobs. The crescent moon was high overhead before the storm within her subsided.

Someone came and sat next to her. Kira was surprised

to see Jaewon staring into the murky waters before them. They sat together for a long while. Kira counted the erratic beats of her broken heart until they steadied to a slow, ponderous rhythm. Her sigh came out in a little hiccup as she looked up at the clear, indigo sky.

"My parents are both in heaven now looking down upon us," she said. Her voice sounded raspy. A cold wind shook the bare limbs of the trees above them. She began to chew on a fingernail, ripping it painfully from its nail bed.

Jaewon finally spoke.

"I, too, have grieved more than I thought I could bear. So much so that I didn't think I could survive."

His eyes were dark and bleak in the moonlight.

"What happened?" she asked.

Jaewon's eyes shone with pain. "It's not something I can talk about. But it haunts me every waking hour of my life. I lost someone I loved very much, and it was all my fault. His blood is forever on my hands. There is nowhere I can hide from my guilt, and I live every day with the pain of his loss."

She couldn't stand to see the suffering in his face. It filled her with a strong compulsion to touch and soothe him. She didn't like the sensation—it was far too confusing.

She jumped to her feet, trying to place some distance between them. Jaewon followed after her, a look of concern on his face.

"Kang Kira," he began.

"I have to go—"

"I'm sorry," he said.

She walked away, trying to forget the sadness she'd seen on Jaewon's face.

23

The group headed north, toward Guru, early the next morning. Mountains rose and valleys dipped, and brightly colored flora flew past their tired eyes.

Taejo was avoiding both of his cousins, preferring to ride with Jaewon and Seung. Since Kwan's outburst, Taejo had withdrawn into himself.

Kira left him alone, understanding he needed privacy. She also stayed away from Kwan, who refused to talk to her, too lost in his own depression. For Kira, it took all her might not to fall into despair. Visions of her parents mixed with memories of Brother Insu and of a forest floor littered with dead monks. She prayed that Brother

Woojin would survive his wounds, for she didn't think she could handle any more guilt.

By midmorning, they arrived in the mountainous terrain of the Oakcho kingdom. On the side of the road, at the foot of a large hill, they passed a group of *jangseungs* planted in a long row. Unlike the stone jangseungs that peppered the Hansong Kingdom, these were long planks of pine with heads carved at the top. The word Oakcho and directions to its capital, Sori, were written on one of the planks.

The well-traveled dirt road behind the jangseungs was teeming with people, walking, riding, or pushing wheelbarrows full of all their belongings. Many of them looked tired, as if they had been traveling for days. Kira saw a couple leading an ox, which carried two small children and a large basket strapped to its back.

So many people, she thought. All of us homeless.

Their arrival caused panic at first, people retreating in fright. It was only as they recognized the colors of the soldiers' uniforms that the travelers returned to their path.

Captain Pak waved down the driver of a wagon drawn by an old horse. In the cart sat an elderly couple, huddled together under a blanket, and a mother with three children, the youngest sitting in her lap.

"Grandfather, where do you hail from?" Captain Pak asked.

The driver gazed warily at the captain. "We come

from the Jinhan Kingdom. The Yamatos burned down our villages and destroyed our lands. They took all our food and left us with nothing. We go north to seek asylum."

As the captain questioned the man, Kira moved closer, noticing the mother's pallor and how the toddler in her arms shivered under a thin blanket. Pulling out an extra blanket from her bag, she rode closer.

"Here, why don't you take this to wrap the baby," Kira said, holding it out to the woman.

The mother's grateful smile changed to horror when she saw Kira's face. She shook her head and turned away.

Kira chastised herself for forgetting her place. People would always hate her.

Suddenly, Captain Pak was by her side. She caught his concerned expression as he took the blanket from her and handed it to the mother.

"Take it," he ordered. "Don't let your silly superstitions harm your baby!"

With a frightened nod, she took the blanket and wrapped it tight around her child.

As Kira and the captain rode away to rejoin their forces, he said, "Don't mind them; it's just ignorance."

Kira let out a bitter laugh. "There seems to be a lot of ignorance in the world."

The captain nodded. "But you can change that, one person at a time."

Kira pondered over his meaning. She'd never tried to change anyone's opinion of her. Was he saying that it was up to her? It seemed an impossible and ridiculous task, and yet his words stayed with her for a long time.

The darkness was absolute and terrifying. Kira lifted her hands in front of her face, but could see nothing. She blinked hard and rubbed her eyes. Still, the dark pressed her from all sides. Never before had she been so blind. She tried to walk forward, taking baby steps, over the brittle, uneven terrain. Tripping, she fell on her knees, her hands landing on hard fragments of what felt like bone. Kira took a deep breath, trying to calm herself. She had no idea where she was.

"Oppa? Taejo?" Her voice echoed. There was no response. On her feet again, she kept moving forward, her hands before her, hoping to make contact with something. It seemed an eternity before she touched the cold, slimy surface of a wall. Grasping at it like a lifeline, she kept one hand on the surface and moved as fast as possible.

The darkness began to lighten as she rounded the bend. Red flickers distorted the shadows that leaped across the floor of the large cavern. A low, rhythmic chanting raised the hairs on her arms. The shadows elongated as something began to approach, disappearing as the flickering lights filled the cavern. Dark and misshapen creatures lurched toward her, red eyes gleaming over fangs bared in openmouthed grimaces.

Kira tried to run away, but behind her, more of the same creatures appeared. They rushed forward, gathering her up with long, pointed talons that dug into her flesh. The creatures raised Kira off her feet and into a prone position, their claws gripping so hard she couldn't move. Screams choked out of her throat as she struggled to free herself. She could see nothing but the shadows that flickered across the walls and ceiling. Her terror was uncontrollable, agonizing. She had no idea where they were taking her or what they were going to do. All she knew was the overriding fear of something worse than death.

Fire shot up from the ground like geysers, and all around them fiendish figures danced about in wild abandon. Kira screamed again, over and over, but her screams excited the demons further, sending them into a rampage as they clawed her clothes and raked sharp talons against her flesh. Ahead, a figure grew to immense proportions in the midst of the dancing creatures. She knew immediately what it was: the Demon Lord.

Grayish-black skin gleamed as it filled her vision entirely, until all she saw before her was a face. Black eyes with red pupils stared at her while the great slash of a mouth turned into a large, gaping hole that pulled itself into a bizarre semblance of a smile. This creature looked nothing like she'd imagined. It was far worse.

Kira looked into the black eyes and found horror and death staring back at her. She tore her gaze away and saw the cavern had changed into a battlefield. Kwan and Jaewon fought Yamato soldiers of incredible speed and strength.

One soldier looked directly at her, his skin melting away to reveal the demon underneath. Grinning, the demon stabbed Jaewon through his abdomen, while other creatures dragged Kwan from view.

The battlefield went up in a blaze of fire and then burned out to reveal Taejo alone, surrounded and outnumbered, but fighting bravely. A horde of half-breed soldiers rushed him all at once, engulfing Taejo until he disappeared.

"Taejo!" Kira screamed. "Taejo!"

She turned to the Demon Lord. "What do you want?"

The monster laughed. Smoke billowed from its mouth.

"The end of you all!" it replied, the voice bellowing as the enormous mouth grew larger and closer, until it surrounded her in darkness.

Kira woke with a scream lodged in her throat to find Jaewon shaking her by the shoulders.

"You were having a nightmare," he said. "I thought it best to wake you."

She wrapped her arms around her knees and buried her face within the hollow.

"Do you want to talk about it?" he asked, still crouched by her side.

Kira shook her head, still frightened by the dream and the darkness all about them.

"I'm scared," she said.

He pulled up a blanket and wrapped it around her.

Slowly, Kira started to relax. They sat close together, staring up at the starry sky above.

"What's going to happen to us?" she asked in a low voice.

"No one can know," he replied. "But I will be there by your side."

Something in the way he spoke brought back the mixed feelings from before, irking her.

"Ugh, you sound so mushy," she said, pushing him away.

He looked offended.

"What do you mean?"

She shrugged. "I don't know. You're acting too nice," she said.

He paused. "I'm sorry. I'll try to be meaner from now on." He shoved her hard, knocking her sideways. "Was that better?"

She grinned as she sat up.

"Pathetic," she scoffed. "I know grandmas stronger than you."

"I'm not offended by that; my grandmother is the scariest woman I know."

"Coward."

"Ya! You're not that tough," he said. "You'd be scared of her, too!"

Kira laughed at his mock anger. Jaewon's face lit up with a smile, his eyes catching the glow of the fire.

"I love looking at your eyes," he said. "They remind me of honey and summer."

She was startled by his compliment.

"You're strange," she said. "Most people are scared of me."

"Idiots!" he said.

"They're not all idiots," she said.

"Yes, they are!" Jaewon was emphatic. "These are the same people who think it's a good idea to treat a wound with horse manure."

"Disgusting!" she said. "So you're comparing me to horse manure?"

Jaewon sputtered in denial, and Kira laughed.

"You should try to go to sleep," he said. "Good night."

Lying down, she closed her eyes, but sleep would not come. She gazed over to where Jaewon lay close by. He had draped his arm casually across his eyes. His firm lips parted slightly as his chest rose and fell.

She couldn't help but compare him to Shin Bo Hyun. They were the same age but vast worlds apart. Yet they both claimed to find her attractive. Kira let out a frustrated groan. She didn't want to think this way. She was a soldier, not a simpering court lady.

She glanced over at Jaewon just as he turned to face her. The light from the fire flickered over his face, accentuating his perfect features. He lay in utter stillness, his eyes filled with the infinite sadness that always seemed a part of him.

"Sleep well, Kang Kira," he whispered.

24

The long and mountainous road they followed north had been a difficult one, but it was the safest leg of their travels. There'd been no demon attacks or sightings, only imp spies that had been taken care of by Kira. Rumors spread that the Yamatos had all retreated south to prepare for a full-scale attack. It explained why Shin Bo Hyun had not come after them.

Along the way, more and more displaced soldiers joined their forces. Men came out of hiding from all over the countryside. Some had been waging guerrilla warfare against the Yamatos. Others had wandered aimlessly until they heard of Taejo's army. They joined by the hundreds, some with full armor and weapons, others with only a sword or a homemade spear, all of them with one mission: to fight the Yamatos. But even with nearly a thousand soldiers surrounding them, Kira kept Taejo close to her at all times.

The second week of the eleventh month brought down the cold winds of the north. Half their nights were spent camping in frigid temperatures that left Kira frozen under her blankets. To keep Taejo warm, she slept next to him, with Jindo on his other side.

Twenty days later, they finally reached the legendary walls of Wando, the Guru capital. Kira was eager to see her mother's childhood home.

Wando was a great fortified city built into the mountains; its perimeter wall stretched beyond their sight. Protruding bulwarks were strategically placed for maximum defense, and the walls themselves were built with interlocking stone blocks, a technique perfected by the Gurus.

Outside the main gates of the capital city, they set up camp. Only Taejo, escorted by Captain Pak, Kira, and Kwan, would enter the city walls. As they approached the gates, Kira peered up at the bulwark. She made out the dark shapes of a dozen sentries.

Captain Pak addressed the palace guards. "The crown prince and heir to the throne of Hansong seeks an audience with his esteemed uncle, King Eojin. He is escorted by his cousins, the son and daughter of General Kang, niece and nephew to your king."

The armored guard bowed respectfully to Taejo before requesting identification. Taejo pulled out a gold chain that he usually kept tucked underneath his inner tunic. On the end of the chain hung a small gold seal bearing the phoenix crescent mark of the Hansong kings.

Inside the city, a soldier escorted them to the palace, which sat nestled into the mountainside.

Wando Palace was designed to suit the nature of the land it sat upon, mountainous terrain that lifted and dipped. It was built in complicated levels connected by flights of stone steps to a hallway that led to the grand pagoda. At the foot of the palace, their horses and Jindo were led away and they parted from the captain, who would return to his men.

Entering the magnificent building, Kira gazed about her. Multicolored tiles covered the entire length of the hallway, while intricately patterned ones adorned the ceilings above. Within the pagoda, the large, well-lit room had but one simple throne on a raised dais. To either side were corridors leading east and west. The wall behind the throne was a painted mural from floor to ceiling of what appeared to be a great battle on one side and a triumphant ceremony on the other.

A voice boomed from their left. "Welcome, my young clansmen!"

They bowed at the arrival of a tall, armored man

with a large entourage of soldiers and advisers. The king removed his gold-inscribed black iron helmet. He wore long vest armor over a black jacket. An ornate jeweled sword was strapped securely to his left side. Except for the mustache and trim beard, the handsome man bore a strong resemblance to Queen Ja-young.

The king came to stand directly before the prince, placing his hands on Taejo's shoulders.

"It's incredible!" King Eojin said. "No one can doubt your heritage!"

Eojin then turned to Kira. "I've heard so much about you. And now I see you in the flesh. The girl warrior who kills demons." He laughed. "You are not as fearful as the rumors make you out to be, but you are as beautiful as your mother."

Embarrassed, Kira flushed and looked down.

The king greeted Kwan with a broad smile. "Now, you are very much like your father!"

Kwan bowed, a look of pleasure on his face.

"Come, let us walk!" Eojin said, steering them down a spacious corridor. "It's been over twenty years since I've seen my beloved sisters, Yuwa and Ja-young." He paused and faced them. "My heart is heavy, as your arrival here confirms the news that I've just received from Hansong. I didn't want to believe it. I thought my sisters would be safe. How foolish I was. No one is safe now that the war has begun."

They followed him down a long corridor that led to a large inner room with a thick rush matting. Kira was relieved to see that it was an *ondol* room, with under-floor heating. She sighed with pleasure to sit on the warm floor, letting the heat soak into her chilled bones.

Eojin sat in the middle of the room with his legs crossed and his back perfectly straight. "We're so far north that word reaches us much slower than it should," he said. "Only recently did we hear of the fall of Kaya and the danger to the Jinhan Kingdom. I was worried for Hansong and thought to send an envoy down, but the Khitans have kept us busy."

"Who are the Khitans?" Taejo asked.

"Nomadic barbarians from the north that keep raiding our villages. They get bolder every year," Eojin said. "I myself have just returned from an extended tour of our northern borders. But before I could send anyone to Hansong, I heard the news. I would like to hear what transpired from the three of you directly."

Kira told their uncle of their return to Hansong and Taejo's rescue. Her throat closed up when she got to her father's death.

"Your Majesty? Will you help me rescue my mother?" Taejo asked.

Eojin patted Taejo on his shoulder. "Do not fear for your mother, my young prince. She is a strong Guru woman; they cannot break her. And this Lord Shin is smart enough to recognize her political importance. An alliance with your mother would mean an alliance with Guru. They won't harm her."

Eojin rose to his feet. The others followed suit.

"All of you must be very hungry. Let's get you some food."

"Your Majesty, is Brother Boyuk here?" Kira asked. "We were told to seek him out."

Eojin shook his head. "He was called away to his temple many days ago. I don't know when he'll return."

Disappointment rushed over Kira. What were they supposed to do now?

Their uncle took good care of them, providing them with luxurious rooms; new, warmer clothes; and even jasmine-perfumed bathing cakes from Cathay. After several hot baths, Kira finally felt human again.

A few days later, at their next meeting with Eojin, Kwan mentioned continuing Taejo's military training.

"Yes, this is very important," Eojin agreed. "In fact, I would like to take over his training."

Kira and Kwan looked at each other in astonishment, while Taejo beamed in excitement.

"If you have the time, Your Majesty," Kwan said.

"I will make the time," Eojin said. "Come, princeling, show me your bow skills!"

Taejo frowned. "I am not very good with a bow. I'm better with a sword," he admitted.

"In Guru, archery is our most prized skill," Eojin said. "Remember, only the gods are perfect, young one. For all others, practice brings mastery."

Kira watched as king and prince left together, easy in each other's company. "He seems to really like Taejo," she mused.

Kwan shrugged. "I think it's because Taejo reminds him of his son who died."

Eojin's first wife was a princess of Oakcho who died in childbirth, along with the baby. Then he married a Jinhan princess who bore him two sons and a daughter, but an influenza epidemic killed them all three years ago, along with the king's younger brothers. The king was spared because he was away battling the Khitans at the time. He returned home victorious, six months later, only to find his entire family gone. His oldest son was only ten years old when he died.

Kira liked her uncle, sensing his sharp intelligence and his aura of power. He was a mix of her aunt's assertiveness coupled with her mother's kindness. But once in a while, she sensed a cold ruthlessness in him. She didn't necessarily think it was a bad thing. After all, he was ruler of the largest kingdom in the peninsula. And it was clear that Taejo already idolized their uncle.

If she were to be completely honest, some of her uneasiness stemmed from jealousy. She felt supplanted by Eojin in Taejo's affections and she didn't like it.

Kira shook off her discomfort and asked Kwan to spar with her.

"I have a better idea," Kwan said. "Let's go train with Captain Pak."

Outside Wando, a huge tent city had been constructed. They found Captain Pak in an open field, where he had set up makeshift training grounds. Soldiers wearing a myriad of colored uniforms representing their different kingdoms sparred and trained in organized groups in every corner of the area.

Catching sight of Kwan and Kira, Captain Pak walked over to greet them.

"As you can see, I am keeping these men busy and ready for battle. We await the day that we march against the Yamatos. Do you bring any word from the Guru king?" Captain Pak asked.

When Kwan shook his head, Pak's face fell with disappointment.

"Well, we will continue to train hard and be prepared," he said. "I see you've both brought your bows with you. Care to train with us?"

Kwan nodded eagerly. "That's what I came down for. I feel like I'm getting soft without daily training. I'd ask to come stay here, but I fear my uncle wouldn't approve."

"That's as it should be," the captain replied. "Come then! You both will be a great help keeping our soldiers fit."

As they walked toward the training ground, Kira stopped.

"Aren't you coming?" Kwan asked.

She shook her head. "I think I'll go look around."

Kwan arched an eyebrow at her. "You mean you'll go looking for someone."

Captain Pak seemed amused. "If you mean your two friends, then I will show you where they are."

Walking to the edge of the field, the captain pointed to a large tent near the forest. Kira thanked him and hurried down, eager to see Jaewon and Seung again.

Inside, the tent reeked of the twenty-odd unwashed bodies packed close together around a small table where a baduk game was in progress. Kira pulled the brim of her nambawi low as she passed empty tables littered with tins of half-eaten food and joined the large group. Jaewon sat with Seung close by his side, both staring intently at the board.

Kira pushed her way to the front, where she had a clear view of the game in progress. As if sensing her presence, Jaewon looked up and caught Kira's gaze. A slow smile spread across his face. She was surprised by how much she enjoyed the play of dimples on his cheeks.

A pile of captured white stones sat at Jaewon's side. His opponent was a wiry man with a long, thin face and hooded eyes, wearing the green-and-black uniform of a Jinhan soldier.

The stench of the tent became overpowering. She was relieved when the Jinhan man conceded the game. Standing, he tossed a small rope of coins onto the table next to the baduk board.

"You are indeed a master-level player," the Jinhan man said with a slight bow. "Where did you say you hailed from?"

Jaewon didn't respond right away.

"Kaya," he finally said.

"Who was your teacher?" the Jinhan man asked.

Jaewon didn't respond. He passed the coins to Seung, who placed them in a small leather pouch that hung close to his body.

"Thank you, Officer Cho. I have enjoyed our game. Please excuse me," Jaewon said with a courteous bow.

"I know of only one great baduk player of your caliber in Kaya. Chief Kim Jaeshik of Wagay," he said, folding his arms across his chest. "I recall he had a son. One he bragged about all the time. Claimed his boy would surpass him."

Jaewon remained impassive, but Kira could see his fist clenching.

"We have been playing for nearly five hours, and I have studied your face as much as I have studied the board. It's been years since I played Chief Kim Jaeshik, but I have no doubt you are his son," Officer Cho said.

Kira didn't like the tension between the two men. Glancing over at Seung, she could see that he was anxious also.

"There have been rumors about you, young master Kim. Disturbing rumors."

Something about the Jinhan man's sly eyes and secretive manner bothered Kira. She moved up next to Jaewon, almost touching him. His tension was palpable.

"I have heard all sorts of terrible things. That you are

a murderer and a thief. That you are a coward. It is hard to distinguish fact from fiction," Officer Cho said.

Kira was shaken by his words. She remembered Jaewon's whispered admission of guilt and loss: *His blood is forever on my hands.*

"But one thing I know to be true," Officer Cho said. "Your father is still looking for you. And there is a reward for information about you."

At these words, Kira whipped out her bow and an arrow, pointing it straight at the other man. Surprised, Officer Cho raised his hands in mock surrender.

"No, you have it wrong; you need not fear me," he said with an amused expression. "I have no desire to turn him in. But it is my hope that one day I will see Chief Kim Jaeshik again. And if that day comes, I will tell him I had the pleasure of playing his son and that his son was indeed a master baduk player."

Jaewon placed a tense hand on Kira's arm, forcing her to put away her weapon. He then bowed and walked off, not waiting for Kira or Seung. As he reached the entranceway, Officer Cho spoke again.

"Strange, you don't strike me as a murderer, but I've been wrong before," he called after him.

Not responding, Jaewon exited the tent. Kira hurried after him, but the baduk player had already disappeared into the crowd.

Kira stopped Seung before he could chase after his master.

"Is it true?" she asked. "Did he kill someone?"

"No!" Seung trembled with anger. "It was an accident, a terrible accident. My master is an honorable man. He never meant to hurt anybody."

Seung took off after Jaewon.

"I believe you," she shouted. "Tell him, I trust him."

Seung turned and waved and disappeared into the woods.

25

When she and Kwan returned to the palace, it was in an uproar. Taejo looked relieved as he bounded up to them.

"Where've you been? The Oakcho and Tongey diplomats have arrived and are asking Guru for military aid. I spent the entire day pleading with our uncle to save my mother. This should help our cause," he said in an excited babble. He led them to a separate building from the main palace while senior Guru military officers and advisers raced through the hallways to join the heated discussions.

The rectangular chamber held several long tables and chairs set along the length of the room, parallel with the walls. A raised dais stood at the front of the room with a formal table for King Eojin and his advisers.

Eojin had not yet arrived, but nearly all the spots on the long tables were filled by the military, diplomats, and their staffs.

Several heads turned sharply at her entrance.

"What is she doing here?"

"Since when have women been allowed in military meetings?"

"It's disgraceful. Get her out of here!"

Kira caught the glare of Lord Yu, the ill-tempered senior diplomat of Tongey.

"Who do you think you are? Away with you, ignorant wench! You have no business here," Lord Yu shouted, pointing his finger at her.

She heard Kwan cursing, ready to confront the ambassador. Kira stopped him with a shake of her head.

"It's all right, Oppa," she said.

Kira fixed Lord Yu with a hard glare. "It seems you believe that you have some authority over me. I fear you are mistaken."

"How dare you! This is a man's world and you do not belong here," Lord Yu shouted. "Guards, remove this creature!"

The Guru guards stationed in the room did not move from their positions.

"As I said, you have no authority over me." Kira inclined her head briefly and walked away.

She returned to Taejo's side and stood behind the prince's chair at the end of the long table. Her cousin looked ill at ease—a boy among men. But he was there to represent Hansong. Kira gave his shoulder a reassuring squeeze as King Eojin entered with his entourage. Within seconds of Eojin's greeting, the ambassadors went on the offensive.

"Your Majesty, I insist that you order that insolent female from the meeting!" Lord Yu demanded.

Eojin raised an eyebrow. "By 'insolent female,' do you mean my one and only niece, daughter of my beloved older sister and the great General Kang? A member of the distinguished saulabi army and personal bodyguard to the crown prince of Hansong?"

He kept his eyes on Lord Yu, causing the diplomat to squirm.

"No, the insolent female stays," Eojin said. "Now let us focus our attention on the matter at hand."

Kira displayed no emotion but she felt a warm glow of pride.

"We were saddened to hear of King Sinwon's death. He is a great loss." Eojin addressed the Oakcho diplomats who bowed in acknowledgment.

"Our king has been murdered also," Lord Yu cut in.

Eojin regarded the diplomat with a grave expression. "Yes, it is a terrible tragedy," he said.

Lord Yu jumped to his feet and pounded the table. "The Yamatos are more than halfway up the peninsula!

What is Guru going to do about it?"

"Kaya, Jinhan, and Hansong have all fallen. Who knows what has happened to Kudara," another Tongey ambassador said.

"Kudara is in league with the Yamatos." Kira spoke in a loud voice. A shocked silence filled the room, and she noticed the surprise on the faces of everyone but the Guru faction. "We saw this with our own eyes."

"Your eyes?" Lord Yu made a derogatory sound. "And who would take your word?"

"I would," King Eojin said. "I would take her word over yours, Lord Yu. She is, after all, my clansman."

There was complete quiet in the room as everyone's attention focused on Eojin and the Tongey ambassador.

"Of course, Your Majesty," Lord Yu said, and bowed.

"If Kudara has gone over to the enemy, then it is clear what we must do." This came from Lord Rah, an Oakcho ambassador who'd remained quiet until now. "We must stop the Yamato advance immediately. The Guru army is the only army large enough to challenge them." His words riled up the crowded room.

"If we had our entire army at our disposal, then yes, it would be feasible. But we will not leave our northern boundaries unprotected," said General Kim, the commanding general of Guru. He was a large, stout man with a powerful baritone.

"What use are your northern boundaries if you cannot stop the Yamatos?" Lord Yu sneered.

The debate raged on for nearly an hour as diplomats from the kingdoms of Oakcho and Tongey argued and pleaded for immediate assistance from the king.

Finally, King Eojin spoke up. "The Iron Army is strong, but we cannot fight alone and we cannot fight without unity. Four kings have been murdered—Hansong, Jinhan, Tongey, and Oakcho. Hansong and Jinhan have fallen and Tongey and Oakcho have no kings. Two leaderless kingdoms will be no match for the advancing enemy. Now is the time to unite. Pledge yourselves to me, and we will fight together."

The angry voices of the ambassadors echoed through the room. The Tongey diplomats were arguing vociferously. They did not want to give up their sovereignty. But they were becoming desperate. Their southernmost fortresses were under siege. It would not be long before they were breached.

Kira eyed her uncle with dawning respect and alarm. He'd sat and listened to the diplomats without saying a word, raising their anxiety to a fever pitch before making his demands. Eojin was smart, powerful, and ambitious. This also made her uncle a dangerous and ruthless leader. Now she understood why she'd always felt a vague distrust of him.

In his own way, he was no different from the Kudara king or the daimyo. He sought to control the entire peninsula. Her admiration for him was muted by her concern for what this all meant to Taejo.

As the arguments intensified, a new voice broke through the commotion.

"Gentlemen, the Dragon King's prophecy is coming true. In order to save our world, drastic actions must be taken."

A tall, stately monk clad in the gray robes of the Dragon Springs Temple stood at the entranceway.

"Welcome back, Brother Boyuk!" Eojin rose to greet the new arrival. The monk bowed deeply before taking his place near the king at the front of the room.

"What nonsense is this?" Lord Yu complained. "Everyone knows the prophecy is meaningless."

Eojin ignored the diplomat as he addressed the monk. "What do you mean? Please enlighten us."

Brother Boyuk did not answer right away; instead, he gazed about the room until he caught sight of Kira, Kwan, and Taejo. He gave them a nearly imperceptible nod, as if he recognized them, before responding to Eojin.

"I have just arrived from my temple, where I met with Master Roshi. The first part of the prophecy has now come true. Seven have become three. Of our Seven Kingdoms, four have now fallen. Oakcho, Tongey, and Guru are the only remaining kingdoms. We believe that Tongey and Oakcho must become one with Guru in order for all of us to survive."

"I thought the One was to be our savior," Lord Rah said.

"The prophecy has a dual meaning. The Seven

Kingdoms must become one, and our savior, the Dragon Musado, will defeat the Demon Lord," Brother Boyuk said.

"Dragon Musado?" Lord Yu scoffed. "That's just a legend you monks made up in your temple. It is a child's story! And now you're asking us to give up our sovereignty on the basis of a fairy tale?"

The monk ignored the diplomat and continued, "If the prophecy is correct, then the downfall of another kingdom may signal the downfall of all."

There was more murmuring debate among the diplomats before Lord Rah stood and addressed the king. "The prophecy has long spoken of a savior. Perhaps that savior is you, King Eojin. Perhaps you are the warrior of the prophecy. You, with your great army, may be the one to lead us into battle and save our lands. I say it is only right that we fulfill the rest of the prophecy."

Kira looked sharply at Eojin, noting his pleased expression at being named the Dragon Musado.

"This is easy for you to say. Oakcho is a tributary of Guru. But we Tongey are a free people and we answer to no other king but our own," Lord Yu cut in.

"You have no king," Lord Rah said.

"We have several contenders."

Kira snorted in disgust. "You'll answer to only the Yamatos if you do not stop this foolishness," she said sharply.

Lord Yu jumped to his feet. "Silence, kumiho! I will

not listen to this nonsense any longer."

He faced Eojin with a bitter scowl. "It seems this prophecy goes two ways. Either you help us, or you doom us all!"

He charged out of the room, a deliberate insult to Eojin. Lord Rah stood in shock.

"I deeply regret Lord Yu's actions, Your Majesty," he said with a bow.

Eojin shrugged. "It is not for you to apologize for him," he said. He let out a deep breath. "We all have much to think about."

He rose and left with his advisers.

"What's there to think about?" Kwan groused. "The entire peninsula is overrun by these cretins, while we sit here doing nothing! How long must we wait before we fight?"

Although Kira agreed with her brother, she knew they had no other choice. There was nothing they could do but wait for the king's decision.

"Oppa, now that Brother Boyuk is here, we must talk to him," she said.

Kwan agreed, his face brightening. "You stay with the prince. I'll go meet with the monk right away."

Kira breathed deeply. Maybe now they could move forward.

26

Kira stood within the hallways of an unfamiliar, deserted building. No servants, no soldiers. The wind blew loud and cold, whipping up piles of debris. A terrible wailing echoed down the corridors, fading in and out to a soft weeping.

The shadows along the walls formed into distinctive shapes that came alive. Demons and imps capered around a pulsing object that uncoiled into a great sea serpent. Kira stood transfixed by the spectacle playing out before her; the frenzy of the dancing figures as they were devoured by the serpent. Larger and larger it grew, a massive sea of black, until it engulfed the entire corridor in darkness.

Kira fled from the shadows down a maze of empty

hallways echoing with the cries of the weeper. Each turn she took seemed to take her nowhere. She thought to go back, but found herself confused and hopelessly lost. Closing her eyes, she decided to follow the sound of crying. It led her to a corridor that ended at a large metal door. The wailing had quieted. Kira pushed the door open into a bitterly cold chamber lit by an array of candles scattered all about the room. As she entered, the weeper began to shriek so loud it was deafening. Kira covered her ears until the screams came to an abrupt stop. The room was empty.

"Where are you?" she cried.

"Kira!" A voice kept calling out her name, over and over. She knew the voice; it was her mother.

She swung around in a wild circle.

"Mother, where are you?" Kira shouted desperately.

Kira followed her mother's voice until she reached the farthest corner. A small shadow near the foot of the wall began to grow at her approach. As she came closer, the shadow grew larger, beckoning her with its arms. Kira pressed her hands to the walls.

"Mother! Where are you?"

The shadow tried to caress her face, its arms reaching wide as if to embrace her.

"I am trapped in the shadow world, my little tiger. I cannot alight to heaven, for my soul and all these others have been cursed by Lord Shin," the shadow of her mother said, waving an arm around as others began to appear.

"He had his shaman curse all who refused to accept him as king," another shadow said.

Kira was in anguish. "What must I do to free you all? Tell me and I will do it!"

The shadows flickered as the wind blew through the room.

"We don't know."

"We are trapped!"

"Help us!"

Kira put her hands over her ears to stop the voices of the shadows until she heard her mother calling to her again.

"Kira, listen to me: you are the key," her mother said. "Somehow, you can save us."

"How?"

"I don't know, but you will discover it. I know you will. Until then, I will come to you in your dreams, for only in your sleeping state can you reach the shadow realm."

"I miss you, Mother," Kira said, trying not to cry.

"My little tiger! I love you so much," her mother replied. The other shadows began to whisper in frightened alarm.

"Quickly, my child! You must wake up!" her mother said. "You cannot stay here any longer, it's too dangerous. The demons will come soon, and all of us must hide!" As her mother spoke, the wailing began again.

"Mother, don't go!"

"You must hurry," her mother said. "If we stay too long in the shadow world, our spirits will corrupt and we will never reach heaven."

Her voice blended in with the voices of the other shadows.

"Never see your father."

"Or our husbands."

"My children, who weep for me!"

"Good-bye, my little tiger!" her mother said.

"Don't forget us!"

"Good luck!"

Kira struck at the wall.

"No!" she shrieked. "Come back! Please, come back!"

But the shadows were gone, and all that remained was the same terrible wailing.

Her dream haunted Kira every waking moment of the next day. She didn't know what to do or who to talk to. She feared telling Kwan about her dream, knowing that guilt over their mother's death was still eating away at him. How would he handle hearing that she was cursed?

If Jaewon were staying in the palace, she would have talked to him first. But with Brother Boyuk's return, she wondered if there was a connection between her dream and the monk. Kira was determined to meet with him.

Learning that he was in the war room with Eojin and his advisers, Kira sat in the drafty corridor, waiting for the king to finish his endless meetings. It was late into the night when the doors finally opened and Eojin stepped out with his entourage and Brother Boyuk.

Kira surged to her feet, with her head down.

"Please, Uncle, it is imperative that I speak with Sunim." She spoke while still bowing, her eyes trained on the tips of Eojin's black boots.

"Would you allow me a few moments with your niece, Your Majesty?" Brother Boyuk asked.

As Kira straightened, she caught sight of her uncle's scowl.

"This is an inopportune time. Especially when we are on the eve of going to war," Eojin replied, waving her away. "Kira, you and your brother will refrain from bothering Brother Boyuk. That is an order."

Kira bowed to hide her frustration and her anxiety. She was tired of waiting. She was tired of playing it safe.

Regardless of what the king said, Kira couldn't sit and do nothing.

She would find a way to save her mother, even if it meant taking on the Demon Lord himself.

Two more nights found Kira dreaming of the same large room where she'd met the shadow of her mother. But no one was there. Anxious and scared, Kira felt her resentment against the king growing. She needed to do something, anything, to help her mother.

"Oppa!" Kira found her brother out in a small courtyard, taekkyon training alone.

"I think I should return to Dragon Springs Temple and speak directly with Master Roshi," Kira said.

"Don't be ridiculous," he cut her off. "It's too dangerous."

"It doesn't matter, I have to go see him," she said.

"Eventually we'll be able to meet with Brother Boyuk," he said. "Just be patient."

"We don't have time!" Kira sighed and explained her dream to him.

Kwan was quiet. "Why didn't you tell me this before?" he asked.

"I didn't want to grieve you more."

"Don't do that again," he said. His response was mild, but Kira knew he was upset.

"I'm sorry."

He wiped his sweaty face on a small towel. "Let's wait a little longer, and if nothing changes, then we'll all leave," he said.

Before she could respond, a guard arrived and informed them that the king required their presence immediately. Outside the king's quarters, they found Taejo waiting for them.

Eojin sat on luxurious silk cushions on the ondol-heated floor, surrounded by a few of his closest advisers.

"Young clansmen!" Eojin said. "Come before me. We must talk."

The three of them bowed and moved to kneel in front of the king.

"The army you have brought to our gates has grown greater in size since your arrival. Now there are approximately three thousand men. Those that came from different kingdoms have given fealty to me and accepted me as their king. But your Hansong men claim they serve only you, Prince Taejo! They pledge their swords, they pledge their support and their service, but their loyalty lies with you," Eojin said.

Kira felt a surge of pride for the prince and their soldiers.

"I admire loyalty," Eojin continued. "However, your men are already running out of supplies and getting soft without proper training. So I ask you, young cousin, a very difficult question. I know you may hope for the return of your lands and to be king one day, but in these times we must put individual desires aside to focus on the good of the people. What we need is a unified army, strong in mind and body, united under one cause and one king. I ask you, will you pledge your men to me and accept me as your king?"

Even though his request was reasonable, Kira could feel her hackles rise. He was asking Taejo to give up his men and to give up all chances of recapturing his kingdom and throne. If they were able to drive the Yamatos out of his homeland, Taejo could never be king. Hansong would be no more. They faced the same troubling dilemma that the Tongey diplomat, Lord Yu, was so upset about.

But Hansong was lost already. Perhaps there was no choice. Taejo looked young and unsure about making a decision that would change the course of his life. Her father's voice slid into her head: Advise him, guide him. Help him grow into a great king.

She faced Eojin once again. "Your Majesty, you have no heirs, and Prince Taejo has lost his father. Will you make him your heir?"

Kira ignored the outraged disapproval of the king's advisers. General Kim rose up to his knees and raised his arm, preparing to strike her. The king caught his arm. He regarded Kira with a look of respect and approval.

"Kira, your loyalty to the young prince and Hansong is truly admirable. I will consider your request."

Kira bowed and gave Taejo a slight nod. There was no real choice here. Taejo's refusal would cause irreparable harm in his relationship with the Guru king.

Casting one last sidelong glance at Kira, Taejo faced Eojin.

"I pledge my loyalty and that of my men to you, my king," he said. He bowed, his forehead touching the firm matting of the floor. Kira and Kwan quickly followed suit. Kira said a quick prayer to the heavens, asking that all would work out favorably. The three cousins rose in unison to face the king.

"Excellent," he said. "Now, let's prepare for war!"

Later that same afternoon, Kira stood outside the city walls with Kwan and Taejo. The army of displaced soldiers that Captain Pak commanded stood at attention, joined by the Guru cavalry and the divisions of the Guru army currently stationed within the city.

Walking around the perimeter of the crowd, her

nambawi pulled low over her face, Kira searched for Jaewon and Seung. She found them following three shamans who patrolled the area. Seung's face lit up when he saw her, while Jaewon greeted her quietly. With all that had transpired, she'd nearly forgotten about the altercation in the baduk tent, but it didn't matter. In her heart she knew that Jaewon was not a murderer.

"Young mistress, what are the shamans carrying?" Seung asked.

The shamans held brass bowls filled with a milky substance in their left hands and chains of bells draped around their right. They sprinkled the area with the milk, the bells ringing with the movements of their arms. From a tree, Kira saw the flash of several silvery-gray imps fleeing into the woods. She whistled under her breath. The power of the three shamans together made for strong magic.

"They call it earth's milk, and it is a secret substance that only shamans know how to create. But it is the basis for all their power," she said. "They use it to commune with the spirit world, exorcise ghosts, find treasures, raise the dead—"

Seung gasped. "They can't really raise the dead, can they?"

Kira smiled. "No, but unscrupulous ones have been known to raise demons who masquerade as the recently departed in order to gouge their families of money."

"That's terrible!" Seung looked scandalized at the

revelation. "I've always revered our shaman. He would never do anything like that."

Kira shrugged. "Shamans are good and bad just like all other humans. But the reason I don't completely trust them is because their magic is too closely tied to demon magic. Even that earth's milk they use—I can smell a slight demon stink to it."

"Young mistress, you are frightening me," Seung said with a shudder. "I may never be able to face our village shaman again."

At that moment, the city gates began to open. King Eojin had arrived, mounted on a beautiful white stallion with an elaborate golden bridle that matched his gold armor. As the sun forced its rays through the overcast sky, it shone down on Eojin as if the gods themselves were blessing him. Kira rolled her eyes at the awed whispers of the crowd.

She made her way to the front where her brother and Taejo stood next to Captain Pak.

"We have received word that Tongey is in danger of collapsing under the Yamato siege," Eojin said. He cast his steady gaze across the field of soldiers before him. "With no king and tremendous infighting between the remaining heirs, the Tongey are ill prepared for this onslaught. In desperation, they come to us, mindful of what it will cost them, but prepared to do what is necessary to save their lands. Oakcho and Tongey have pledged their armies to Guru also. So today we fight as a united nation. Today we fight for Tongey, which is now part of the Guru Kingdom. They have pledged fealty and accepted me as their king. Their fate is now tied to ours. And what is ours, remains ours!"

The men stamped their feet and pounded on their chests as they chanted his name. Suddenly, General Kim stepped forward to stand at Eojin's side. Throwing up his arms, he bellowed for their attention.

"The Dragon King's prophecy has come true. Seven have become three. Three have now become one. One will save us all." He faced Eojin and bowed deeply. "King Eojin, you are the one that the prophecy speaks of—the Dragon Musado. All hail King Eojin!"

The mass of soldiers went wild, and shouts changed from "Eojin" to "the Dragon Musado." Kira was stunned. They hailed Eojin as the "one" of the prophecy. She could see Taejo's look of relief along with a glazed, starry-eyed hero worship that she was becoming familiar with.

Kira gritted her teeth, overcome by irritation. It vexed her to see how easily people believed Eojin was the Dragon Musado. She turned to her brother and could see his own conflicted emotions. Catching her eye, Kwan shrugged.

"He'd make a better Dragon Musado," he said. "And at least now we'll fight those Yamato bastards!"

Kira's lips tightened as she felt the throbbing of a headache. It was bad enough knowing they'd given up Taejo's throne to Eojin, but for him to also fulfill the prophecy was too much. She wanted Taejo to have this future before him. She didn't want that stolen from him also.

Her gaze swept up to meet Jaewon's. His eyebrow arched in question. She shook her head and pushed her way through the throng of soldiers. She needed to get away from the screaming crowds around her.

She cut through the left side, shoving past shouting men all the way to the edge of the crowd, and stomping toward the forest. From behind, she heard Jaewon calling her name, but she didn't stop until she reached the protection of the trees. Sitting on a fallen log, she waited for him to arrive.

He collapsed at her feet on the leaf-covered ground. Rolling over to his side, he gazed up at her. "What is troubling you now?" he asked, wiggling his eyebrows at her.

She laughed at his silliness but didn't respond. She didn't feel up to talking about Eojin.

Kira realized that they hadn't spoken since the day he'd rushed away from the baduk tent. Regardless of what Officer Cho had said, she knew Jaewon was not a murderer. She didn't know how to raise the issue nor did she want to pry, no matter how curious she was.

"I have something for you," he said. He sat up and rummaged within his inner pockets. "I won it at a game a few nights ago and have been saving it."

He pulled out a small cloth and unwrapped it. Within

were several small, hard balls covered in sesame seeds.

"What are they?" Kira asked.

"They are a sweet from Cathay. Made from toasted sesame seeds and honey. Here, try one." He pressed one to her lips. Her eyes widened in delight at the combination of the sweet honey and the nutty flavor of the sesame seeds.

She watched him as he enjoyed his sweet. She liked the way the muscles of his jaws moved, flashing the deep dimples in his cheeks. The way a lock of his hair fell out of his braid and waved over his brow. The way he crinkled the bridge of his nose in enjoyment.

He caught her peeking at him and grinned. Affection and something more glinted in his eyes. Embarrassed by her awareness of him, she moved back, feeling warmth creep up her cheeks.

"Why are you still here?" she asked. "I thought you and Seung would have continued north by now."

"Brother Woojin said our fates are intertwined."

"Brother Woojin's not here," she said. Her voice was harsh as she held in the guilt and grief that always came with thoughts of the little monk. "Nothing is holding you back now."

"You asked me to stay. I will always do whatever you ask."

"I didn't actually ask you to stay," she said. "You and Taejo tricked me into saying that."

Jaewon patted her on the head. "That counts for me."

With a shrug, Kira pulled her knees up, wrapping her arms around them.

"I don't know what to do anymore," Kira said.

Jaewon's eyes narrowed in concern. "What is it? Is something troubling you? Please, tell me."

It felt good to unburden herself, releasing all the frustration, fear, and anger that had built up inside. Jaewon listened intently as Kira described the shadow land and her mother's suffering. When she explained the situation with Brother Boyuk and how the king refused to allow her to meet with him, Jaewon's eyes narrowed, but he remained silent until she was done.

She shuddered at the end of her tale, bereft of emotions. It was a long moment before Jaewon finally spoke.

"I've no doubt that you are right about the king. But if his intent is to keep you from the monk, then there must be some reason for it," he said.

"I know his reason: to keep Taejo from becoming the Dragon Musado," Kira said bitterly.

Jaewon put a comforting arm around her. "Maybe," he said. "Or maybe he just wants to protect the prince."

She shrugged and tried to pull away, but Jaewon made her face him.

"You may not trust his motives completely, but you know he wouldn't harm your cousin."

"I don't know that!" she snapped.

"Yes, you do," he said, shaking her gently. "If you'd thought for even a moment that the prince was in danger, you would have dragged him away at your first opportunity."

Kira knew Jaewon was right, but she didn't want to admit it.

"Get off me," she groused, slapping his hands away. "Regardless of what the king does, I'm going to see Brother Boyuk and I'm going to help my mother. I have to."

Jaewon nodded. "And I'll help you. No matter where you go or what you have to do, I'll be there for you."

"Why?" she asked bluntly.

"Because I'm your friend," he replied.

Taken aback, Kira was silent.

"What, am I not good enough for you?" he asked.

"No, don't be silly," she said with a wide smile. "You're a good friend."

His words warmed her inside—she felt happy. In seventeen years, no one had ever called her friend, although she'd always wished for one. She hoped that he would never regret his words.

28

It took seven days to prepare the Iron Army for battle. On their last night in Wando palace, Jaewon and Seung were allowed to stay at the palace with Kwan in his quarters. Kira joined them for a private dinner in the prince's chambers, discussing Eojin's battle preparations for the attack on the Tongey port city of Wonsan.

"Didn't we spend all this time heading north to get away from the enemy?" Jaewon complained.

They sat on the floor of the prince's sitting room, each person eating off a small round table set with individual portions of meat, vegetables, soup, and rice. Kira sat next to Jaewon, noticing that he'd eaten all of his soy-sauce potatoes. She surreptitiously placed her plate on his table.

"Now is the time to fight. No more running," Kwan replied. "No more running." His expression was as hard as granite.

"We are going to save my mother," Taejo said.

Jaewon nodded in agreement. Looking down at his meal, he noticed the full plate of potatoes. Kira smothered a laugh as he eagerly demolished them.

The great Iron Army in motion is an intimidating sight, Kira thought. With the addition of more Guru recruits and displaced soldiers to his army, Eojin marched with a force of one hundred thousand men.

As Taejo's personal guards, Kira, Kwan, and Captain Pak rode with the king's cavalry. Upon Taejo's request, Jaewon and Seung were added to his escort.

They were the only ones to ride fully armored horses. The infantry marched in platoons, while supply transports set off to set up camps at prearranged locations. The dirt roads were in poor shape from the winter storms, so that it was commonplace to come across broken wheels and even abandoned wagons all along their route.

The king's cavalry reached Oakcho five days later. At the border, the Oakcho generals pledged their allegiance to Guru, adding an additional ten thousand men to their numbers.

It would take the massive army another ten days to

reach the Tongey borders, while scouts brought daily word of the enemy onslaught.

Kira hated their slow pace. At this rate, the new year would be upon them before they saw any action. And with the start of the twelfth month, the frigid air tasted of the coming snow.

To be truthful, she didn't care about the war effort. She spent nearly every waking moment thinking about Brother Woojin and Master Roshi's words. They'd said the first Dragon King treasure was located somewhere in the Diamond Mountains. After she'd finally told Kwan about her shadow-land dreams, he'd redoubled his efforts to meet with Brother Boyuk, but to no avail. It was as if the monk had disappeared. Frustrated and anxious, Kwan finally agreed that they should make the trek to the mountains themselves. They would discuss it with the others at the next opportunity.

At night, the army would sprawl across the landscape, separated by their divisions. Hundreds of women followed on foot behind the infantry. Kira stayed away from all of them, aware of the fear and loathing she caused. But when she sensed a demon presence among them, she was compelled to investigate. The shamans should have put up wards all around the entire perimeter of the camp. But it was hard to keep the men from straying out of the protected areas. When Kwan and Jaewon insisted on going with her, she agreed. This was not Hansong, and she could not easily move about unrecognized. She would be safer with them.

They passed a large and rowdy crowd surrounding a wrestling match. Kwan and Jaewon stopped for a moment to watch the wrestlers. Kira walked past. She'd never been interested in wrestling, despite its popularity.

Sensing something in the air, Kira whirled around and bumped into another soldier. He wheeled back, off-balance, falling against several onlookers. They pushed him away, cursing at him. Furious, the soldier rushed at Kira.

"Watch where you're going, dog spawn!" he shouted. He shoved her hard on the chest. Kira rocked back from the blow as her fist shot out reflexively, knocking the soldier onto his rear.

"Son of a whore!" the soldier sputtered as he jumped to his feet. When his eyes met hers, he stepped away in fear and disgust.

"Get away from me, Demon Slayer! We don't want your kind here!" He spit on the ground, barely missing her boot.

Kira contained the fury that threatened to erupt within her. "What do you mean by that?" she asked.

"You don't fool me," he sneered. Kira smelled the alcohol fumes emanating from him. "Acting like a man when there's naught between your legs or your ears. Women don't belong in the army. You don't belong here!"

He pulled out a dagger and slashed at Kira's face. Instinct saved her. With a quick side step, she dodged the blow and grabbed her sword. She dashed the pommel onto his head, knocking him unconscious.

Leaving the fallen man, she tried to find the odor trail she'd sensed before. Many soldiers were now glaring at her. Ignoring them, she pushed past those who deliberately stepped into her path. She had detected the foul scent of the demon she was tracking. It led her back to a group of men who knelt around the drunk who had attacked her. A flash of silvery-gray skin clung to the neck of a large, bearded soldier.

An imp. So bold. She thought. It peered at her with hungry eyes as it sank sharp teeth into the bearded soldier's dirty neck.

Kira raised her sword and approached the group.

"Demon!" the bearded soldier shouted. "Kumiho! She wants to kill us all!"

Kira stopped in confusion. Before she could explain about the imp, a rock flew out of the crowd, glancing off her forehead. Dazed, Kira touched her face, feeling the wetness of blood trickle down her cheek.

"Send her to the underworld where she belongs!" someone shouted.

Dozens of stones flew at her as she covered her head. Her sword fell from her hand as she ducked down and pulled herself into a ball. A cry broke through her lips as searing pain dropped her to her knees. The missiles pounded her back and arms, ripping into the tender flesh unprotected by her armor.

Over the thudding in her ears and the maddened cries of the mob, she heard the outraged shouts of her brother.

Kira couldn't move; her limbs had stiffened with pain. Someone pulled her gently up, steadying her. Jaewon held her against his chest. She could feel his heart thumping erratically.

Kwan stood over several dead soldiers, his sword dripping with blood.

The mob scattered with the arrival of the military police officers, who surrounded them and shouted for Kwan to drop his sword. He threw it down and spit on the nearest body. Kira noticed the gray, atrophied form of the imp steaming its black gunk into the ground.

"Lower your weapons—he's the king's kin!" an officer said as he bowed before Kwan. He ordered one of his men to retrieve Kwan's sword and wipe it off before returning it to him. Kwan sheathed his weapon and went over to Kira. He held her by the arms, his jaw tight with rage as he took in the sight of her bloody and bruised face. Kira bit back a cry as he pressed against her injuries.

"I will deal with these men. You go get some rest," he said. With a nod to Jaewon, he returned to the officers.

Jaewon offered Kira his arm, but she shook him off. She was keenly aware of all who watched their progress— cursing her, hating her. She refused to let them see her weakness.

All her life she'd dealt with prejudice and hate. All her life she'd lived knowing people despised her for being different. It was her parents who kept Kira from turning her back to the world. They'd taught her that every life was precious and worth protecting. Without them, Kira could feel her control breaking down. Rage consumed her. She'd never understood why people could hate so unconditionally.

But now she knew. Now she burned with hatred.

29

The pain was agonizing. Her leather armor had protected her back from the brunt of the stoning, but there were numerous cuts and bruises on her arms, neck, and face. Her right eye was swollen and her face black-and-blue from her ear to the bridge of her nose.

She didn't respond to anyone. Not to her brother's questions as he cared for the worst of her wounds. Nor even when Taejo cried to see her so battered and bruised. Fear of what she would say kept her quiet. But on the inside, her emotions were in turmoil. She thought of her mother and the other trapped shadows and her inability to help them. She relived the attack, letting guilt seep into her thoughts, wondering if she should have warned the men of the imp first, wishing she hadn't pulled out her sword.

Lying alone in her tent, she felt the warm embrace of a tiger curled up by her side, purring gently. It emitted a golden light that surrounded them both. She could feel how its *ki*, its pure tiger energy, transferred into her body. Kira touched its soft fur. Powerful muscles rippled under her fingertips. The energy was giving her strength again.

"My father was right," she said. "I always thought you were just a dream. But you're real. You are my tiger spirit."

The tiger purred in response.

"Thank you," she said.

It opened its eyes, which were golden in color, just like Kira's.

Don't despair, my child. I am always with you.

She heard its words in her mind, and the hate and anger released itself. It didn't matter what the world thought of her. She was the girl with the tiger spirit. Finally at peace, she buried herself deeper into the tiger's embrace and fell asleep.

She didn't wake until the following evening, when hunger forced her to leave the tent. Outside, she saw her brother, Taejo, Jaewon, and Seung, sitting on furs spread across the ground. They stood up at her approach.

"Noona!" Taejo rushed over to grab her hand and pull her over to sit by his side. "I've been so worried about you," he said.

As she sat, she could see that more than half of the

campsite was empty. Kwan caught her look.

"They left this morning. We will leave tomorrow," he said.

She nodded and thanked Seung for the bowl of rice gruel he'd brought over. It was thick and flavorful, filled with small pieces of chicken and vegetables. She ate slowly, avoiding everyone's concerned looks. Taejo sat close to her, occasionally patting her knee or arm. She tolerated it, more for his sake than for hers.

"How are you feeling?" he asked, peering up at her.

She could hear the fear and concern in his voice, and it reminded her of how important he was to her.

"I'm fine," she said, ruffling his hair. "You know I'm a fast healer."

Except for the bruises on her face and arms, and a lingering stiffness, she was pain-free.

"Are you sure you're all right?" Jaewon asked. His face showed his disbelief.

Kira cracked her knuckles. "You want to fight me and see?"

"No way! I believe you." He laughed.

Kwan leaned over to command her attention. "Kira, I tried one last time to see the monk. He must know by now how badly we need to talk to him. It's been so frustrating!" He slammed his fist into his hand. "I say we head down to the Diamond Mountains and seek the first of the Dragon King treasures on our own. Maybe the treasures will help. . . ."

He trailed off, but Kira knew he was thinking about their mother's spirit. Kira nodded grimly. They needed to get going.

"But we don't know where to go," Taejo burst in.

Jaewon nodded. "I must agree with the prince on this. We can't go blindly into the mountains. They say there are over ten thousand peaks. Without knowing where to look, we'd be hopelessly lost."

Kwan stood and paced about. He picked up a few pieces of wood from a nearby pile and began to fling them into the fire, shooting up sparks all about them.

"We can't stay here forever! We must act now!" he said.

Jaewon crossed to Kwan and took away a large branch from him before he could throw it.

"I thought that King Eojin was the Dragon Musado?" he asked.

"He's not," Kira said sharply. "Sunim said it was Prince Taejo."

Jaewon shrugged. "Maybe he was wrong?"

"He wasn't wrong!" Everyone froze at her outburst. Kira sighed. "I'm sorry. I can't explain it, but I just have a strong feeling it isn't my uncle."

Suddenly, they heard the sound of shuffling steps along with an even thud. Brother Boyuk was approaching with the help of a stout walking stick.

"Young mistress is right. My esteemed brother was not wrong," he said. He placed his hands together and bowed.

"King Eojin is a good man, but he is set in his ways

and immovable once his decision is made. When I arrived, I explained to the king the mission you and your friends must embark upon. But he refused to let me speak with any of you, for it is a long and treacherous route back into enemy territory for such youngsters, and not a one among you has yet to see twenty years."

"That wasn't his decision to make," Kira said.

"I agree," he said. He bowed in thanks as Seung set out a fur rug for the monk to sit on. "But remember the king's tragic history. He doesn't want to lose any more of his family."

Kira shuddered as a cold wind whipped through their campsite. She stared into the fire, thinking of what the monk had said. It explained much, but Kira still couldn't forgive the king.

"I know, young mistress, that you and your brother have been seeking me," Brother Boyuk continued. "Forgive me for being unavailable, but I have been waiting for the right moment. If you will follow me, I will show you."

He grabbed a nearby torch and began to leave the campsite. Mystified, Kira rose to her feet and followed the monk to the edge of the forest. The others were close behind.

As they reached the forest line, Brother Boyuk spoke a few words to the guards, who then let them pass. Within the forest, Kira followed the monk until they reached a clearing, where a lone figure sat quietly meditating before a campfire.

"Sunim!" Taejo shouted.

Brother Woojin rose to his feet, a wide smile creasing his entire face.

"Sunim, you're all right!" Kira said as she rushed over. "It's so good to see you!"

"Yes, yes, I'm all right," Brother Woojin said, laughing at their joy at seeing him. "I am quite durable, you see. I may be old, but I am tough."

Kira was relieved to see Brother Woojin again. He was someone familiar and comfortable. He brought back a sense of balance she hadn't even known she was missing.

"Your Highness, now that we are together again, we must discuss our course of action," Brother Woojin said.

Kira nodded. This was the moment she'd been waiting for.

Brother Woojin sat down again. "It is time for us to seek the first of the treasures. Master Roshi is concerned about how much time has passed already. We must be at the Dragon King's birth cave before the New Year is upon us. We have twelve days left. Time is running out."

Taejo started in alarm. "No! We go with my uncle! We need to save my mother!"

"That is not your mission, my prince. The time has come for you to seek the tidal stone."

"But my mother . . . ," Taejo pleaded.

Kira put an arm around Taejo's shoulders and gave him a hug.

"We need to do this," she said. "It'll be OK. We'll be

with you. I'll be with you."

Taejo leaned his chin into his hands with a heavy sigh. "What does the tidal stone look like? And how are we to seek it?"

"They say it is a ruby larger than a chestnut," the monk said. "Don't worry about how to find it. If you are the true Musado, then the tidal stone will present itself to you."

"But what if I'm not?" Taejo asked.

Brother Woojin was quiet. "Let us just worry about getting to the Diamond Mountains for now."

Kira bit her bottom lip, considering the foreseeable problems. "We will need a good plan on how to slip away without notice."

"Yes, and you'll need to prepare supplies for the trip," Brother Boyuk said.

"This is insane!" Jaewon interrupted. "The Diamond Mountains are on the eastern shore of Tongey. The whole southern peninsula is now under enemy control. The battle we're now heading toward lies right between us and the mountains. How by the gods are we to make it through?"

"By having faith," Brother Woojin answered. He bowed and raised his clasped hands to the heavens.

"And a huge diversion." Brother Boyuk grinned. "What better diversion than an advancing army of a hundred thousand men!"

The plan was to sneak away as Eojin and the Iron Army attacked the port city of Wonsan, where Yamato was waging a full siege. With his focus on his battle plan, Eojin ordered Taejo to stay close to camp with his cousins, guarded by Captain Pak and his men. Brother Boyuk would stay close to Eojin and keep him away.

At night, the element of surprise would be strongest for the attack and for their escape also. Kwan would create a distraction while Jaewon and Seung readied their horses for the long journey.

Inside the tent, Kira and her cousin sat fully clothed and armed, waiting for Kwan to signal for them.

"Do you think we'll see our uncle again?" Taejo asked. "Will he be angry? Will he forgive me? I mean, he won't think I ran away because I'm afraid, will he?"

"If anything, you are running toward more danger, so it isn't a lack of courage, and he'll know that. And yes, we'll see him again. Besides, you wrote him that long message."

She'd agreed to let him leave a scroll with Captain Pak, to be delivered in the morning, once they were long gone.

A soft whistle trilled nearby, the slight vibrato indicating Kwan was ready for them. Kira pulled out her knife and slit the back of the tent wall. She slung several bags of provisions and their water sacks over her shoulder and stepped through the slit, Taejo right behind her. They marched quickly along the path, joining up with Kwan.

Once clear of the tents, they headed to the latrines,

waiting for the night patrol to pass before ducking into the dense line of trees behind them. Another low whistle alerted them to the others' presence. They followed the signal to a clearing where Jaewon, Seung, and Brother Woojin stood with their horses. All their weapons had been hidden and loaded earlier. Jindo dashed over, happy to see Taejo.

"Let's go," Kwan said.

They rode slowly through the forest by the dim light of the moon and stars, Kira in the lead. They traveled southeast, stopping only to rest their horses when the fog became too dense to ride.

Six days later, they glimpsed the glistening peaks of the Diamond Mountains.

Kwan led them out of the forests and onto a rocky trail along the seashore. He was cautious, stopping often and keeping careful watch up ahead. They'd already been in numerous run-ins with demons and imps and avoided one close call with a Yamato patrol. Each time, Kira's nose warned them of danger. Since reaching the Diamond Mountains, there'd been no demon sightings at all, as if the mountains themselves were protected.

Kira breathed in the cold, briny air. She gazed at the white-capped sea. Large boulders jutted out of the waters like small islands, stepping stones for the gods. The wind was harsh, buffeting them with a cold spray from the sea.

Taejo rode next to her, hunkered down as close as he could get to his horse, his breath blowing in white clouds before him. She watched as Jindo ran off onto the beach, chasing the receding waves and racing away from oncoming ones.

The rest of the day, they traveled along the sea road as the peaks and spirals rose and fell to their right. By late afternoon, they reached a bay where a large white-sand beach encircled a portion of the turquoise sea gently lapping at the shore. The water was calm here and gave them a brief respite from the harsh winds of the sea. The road suddenly veered away from the shore and turned west into the mountains.

They crossed a wooden bridge over a fast-flowing creek and found themselves not far from a small but picturesque temple with several larger buildings surrounding it. Numerous statues of small animals lined the corners of the temple roof, like tiny guardians. Next to the temple, a small wooden pagoda housed a large bronze bell, while behind it stood a narrow and very pointy seven-story stone pagoda.

The bright-red doors of the temple opened at their approach, and several young monks in gray robes with yellow sashes came to greet them. Brother Woojin dismounted first, placing his hands together and bringing them to his forehead. The younger monks responded in kind and invited the party into the temple. Three small boys with the shaved heads and light-gray robes of young disciples rushed over to care for the horses.

Seeing Jindo, one tiny boy shyly approached Taejo and

asked to pet his dog. Smiling, Taejo sent Jindo off with the delighted child, who patted the dog and promised him plenty of treats. Kira waited for Taejo to hug Jindo in farewell one last time before following the others into the warmth of the inner temple.

"Welcome, welcome to Singing Temple!" A wiry old monk stood at the temple sanctuary before a large golden statue of San-Shin, the mountain god. Brother Woojin bowed and greeted the head monk while Kira and the others waited with the young monks.

"I wonder why it's called Singing Temple," Kira mused.

One of the monks heard her question and cleared his throat, motioning her closer.

"We are called the Singing Temple because at certain times of the year, the voices of singing angels surround us from the mountains," he said.

"Angels?" she asked.

"Yes, angels singing glorious music such as you have never heard before."

"Have you actually heard the voices yourself?" she asked.

The monk nodded, a dreamy expression on his face. "It's hard to explain what it sounds like, but now that you are here, perhaps you will experience it for yourselves."

Kwan interrupted abruptly. "What I want to know is why the Yamatos didn't come here."

The monk gazed at Kwan with a puzzled expression. "But these are holy grounds," he said. "No evil can enter the sacred mountains."

"How could they be stopped?" Kwan asked.

"By the angels," the monk replied. "They would not allow an enemy army into their mountains. War does not enter our realm."

Before Kwan could question him further, Brother Woojin arrived and introduced the temple's head monk, Master Hong, to the group. The old monk peered closely at them, his wrinkled face alive with curiosity.

"Greetings, my children! We welcome you to stay the night at our monastery," he said in a high-pitched, wavering voice. "I am aware of your task, and you will need your energy, for we do not know how long you will hike through our sacred mountains to find what you're looking for. After all, there are ten thousand miracles here, and Brother Woojin tells me you have no idea where to start!"

Master Hong chuckled as if this was the most hilarious thing he had ever heard. Kira gazed at the others in alarm. They'd all taken for granted that Brother Woojin knew where they were to go. Did he expect them to wander the mountain cliffs in the dead of winter, blindly seeking something that had been hidden for centuries?

"Do not fear, young ones," Brother Woojin said. "The path will find us if we keep our eyes open."

Kira was troubled by the monk's words. How could they plan what to do without knowing where to go?

"Sunim, are you trying to tell us that you have no

idea where to start?" Kira asked.

"That's not entirely true," Brother Woojin corrected. "I believe we are to head to Nine Dragons Waterfall and the Eight Jade Fairy Pools. It is the beginning."

"The beginning of what?" Kira asked.

But the monk didn't answer.

30

They left early the next morning for Nine Dragons Waterfall. Master Hong shook his head in concern as he described the hours of hiking it would take them to reach their destination. The series of directions he gave Brother Woojin were incomprehensible to Kira, but Brother Woojin just nodded. The monks provided them with tents, extra blankets, heavy coats, boots, and food needed to sustain their hike. Faced with snow-covered terrain, Kira was sorry to leave the warmth and security of the temple.

The trail followed the course of a river, but the river itself was only at a fraction of its normal flow. Jindo jumped off the dirt trail and down the rocky side to drink from the trickling water.

It snowed heavily for several hours. The drifts came up to their knees, making the hike slow going. They traveled single file. Kwan led the way, followed by Brother Woojin and Taejo. Kira walked behind Taejo, with Jaewon and Seung taking up the rear.

She watched as Taejo struggled to lift his feet and trudge through the high snow. Even Kira found it hard to resist the inertia creeping over her, making her eyes heavy. Shaking it off, she pushed on, keeping a sharp eye on Taejo.

They'd been walking for another hour when she saw her cousin fall onto his hands and knees. Jindo whined, nudging him.

Kira grabbed Taejo by his elbow as Jaewon came over to help him on the other side. Taejo's head lolled forward.

"Just a little farther and there is a clearing where we can set up camp for the night," Kwan said.

Kira nodded and gripped Taejo about his waist, overlapping arms with Jaewon as they carried him. At the clearing, Kira held him upright on a rock as the others quickly prepared their campsite. Once a tent was up, Taejo crawled in and buried himself with blankets, Jindo pressing next to him. He fell asleep immediately.

"He'll be all right," Jaewon said to Kira.

Kwan and Jaewon built a large campfire as Seung and Brother Woojin prepared a meal. Kira paced around the perimeter, to check for any dangers, before returning to the fire. She sat next to Jaewon, noting the shadow of grief that passed over his face as he studied the fire.

"You said you lost someone you loved," she said. "What happened?"

Jaewon didn't respond. Kira watched his frosty breath fill the air between them. She had nearly given up when his voice came to her ear in a soft whisper.

"I was thirteen when it happened. We were visiting the mountain god shrine in preparation for the coming harvest. My brother was seven years old, given to running wild, as young boys will do." He gave a soft chuckle. "I still remember how he loved to wrestle with anyone or anything he could get his hands on, even a neighbor's pig!"

He held his face up to the skies. His breath caught as he spoke. "The steps to the temple were steep and treacherous. I had brought my new bow with me, the one my father commissioned for my birthday. I shouldn't have brought it, but I was proud and unaccustomed to being refused. My brother was anxious to see my bow. He kept asking to hold it, and I kept saying no. We were halfway up when he grabbed it from my hands, breaking it in the process. I was so mad! I wasn't thinking when I . . ." He stopped and ran a shaky hand over his face. He stared blindly into the fire before him. Kira noticed suddenly that Seung and Kwan sat nearby, listening to his every word.

"I hit him, forgetting that we were on those steep

steps. He fell all the way down. I tried to catch him, but it was too late. When I reached the bottom, his head was bleeding and his eyes were still open. I knew he was dead."

A bleak smile creased his lips. "It was my mother who called me a murderer. Sometimes at night, I can still hear her crying."

"It was an accident," Kira said. Her heart hurt and her eyes burned with tears.

"It was my fault," he replied. "And I must live with it." Rising, he walked away into the woods. Kira looked at the others, who'd sat listening quietly as Jaewon spoke. Seung continued to prepare their meal, his usual cheer replaced by melancholy.

Kwan sighed. "Poor fellow."

"He carries a heavy burden," Brother Woojin said. "I hope one day he will be able to forgive himself or else—"

"Or else what?" Kira asked.

"Or else it will destroy him."

31

She woke in the middle of the night. Darkness blanketed the Diamond Mountains all around them. Within the tent, she lay next to Taejo, with Kwan on his other side. They were rolled tightly within their furs and lying as close together as possible. Jindo lay at their feet, providing them with some additional warmth. Kira could see the flickering flames through the tightly closed canvas of their tent. She watched the silhouette of a stocky figure throwing more sticks into the large fire.

That must be Seung standing guard, she thought.

She heard the wind shaking the bare limbs of the trees as if searching for the leaves it once rustled through. She dozed again.

It was the sound of singing and lighthearted laughter that woke her. At first, she thought she was dreaming. Then she saw Taejo sit up and look around in bewilderment. Kwan jumped to his feet and rushed out of the tent. The singing grew louder.

Putting on their heavy coats, she and Taejo joined Kwan, Seung, and Brother Woojin; all of them stood staring at a golden, shimmering light that lit up the forest, exuding warmth and invitation. Taejo began to move toward it when Kwan called to him.

"Stop! I don't want you going near it until I know what it is," Kwan said.

"No, Lord Kang!" Brother Woojin waved him back. "This is the sign we've been waiting for. We must follow the prince."

Jaewon appeared behind them.

"What is it?" he asked.

Taejo shook his head and shrugged. "I don't know, but I think it wants us to follow it."

Jindo trotted toward the light, stopped, and looked at them. He barked once and ran down the trail. Taejo followed, with Kira and Brother Woojin right behind him. From a distance, she heard Seung announce that he would stay behind and guard their campsite. She even heard Kwan shout after them to wait, but neither she nor Taejo stopped. She found the pull of the light too alluring to fight.

Within the forest, the light changed night into day. No longer did her boots crunch on newly fallen snow. Instead, she wondered at the green grass beneath her feet and the warmth of a beautiful spring morning. This was powerful magic.

Glancing back, she saw that her brother and Jaewon still stood in the knee-deep snow, their breath frosty in the air before them. Just ahead of her, Brother Woojin and Taejo were taking off their coats, leaving them on a large boulder as they lifted their faces to the warm sun. Kira took off her heavy coat and placed it on a nearby boulder also.

"What are you doing?" Kwan asked sharply. "You'll freeze to death!"

"Don't you feel the sun?" Taejo asked in surprise. "It's springtime here."

Kwan looked alarmed. He stepped forward and stopped. Putting his hand in front of his face, he pounded at the air, as if there was an invisible wall.

"We can't go through," he shouted as Jaewon, too, began to push on the barrier.

"I don't think you are supposed to come with us," Brother Woojin said. "It is why you cannot see the change in the weather here. But don't worry. We will be safe."

"No, I can't let you go without me!" Kwan was furious.

"Oppa," Kira said. "It's all right. I'm here."

Kwan calmed down and put down his fists. He nodded and crossed his arms. "Be smart, Kira."

She inclined her head. As she turned away, her eyes caught Jaewon's.

"Be safe," he said.

She walked after Taejo and the monk as they followed the trail. The sharp peaks, which had glistened with snow and mist, now glinted like the jewels they were named after. All around, the forest bloomed vibrant and lush.

They walked along the course of blanketed green, the sweet smell of honeysuckle and peach heavy in the air. The music was louder now, as were the laughter and melodic singing of the unseen beings.

"What is this place?" Taejo asked.

"We are walking into the playground of the gods," Brother Woojin said. His excitement was palpable and contagious. "When they first appeared in our world, they came here to the Diamond Mountains and pronounced it the most wondrous place."

The trail snaked around a jutting mountain. Across a large river, an elaborate golden bridge encrusted in jewels stood near the tallest waterfall she'd ever seen.

"Nine Dragons Waterfall," Kira said with an awestruck breath. "It must be nearly a quarter of a li high!"

A heavy ribbon of water coursed between the shadows of two large mountains. Mist sprayed up into Kira's face, soothing and refreshing.

"Sunim, why is it called Nine Dragons Waterfall?" Taejo asked.

"Legend has it that nine young sea dragons left their

ocean home to seek wives. They flew all over the world but couldn't find anyone that took their fancy. Until they reached the Diamond Mountains. Here, they came across eight Heavenly Maidens, each more beautiful than the other. But there were eight maidens and nine dragon suitors. Unable to choose fairly and unwilling to fight one another, the dragons decided that they would take no wives. Instead they would guard the pool of the maidens so that no one would ever disturb them while they were bathing. It's rumored that the nine dragons live here in this waterfall, always ready to protect their maidens."

"I wish I could see them," Taejo said. "I've always wanted to see a dragon."

Kira shook her head. "Yes, but nine of them at the same time? I think that would give me heart palpitations."

As they crossed the bridge, Kira leaned her face into the spray, enjoying the tingling sensation of the cool water before hurrying after the others. She missed the warm weather terribly. Camping out in the winter elements taught her one thing—she hated the cold.

They stopped short before a staircase, as ornate as the golden bridge they had just crossed, that appeared magically before them in a steep incline straight up the mountainside, each step made of pure crystal and framed with gold.

"Is it real?" Taejo asked.

Kira stepped forward and ran her fingers over the ornate handrail. She grinned. "Come on, let's climb!"

Jindo barked and whined. The big dog cowered away from the stairs.

"It's all right, boy. You stay here!" Taejo said. Without any hesitation, he began to climb after her.

Kira felt the music pull at her, giving her the confidence to ascend the delicate stairs. For a brief moment, she looked down and felt an intense wave of vertigo. Gripping the golden handrails tightly with both hands, she continued to climb. No one spoke, but it wasn't quiet. The air filled with the roar of the waterfall and the music from above. All she could see were clouds and mist. She walked out into a valley where a series of jade pools, linked together like beads on a necklace, fed the waterfall.

A narrow trail ran alongside the pools. Taejo hesitated, looking to Kira as if uncertain of what to do.

"I'm scared," he said.

"I think we'll be fine," she said. "Come on, let's see where this leads."

The path curved around a bend and brought them to a large pool.

Kira stopped short in astonishment. Beautiful women dressed in lavish robes of jewel-tone colors sat on the edge of the pool, their small, delicate feet dipped in the water. Some held instruments, while others just lounged, singing along to a melody unknown to Kira. Their long, flowing hair shone in colors she had never seen before, and their skin tones were as varied as their hair. One maiden had skin as dark as night, while another had hair as white as snow. Behind them, the valley stretched around the mountain bend with more pools connecting to one another like shimmering jewels.

The music stopped abruptly as the women became aware of their presence.

"You have arrived!" one maiden said as she rose to her feet and approached them. She was very tall with long black hair, which shone as if lacquered.

"Welcome, Prince Taejo, Lady Kira," she continued. "I am Lady Mina. We have been expecting you."

32

Kira eyed the creature before her, not quite sure if she was real. Who was this beautiful woman, and how did she know their names? Were these the Heavenly Maidens of Brother Woojin's story?

Still dazed, Kira followed as Lady Mina led them toward the now silent and motionless group. She was relieved to hear Brother Woojin coming up behind them. Although she sensed no danger, she was nervous and intimidated by these strangers.

"Is this who we have delayed our trip home for, Sister?" an arrogant-looking maiden asked.

Lady Mina nodded. "They come in fulfillment of the prophecy."

"Oh, our saviors!" the other maiden mocked as she idly plucked at her zither. Taken aback by her coldness, Kira decided she did not like the arrogant maiden.

"Don't mind Lady Mei," Lady Mina said. "She's tired and wishes to return home. We've been waiting here for nearly a month."

"I'm sorry," Taejo stuttered in reply.

She laughed and clapped her hands. "But you are here now, and that is what matters!"

Lady Mina said, "I'm so happy to meet you both. Especially you, Lady Kira! You must be the prettiest warrior I have ever seen!"

Several of the other maidens burst into laughter at her comment, causing Kira to flush in angry embarrassment. They were so beautiful and graceful, and yet Kira could sense the power they possessed. It flowed through the air, a sort of magnetic pulse that made Kira aware of her own humanity.

Lady Mina placed a comforting arm about her shoulders and gave her a gentle squeeze. A tall, dark-skinned maiden approached them and embraced Kira.

"Never be ashamed of what you are, child," she said in a voice of deep authority. Her handsome carved face did not smile, but she radiated kindness and compassion.

"Lady Morrell is a warrior-queen in her own lands," Lady Mina said.

"In her own lands?" Kira repeated.

"We are the Eight Heavenly Maidens, sent down to care for our lands. The natural world is our domain, and each of us is responsible for different regions. Lady Morrell's lands are vast and hot, where part of the region may be desert, while another part may be rain forests. There they worship her as a warrior-queen and protector of the wild."

Lady Mina pointed to a maiden with snow-white hair and skin, and eyes as blue as the sky above. "Lady Rowena oversees the far northern lands, where ice and snow are daily concerns. Lady Mei is Cathay's maiden, while Lady Gwen is in charge of a faraway land you have never even heard of."

Lady Mei was the maiden Kira did not like, while Lady Gwen was a petite maiden with yellow hair the color of ripe grain, who played a lovely melody on a bamboo flute.

"You are the angels the monks talked about!" Taejo exclaimed.

Lady Mina laughed. "Yes, we've been called that, too. Come," she said. "You must be hungry."

They followed her to a path that led to the other side of the mountain. In an outdoor pavilion, a lavish spread covered a large banquet table set with delicate china, golden chopsticks, spoons, and jeweled goblets. The feast held many familiar and unfamiliar items. Roasted meats piled high on platters surrounded by vegetables. Mounds of rice and noodles sat next to plates of whole fish and hot pots of spicy, simmering stews. At the far end, platters of rice cakes, pastries, and sweets sat next to bowls filled with peaches, apricots, oranges, strawberries, and other fruits, many of them strange and unfamiliar.

At the banquet table, three other maidens approached them.

"I am Lady Mari, and am so happy to see you!"

Kira blinked several times in awe of the three maidens before her. Lady Mari seemed to be awash in golden tones. Her hair, skin, and eyes were the color of rich honey. She introduced Lady Sara, with hair as red as a pomegranate, and Lady Minot, a dark-haired woman with eyes of jade green. Their warm welcomes more than made up for the indifference of the other maidens. But what captivated Kira the most was to see Lady Mari's golden-yellow eyes, so similar to her own. For the first time in her life, Kira didn't resent her differences.

Everyone sat at the table, the Heavenly Maidens all on one side, their backs to the jade pools. The smell of the food was intoxicating, and at Lady Mina's invitation, Kira began to fill her plate with roasted meats and vegetables, sticking to dishes she recognized.

As they ate, Lady Mina addressed Brother Woojin.

"You have done well to bring your charges here," she said. "Another day, and it would have been too late."

"My apologies, my lady," he said.

Lady Mina waved a slender hand. "It doesn't matter. For a Dragon King's descendant is here, and tomorrow is the winter solstice."

"Dongji," Kira whispered. The day of the shortest sunlight and the longest night. The Dongji festival was always her favorite time of the year, when her mother and aunt, uncaring of their royal dignity, would chase the kitchen servants away and make her favorite dish, sweet red-bean-and-dumpling porridge. She felt homesick and noticed Taejo's downcast face.

"Never fear, Prince Taejo; you will see your mother again," Lady Mina said.

Her words caused him to sit up straighter. He began to attack his food with vigor. Kira felt a sharp pang to know that Lady Mina could not say the same to her.

Upset, Kira crammed a large bite of clear rice noodles into her mouth and tried to pay attention to the conversation.

"It is of grave concern to us," Lady Morrell was saying. "Each day, the Demon Lord's powers grow stronger in the human world. Death and conquest feed him. The heads of his enemies, brought back by the shipload in tribute, strengthen him."

Lady Mei sat forward, her hooded eyes staring straight at Taejo. "If the Seven Kingdoms fall, then Cathay is next!"

"You only worry about Cathay?" Lady Morrell scorned. "If the Seven Kingdoms fall, the world is next, or have you forgotten the power of these sacred mountains?"

Mei subsided as the other maidens grew restless.

"These mountains are vital to us. As long as a Heavenly Maiden is here, nothing can enter these mountains without our permission. Four times a year, all eight of us gather here from our lands and revitalize for one week. But once a year, on the day of the winter solstice, we return home to the heavens for one month," Mina said. "Within the human realm, we have magical abilities and may move about the world with the wind. But we cannot return home from anywhere but here, for the entrance to the heavenly palace lies directly above these mountains."

"That means, as of tomorrow the mountains will be unprotected," Kira said.

"That is not entirely true," Lady Mina said. "These mountains have many protections themselves; do not fear. And the true danger only occurs if and when the Demon Lord sets foot in these lands."

"So all we have to do is drive the Yamatos out and kill the Demon Lord?" Kira asked.

Lady Mei laughed. "Kill the Demon Lord? You cannot kill him. He is indestructible; only his human portal can be harmed."

Kira gritted her teeth and nodded. "If we find a way to kill Daimyo Tomodoshi, then that will keep the Demon Lord in the underworld?"

The maidens nodded. Kira repressed a sudden shudder. How could they fight the Demon Lord? One glance at Taejo, and she knew he was in complete panic.

"Do not let fear overtake you, young prince," Brother Woojin said, his soothing voice breaking through the tense quiet. "The Heavenly Father will not desert us in our greatest time of need. That you must always have faith in."

Taejo asked, "What is it we must do?"

The maidens all turned to Lady Morrell, who was clearly their undisputed leader. The maiden rose from her seat, appearing every inch a warrior-queen, and swept her arm over a portion of the table. Immediately the food and drink at the center vanished. In their stead appeared a miniature map of the Diamond Mountains. Small peaks rose up from the table, and waterfalls and rivers flowed throughout. The detail was exact, down to three small figures located beside the string of pools above Nine Dragons Waterfall. Kira realized that the figures were of her, Taejo, and Brother Woojin. Tracing their steps backward, Kira found Jindo waiting at the foot of the waterfall and then their tents with three tiny versions of Kwan, Jaewon, and Seung standing guard in the cold. Unlike their current surroundings, the map showed the true weather, as snow blanketed the entire region.

Her breath caught as she found herself wishing the others were with them now. It seemed so unfair that they could not see this magnificent place or meet these earthbound goddesses.

"What wondrous magic!" Taejo said. He reached out a hand to touch the map, only to see his hand pass through it like water.

Lady Morrell pointed to the waterfall and, with a flick of her finger, lifted the ribbon of water to expose a cave at its tail.

"There is a path behind the waterfall that will take you to a cave. Tomorrow, before the last ray of the sun sets on the winter solstice, a descendant of the Dragon King must enter the cave and find what has been lost."

"Alone?" Taejo asked.

"You may take one companion with you."

"But what am I looking for?" Taejo asked.

"Only when you are in the cave will you know what you seek," Lady Morrell intoned. "Good luck to you. Perhaps someday we shall meet again."

Kira wanted to ask more questions. What were they to do with what they found? How would it help them? Why did the Heavenly Maiden have to be so mysterious? But Lady Morrell's stern face intimidated her as much as it did her cousin. They shyly nodded at the warrior-queen.

Lady Morrell inclined her head as a shimmering light haloed above her, blinding Kira and the others with its brilliance. Peering up, she saw Lady Morrell place her hand on a brilliant rope of gold, which lifted her straight up into the sky. Each maiden moved forward, waving a hand in farewell, and they, too, caught hold of the rope and disappeared into the heavens. Even Lady Mei offered them a smile and well-wishes before disappearing into the clouds. The last to leave was Lady Mina.

"Your paths lie intertwined with a greater destiny. What will happen none of us really knows, for far too many factors can affect the outcome," Lady Mina said.

The musical voices could be heard from above, urging her to hurry. As the maiden glided toward the rope, Kira ran up to her.

"Please, my lady," Kira cried out. "What of my mother? She is trapped in the shadow realm! Please, what must I do to save her?"

"You must destroy the one who cursed her," the maiden replied. She gazed at Kira with eyes that seemed to gleam with a deep knowledge. "But remember, revenge for the dead should never occur at a price to the living. Don't give up on the world. Trust in yourself and others. Trust in the heavens that you are on the right path."

Kira was so shaken by the maiden's words that she forgot to thank her. Lady Mina placed her hand on the rope and waved good-bye.

"My Heavenly Father awaits me. Blessings to you all. We shall meet again. . . ." Her voice trailed away as her form disappeared with the rope, and the light faded.

Kira gazed up at the heavens, when suddenly she heard the maiden's voice. "Do not forget your vow to your father; protect the prince with your life, for he is the One."

She started in alarm, but no one else seemed to notice the maiden's voice.

"He will be the true king—the one who will reunite

the kingdoms." Lady Mina's lovely voice rang loud in her head.

"I won't forget. I will protect him with my life," Kira whispered. The voice faded, leaving her mind clear.

"Quickly, children, we must leave now!" Brother Woojin said. Kira looked to see the monk pointing at the roof of the pavilion, which was beginning to slowly fade.

"It's disappearing!" Taejo said.

Without stopping to think, Kira ran to the banquet table and grabbed a bowl of fruit, which she piled high with more food.

"What are you doing? We have to get out of here!" Taejo shouted.

Kira threw in the meats and vegetables in a big pile, picked up the bowl, and ran after them. They raced back to the waterfall staircase, which had not yet begun to disappear. Kira looked behind her to see the pavilion had become a mere shimmering mirage. Through it, the winter-clad mountains could once again be seen.

Taejo and Brother Woojin scrambled down the steps first, cautious not to fall. Kira found it hard to maneuver with only one hand, but she was determined not to let go of the bowl. At the bottom of the staircase, Jindo stood, barking and waving his tail madly. Taejo and the monk jumped down and raced for the bridge.

Kira held tight to her bowl and crossed the flickering structure. Once all of them were safely over, it disappeared in a shimmer of light, leaving behind an old rickety bridge in its place. Spring melted back into winter, and the cold wind pierced through their flesh. They trudged through the snow until they reached the boulder where their winter coats lay in neat piles. With freezing fingers, they pulled on their coats and returned to camp.

As they emerged from the forest trail, they observed the glow of the large campfire and three people racing toward them.

Kwan reached them first. "Thank the gods! I was so worried about all of you!" he said.

Jaewon and Seung looked relieved to see them. Seung's eyes lit up.

"Where in the world did you get that food?" he asked. Kira pushed the large bowl into his hands and sat down before the fire. Delighted, Seung hugged the bowl to his chest. He passed out several large yellow pears to Kwan and Jaewon, who eyed the fruit in bewilderment.

Seung began to eat as the others collapsed before the fire.

"What happened?" he asked around a mouthful of juicy pear.

Kira closed her eyes as Taejo and Brother Woojin tried to explain the wonder they'd observed.

Mother, I know what to do now. I will not fail you. She took a deep breath. *I swear to you, I will not fail you.*

33

Breakfast consisted of a hot rice porridge mixed with meats and vegetables, and a meatless version for Brother Woojin, from the food Kira had brought back. Everyone ate with gusto except Taejo.

"What's the matter? Is it not to your liking?" Seung asked with a worried expression.

"No, I'm just not that hungry," Taejo replied.

"Today is a momentous day. It is important that you be well nourished," Brother Woojin said.

Taejo shoved a large scoop of food into his mouth with his small, flat-headed spoon before putting the bowl down.

"Who will you choose to go with you?" Brother Woojin asked.

Taejo's face scrunched tight and his lips pulled into a deep frown. It was clear he didn't want to go.

"I'll go with him," Kwan said. "I'll watch out for you, little cousin!"

"No!" Taejo said. "I'm taking Kira."

Kwan's face fell in disappointment. "Of course, Kira is a good choice."

"Apparently, the prince feels safer with your little sister than with you," Jaewon teased.

Kwan glared at him and stalked away, causing Jaewon to laugh.

Kira ignored them. She was thinking of the journey and wondered what they would need to bring along. The Heavenly Maidens had been obscure, and Brother Woojin was typically unclear. She worried that without any knowledge of what was ahead for them, she couldn't adequately protect her cousin.

But more distracting was that she now knew how to free her mother. Last night she'd dreamed of the shadow room again. Her mother and the other shadows had appeared, but they didn't know the name of the shaman who had cursed them.

"He is a Yamato. A soldier close to Shin," her mother had said. "You will find him, little one. I have faith."

It was the last she heard before all the shadows faded away. She woke up and joined Kwan on the early-morning watch. They'd spoken at length about what to do, and they agreed that they must return to Hansong.

But for now, she had to focus on the task before them. She willed herself to forget about Shin and the shaman, smothering the hot anger and grief that simmered within her.

"What do you think we will need?" she asked Taejo.

Taejo hunched his shoulders and huddled down by the fire. Part of her wanted to hit him and make him snap out of his fog; the other part wanted to lock him away from danger. Now that she knew the Heavenly Maidens had marked him as the Dragon Musado, she could feel the weight of her responsibility. She'd vowed to keep him safe. It was a vow that she would keep at all costs to herself—and others.

She picked up her water bag and her leather satchel, throwing in a few wrapped packages of food and dried fruit before rising to her feet. Strapping on her sword, she hesitated over her bow and arrow case.

After a long moment, she asked Jaewon to hold them for her. He nodded in reply and slung them over his shoulder.

"Come on, let's go!" she called over to Taejo.

Once again Seung stayed at their campsite, wishing them luck on their journey.

They traveled the same path they had taken the previous night. This time, however, the way was treacherous with snow and ice. When they reached the waterfall where the wondrous golden bridge had stood, only the rickety wooden one remained. They crossed it one at a time, taking care not to step too heavily on any one slat. Unlike before, the waterfall was quiet, mostly frozen. The trail was rocky and slippery. They observed a large gaping cavern clearly through the narrow flow of water. Brother Woojin lit a lantern and passed it to Kira, who waited patiently for Taejo.

"What am I supposed to be looking for?" Taejo asked.

The monk placed his hands on Taejo's shoulders and patted him. "What you seek will come to you."

Kira rolled her eyes, exasperated. She carefully climbed up the rocks to the edge of the waterfall. Stepping behind a curtain of water, she was enveloped by a dank, musty odor with faint undertones of sulfur and mold. The contrast of the light shining through the waterfall and the darkness of the tunnel behind it unnerved her. It was not merely the idea of going deep into the mountain itself that made her throat tighten up, but the thought of what they would find in the cavern below.

Taejo reached her side, an alarmed expression on his face. Jindo leaned close to him.

Unsure of how to calm her cousin, Kira held the lantern high, shining it down into the dark tunnels before them. Jindo took one look down the passageway, whined, and retreated. Taejo tried to command the big dog to come with him, but Jindo refused to enter, hiding behind Brother Woojin. No matter how much Taejo pleaded, cajoled, and commanded, he wouldn't budge.

"You're not a dog! You're a great big chicken!" Taejo yelled.

Brother Woojin laughed and said, "Jindo is embracing his cowardliness. Leave him be, young prince. It is not in an animal's nature to go where it senses danger."

Taejo swallowed hard and muttered, "Lucky dog."

"Come on, it'll be all right," Kira said.

As they entered the cave, Jindo let out an encouraging bark that echoed into the darkness after them. The tunnels were narrow but tall, with crevices that glowed eerie green.

"Let's go back," Taejo said. "I don't like this place."

"We can't," Kira said over her shoulder. "We've come too far to turn back now. I'm sure we're close—I can hear water running." Sniffing the air, she was surprised to note that it smelled briny, like seawater.

Something skittered by, brushing against her foot and running behind her. Taejo jumped and let out a loud yelp, grabbing her arm. Kira shone her lantern on the ground, illuminating the tail of a large rat.

She sighed in irritation at the frightened and disgusted expression on his face.

"You need to calm down and stop acting like a baby," she said.

Hot anger flared in Taejo's face. He grabbed the lantern from Kira's hand and pushed past her to take the lead and stalked down the tunnel.

"Hey! Wait up!" Kira cried out behind him. Suddenly, she heard a surprised yell and a rolling and thudding sound. The tunnel took a sharp turn to the right, causing her to slip. It sloped down at such a steep angle she had to hold on to the wall to keep from falling. Toward the end of the tunnel, she glimpsed the glow of lights, but no sign of her cousin.

"Taejo, are you all right?"

Taejo shouted, and then there was a loud splash. She half ran, half slid down the rest of the way and entered a large cavern with an enormous underground lake bordered by a low retaining wall. Taejo was sputtering and splashing, trying to keep afloat in the murky lake waters. Already, a current was pulling him farther away.

"Kira!" he shouted before going under. Flailing, he bobbed back up. "Kira, help me!"

"Keep swimming!" Kira yelled. She tore off her bag and sword and her heavy outerwear.

Taejo's head went under again and he struggled to fight his way to the surface. Before Kira could jump into the water, a great surge rippled across the surface, pushing Taejo up and out of the lake. Below him swam a massive turtle, its ridged shell glinting like polished jade. The turtle's powerful strokes took Taejo to the wall in a few glides. He grabbed Kira's outstretched hands and clambered off awkwardly, trembling from the cold.

Only then did she notice the turtle staring at them from large onyx eyes.

"She's beautiful," Kira whispered. She bowed with deep reverence to the turtle. "Thank you for saving my cousin," she said.

"Yes, thank you very much for saving me." Taejo bowed also, his body shaking from his drenching. "How do you know she's a she?" he asked.

Kira smiled, still staring in awe at the creature. "I don't know. Just a feeling."

She couldn't explain. She sensed a warmth and infinite patience that made her think it was female.

Taejo shivered violently.

"You're going to get sick," Kira exclaimed. "I don't have an extra change of clothes for you, but undress as much as you can." Taejo quickly peeled off all his layers until he stood in an undershirt and trousers. She wrapped her quilted jacket and heavy coat around his shaking form and sat him on the low retaining wall.

The turtle continued to float in the water, watching, waiting.

"Wonder what she wants," Taejo said.

Kira shook her head in wonder.

Suddenly, the turtle dived and resurfaced mere inches from them. Taejo pulled away in alarm, but Kira leaned forward. The turtle opened its jaws wide. Nestled on the center of its black tongue was a ruby the size of a plum. Kira sucked in her breath, her mind flashed back to Dragon Springs Temple. She could hear Brother Woojin's voice telling them of the three treasures—one of which was the sacred ruby tidal stone that controlled the seas.

"It must be the tidal stone!" Kira said. "Quick, Taejo, grab it!"

Taejo hesitated.

"Hurry up!"

He jumped away from the wall, breathing hard. Kira looked at him in disbelief.

He covered his face. "Make it stop staring at me!"

"But you're the Dragon Musado!" she said, even as she realized it would do no good.

The turtle remained frozen in position, its mouth hinged open. Kira reached in and took the ruby, surprised to find it pulsing with warm heat. As soon as she withdrew her hand, the turtle closed its mouth with a loud snap and slowly began to submerge into the recesses of the lake. Kira waved in thanks and farewell, watching until the last bubbles faded and the lake was calm once more. Staring at the bloodred jewel, she sensed a latent power within it, which reached out to her and spoke of tidal waves, hurricanes, and monsoons.

"I knew it. Take a look at this!" she said as Taejo finally approached.

Standing on top of the retaining wall, Kira held her hands over the lake, letting the ruby speak through her and into the water. The ruby began to glow brightly as the calm surface frothed and a large wave formed before their eyes. With a sweep of her arms, Kira aimed it at the farthest shore. The water crashed against the wall with a thunderous clap before becoming tranquil again. The Dragon King's sacred ruby tidal stone, which controlled all the seas, pulsed softly in her hands.

"Let me try!" Taejo snatched it away, but what was once bright and warm, with a radiant inner light, dimmed in his hands.

"What happened?" he asked.

Kira shrugged and took the ruby. It began to glow and pulse, as if it were alive. He grabbed it again, only to find the stone cold and lifeless.

"I don't understand. I thought I was supposed to be the Dragon Musado?"

"You are! I think you were supposed to take it when the turtle first offered it to you. Why didn't you?" Kira asked. She wondered if their actions had changed the course of both their futures.

Taejo shook his head.

"I saw something in its eyes. Something terrible. I can't explain. Maybe it means you're the Dragon Musado," Taejo said, puzzled. "But you can't be! You're a girl."

She glared at him. "Why do you think that would make a difference?"

"But that is the way of things. You know it, too."

Kira shrugged, aware of the truth of his words. How she hated that phrase, *the way of things*.

Taejo's refusal to take the stone might have transferred its powers to her, but it still didn't change the fact that the Heavenly Maidens had named him the One. That must mean he was the Dragon Musado. The thought dimmed some of her joy at finding the tidal stone.

"I don't understand. Why doesn't it work for me?" he said.

"You should have grabbed it when you had the chance," she retorted. Then, less harshly, "I don't know. Maybe I just need to hold it for you until you get the other two treasures. Think of me as just the keeper."

He nodded, but Kira caught the angry frown on his face.

"Come on," she said. "Let's go."

She pulled out her small leather pouch that hung around her neck. Opening it, she placed the ruby next to her little haetae statue before tying it closed and tucking it under her shirt.

She gazed down into the water and reached her hand in, grabbing a small rock covered in green, glowing algae.

"Look! These rocks glow, even in the water!" she said.

Taejo glanced indifferently at her find. But Kira was intrigued. She leaned into the water and gathered several more glowing stones, which she placed in her bag. Catching Taejo's moody gaze, she smiled.

"They might come in handy," she said.

Without answering, Taejo ran up the sloping tunnel. They trudged back, neither speaking, too caught up in their own thoughts.

The warm, pulsing sensation of the ruby stone against her chest was pleasant. The power of it made her heady.

Kira could use it to destroy Shin and the Yamato army. She could find the shaman who had cursed her family and kill him. Kill them all.

The stone grew warmer, pulsing against her skin, in tandem with the rapid beating of her heart.

34

"I don't understand," Brother Woojin said. "Why do you have it?"

Kira could see the shock and confusion on everyone's faces.

"I am just the keeper of the stone for the prince," she replied. "He was in an accident in the cave and was unable to retrieve it. That's why he's all wet and should change his clothes now." Taejo moved away, avoiding Brother Woojin's questioning gaze.

Brother Woojin gasped with reverence when Kira placed the stone in his hands. He held it up to the light and watched it catch the rays of the sun. The stone remained dormant in his hands. With a heartfelt sigh, he put it back into the leather pouch and hesitated.

"Perhaps I should hold it for the prince?" he asked, turning toward Taejo.

Kira clutched the bag.

"It's my job to keep it safe," she said. She tucked the precious parcel under her jacket.

"Keep it near you at all times," the monk said.

Kira nodded. Of course she would keep it near.

She shivered in the cold. Taejo was still wearing her coat. She was wishing she had another layer to put on, when someone placed a warm blanket around her shoulders.

"We can't have you freezing to death," Jaewon said.

Kwan came between them, sending Jaewon an untrusting look. "Thank you very much, but my sister doesn't need yours. I'll give her mine."

He pushed off Jaewon's blanket and replaced it with his own. Jaewon shrugged and gave her a rueful wink before handing back her bow and arrows. Kira barely noticed the tension between the two. For once, she was really happy. She'd found the legendary tidal stone. And it had worked for her and not Taejo. For a brief moment, she wished that she could be the Dragon Musado. But it just wasn't possible.

They headed back to their campsite, Taejo setting off before them with only Jindo for company.

"Taejo, wait!" Kira said, starting after him.

"Leave him be," Kwan said. "He needs time to himself without you mothering him."

She halted, shocked at his words. "I don't mother him!"

"Yes, you do. You're worse than a dog with a bone, always all over him, checking up on him, coddling him. Give him some space! Leave him alone," he groused. "I know Father asked us to protect Taejo, but you have to let him make his own mistakes, or he will never become the man he is destined to become."

Kira winced.

"I'm not trying to hurt you, little sister." Her brother softened his tone. "I'm just saying, let him have some room to grow into himself."

She pushed past him, unsure of what to think. Her vow was always first and foremost in her mind, and the Heavenly Maiden had also confirmed her duty.

Regardless of what Kwan believed, she would continue to protect her cousin to the best of her abilities. But she would give some thought to Kwan's words.

Just as she made her decision to run ahead, Jindo came crashing through the woods, barking. The hair on the back of her neck rose.

"Something is wrong," she said.

Jaewon pressed a finger to his mouth for silence. In the sudden quiet, they heard the crackling and shuffling sounds of many heavy boots tramping over snow and ice. Kwan signaled for everyone to disperse, and Kira took off, Jindo right at her heels. She raced deeper into the woods, away from the approaching men, and then began to cut diagonally toward their campsite. As she ran, she noticed Brother Woojin keeping up with her. There was no sign of the others.

Through a break in the trees, she peered below into an open clearing alongside the river. Taejo and Seung were prodded forward by Yamato soldiers with drawn swords. Shin Bo Hyun walked in the lead.

"Where the hell are they?" he shouted. "They should have found the others and caught up to us by now!"

Kira pondered her next move, when the familiar sound of arrows whistling through the air dispatched the rear guard and two more Yamato soldiers. She raised her bow to fire, but Brother Woojin stopped her.

Shin Bo Hyun shouted into the woods for backup. Within minutes, a horde of enemy soldiers charged from the woods, swords held high. Kira gasped in horror. Where had these men been hiding? How could their group of six fight an entire troop of over a hundred enemy soldiers? She wanted to shoot, but again, Brother Woojin kept a firm grip on her bow, shaking his head.

"We must wait for the right moment," he whispered.

They slunk into the shadows of the trees and watched as Kwan and Jaewon were dragged out.

Her brother head-butted a soldier. With a slight pivot, Kwan reverse side-kicked, sending the soldier who was holding him flying back. Freeing his right hand, he struck an attacker in the chin with an upward thrust of the heel of his palm, knocking him unconscious. Kwan took down five Yamato soldiers before Shin Bo Hyun bashed his forehead with the pommel of his sword. Kwan fell to his knees as soldiers tied his hands. He was hauled next to Jaewon and Seung, both of them battered and bound.

Kwan spit at Shin Bo Hyun, hatred blazing hot on his face. "You filthy traitor! Cowardly swine! Come on and fight me yourself! Give me my revenge!"

The soldier next to Kwan punched him hard in the mouth repeatedly.

"That's enough," Shin Bo Hyun said. The soldier stepped away.

"Where's your sister?"

Kwan coughed up blood and spit on the ground.

"She's not here. We left her with our uncle in Guru."

"Please don't insult me. Kira would never leave the prince's side. She must be nearby," Shin Bo Hyun said.

"You leave my sister alone or I'll rip you apart and feed you to the dogs like you deserve!" Kwan shouted.

"Tut, tut. So much anger!" Shin Bo Hyun said. "It isn't good for you. Unhealthy." He paused. "Of course that's a moot point right now, unless your sister, my lovely bride-to-be, would be so kind as to trade herself for you. All three of you."

He raised his voice, letting it echo over the ridge. "What say you, Kira? I know you're out there. You're not doing a good job of protecting the prince. I think your father would be very disappointed in you."

Kwan was shouting profanities, but Kira could no longer hear him over the ringing in her ears. She closed her eyes and tried to think of what to do.

"I wonder, will you continue to hide and watch as your brother and his friends die?"

Suddenly, Shin Bo Hyun hauled Jaewon away.

"No," Kira whispered.

Shin Bo Hyun shoved Jaewon into the middle of the clearing before several archers.

"Kang Kira!" he shouted. "Don't keep me waiting."

Brother Woojin stopped Kira from rushing down. "No, young mistress, not that way. Use the tidal stone."

The soldiers raised their bows. All Kira could see of Jaewon was his back—but he stood tall and proud. She could hear Taejo screaming at Shin Bo Hyun to let them go.

"No!" Taejo screamed. "Don't hurt any of them! You've got me. I'll go with you. Just let them go."

"I'm not leaving without my betrothed!" Shin Bo Hyun answered.

She heard Jaewon's calm voice. "It'll be all right, my prince."

With shaky hands, she pulled out the tidal stone. The ruby began to warm, glowing brightly as she concentrated all her thoughts on it. The stone seemed curious, asking her what she wanted from it. Her thoughts were too frenzied to be coherent. All she knew was that she needed to save them and that it had to be something really big.

"Kira!" Shin Bo Hyun shouted; a hint of desperation sounded in his voice. "His blood will be on your hands!"

Please, right now! she screamed inside.

"At my command!"

The archers were drawing their bowstrings when the river surged and bubbled, exploding into a huge tidal wave and knocking them off their feet. The water formed a large column that rose straight up into the sky. The soldiers panicked. Shin Bo Hyun shouted for his men to hold their positions, but all deserted their posts.

Kira's hands were burning from the heat of the stone. The ruby prodded at her mind, but Kira didn't know what it wanted.

Just save them, she begged.

Within the column, a figure materialized, obscured at first by the water seething about it. A large triangular-shaped head formed over an elongated neck as legs, claws, and a tail formed. It was a dragon, made entirely of water, that towered above the men on the river's edge. The dragon lowered its head until it faced Shin Bo Hyun. It opened its mouth and let loose a torrent of water that swept him and his men into a wild and raging flood. The tidal stone knew to protect Taejo and the others, listening to Kira's directions as it set the water dragon loose.

With the threat gone, Kira fell to her knees, exhausted. She carefully packed away the ruby as a gentle hand pulled her up. Brother Woojin held her steady as she felt the ebbing of the stone's power. Releasing her, he clasped his hands together and bowed in respect, acknowledgment of her power over the tidal stone. Kira bowed in return and raced down the ridge.

At the river's edge, Seung knelt before the water dragon and prostrated himself. It began to diminish, reducing in size until finally it disappeared completely. Kwan limped over, still groggy from his injuries, and wrapped an arm around Kira's shoulders.

"That was you, wasn't it, little sister?" Kwan asked. Taejo stood at his side, grinning broadly.

"That was spectacular! I can't believe you made a water dragon!" Taejo said.

"How in heaven's name were you able to do that?" Jaewon asked in astonishment.

Kira was still dazed by the power that had flowed through her body. "I asked the tidal stone for something really big to save you, and that's what happened."

"Whatever it was, it was amazing!" Kwan said. He gave Taejo an affectionate cuff to his shoulder. "Hey, maybe Kira's the Dragon Musado!"

Jaewon nodded in agreement, his eyes shining with open admiration.

"No, I'm not!" she said sharply. "Lady Mina told me Taejo is the One—the true king who will reunite the kingdoms."

She faced her cousin. "Listen, I know you doubt yourself. I mean, we all did. But now, I know what I must do and what I believe. I believe you are the Dragon Musado, and I am meant to protect you with my life."

Taejo's face was solemn. "If you say so, Noona. I trust you."

35

They returned to Singing Temple to find it deserted.

"Oh no," Kira said. "Was this Shin Bo Hyun's work?"

"No, they are safe," Brother Woojin said. He headed for the wooden pagoda and rang the temple bell thirty-three times.

With the last toll of the bell, Taejo turned to Kira and asked, "What is he doing? What is the meaning behind the number of times the bell was struck?"

"It represents the monks' belief in the thirty-three steps to enlightenment," Kira replied.

At that moment, a hidden door opened from underneath the temple, and the monks came rushing to greet them.

"I knew you would return safely," Master Hong said. "Which is why I made your soldiers wait with us in the underground tunnels rather than have them get lost in the mountains trying to find you."

"Our soldiers?" Kira asked.

They were astonished to see Captain Pak and a company of Hansong soldiers leading their horses from underneath the temple.

"Master, just how big are your underground tunnels?" Kwan asked in awe.

"We've been known to lose a couple of novices down there every so often," Master Hong chortled.

"He's not serious, is he?" Kwan asked Brother Woojin.

"It's hard to know," Brother Woojin replied. "He has an unusual sense of humor."

Captain Pak hailed them. "I am grateful to see that all of you are safe," he said. "I admit to having quite a few nightmares while you were gone."

"King Eojin was successful?" Kwan asked.

The captain grinned. "The Iron Army easily defeated the Yamatos and has been chasing them back down the peninsula."

"That's excellent news!" Kira said. "Where is he now?"

"How is the king?" Taejo cut in anxiously. "Is he angry at us?"

"Well, King Eojin was not happy with me," the captain replied. "For a moment there, I thought he was going to throw me in prison. But then he decided to send me after all of you with a message instead. He asked that you all rejoin him at our next rendezvous point as the Iron Army is heading to Hansong."

Kira and Kwan looked at each other in relief. This was where they needed to go.

"He's going to save my mother!" Taejo said.

After several more minutes of conversation, the captain left to address his soldiers, leaving the cousins to plan their journey. Brother Woojin intervened.

"I'm sorry, but we cannot afford to go to Hansong at this time. We must press on and find the other two treasures," Brother Woojin said. "It is our first priority."

Kira caught sight of Taejo's crushed face and thought of her own family.

"Sunim, I beg your pardon, but our priority right now is to save what remains of our families."

The monk raised his eyebrows.

"And what good is it if the Dragon Musado is killed or captured before we're able to find the rest of the treasures? You vowed to keep the prince safe!"

"My first and most important priority is to keep Taejo safe. But no less important is my responsibility to save my family. My mother is trapped in the shadow realm. If I don't do all I can to save her, then she will be trapped there forever. She will be a lost soul. I can't let that happen," she said. "My brother and I must return to Hansong. You and the prince can continue without us."

"No!" Taejo shouted. "I'll run away and follow you! I swear it! You know I will!"

"Hush, be quiet," Kira said.

The monk rolled his prayer beads between his palms and stood in deep repose. After several minutes, he nodded at her.

"We can't let that happen," he said.

Kira bowed in thanks.

"But I caution all of you to keep the discovery of the tidal stone secret. Even from King Eojin!" he said.

Ten days later, Kira and the others were reunited with the Guru army. They were camped within the mountains that stretched north of Hansong City. When they arrived, Eojin swept the cousins and Brother Woojin aside, where he took all of them to task for sneaking away and leaving him with only a note.

"I should be very angry with you all. But I find I cannot hold onto my anger when I see you standing safe before me," Eojin said, his eyes lingering on Taejo. He cuffed the prince on the cheek and smiled. "Come and tell me about all your adventures."

Kira could see Taejo's happiness to be reunited with their uncle. It was clear to her that they had developed a close bond. She was relieved to know that she could count on her uncle to protect Taejo.

The next morning, they attended a meeting with Eojin and the Guru commanding generals. Captain Pak was reviewing the plan to recapture Hansong.

"There is an old tunnel entrance into the palace compound, which is now completely submerged underwater," the captain said, pointing at a detailed rendering of Hansong Palace. "It was once a private underground pier for escorting the royal family to safety in case of a siege. The water levels rose years ago, and the entrance is long forgotten. The only way to access it is to swim under the palace wall for a distance of twenty to thirty horse lengths, through the entrance, and up into the underground pier."

"How do we know this is viable and not a death trap for our men?" one of Eojin's generals asked.

"Because my father did it once years ago," Kwan answered. He stepped forward and took his place next to Captain Pak. "He said he was underwater for at least two minutes, possibly three, before he reached the entrance. It's doable, but it is only for the strongest and fastest swimmers."

Captain Pak continued. "The first problem is that there will be no light. Fortunately for us, our young mistress Kang brought back these stones." He placed one of the glowing stones on the table, where it pulsed weakly. The men all looked at Kira in surprise.

"It doesn't emit a strong light, but it's enough to see where you're going," Kira said with a shrug.

"It's excellent. This plan wouldn't work without them," Pak responded. "Once inside the palace, the group will rendezvous with our spymaster, proceed to the northern gates, and wait for the signal."

"Who is leading this group?" General Kim asked.

"I am," Kwan said. "I'll take my sister and four additional men."

Taejo started in surprise. Kira avoided his gaze, guilty that she'd hidden their plans from him.

King Eojin placed a new map on the table. "We will attack at dawn. Our armies will approach from three directions. The main charge will proceed southwesterly, down the line of fire. General Kim will command the special units and approach from the west. They will lay siege upon the city walls."

"How will special units bring their equipment through the mountains?" a heavily armored general asked, frowning down at the map.

"Piecemeal," Eojin replied. "They are carrying parts of the catapults over the mountains. Most are already on their way. The shaman went first and killed all the imp spies in the area. Our spymaster tells us that Lord Shin has become complacent. He doesn't believe an army can come over the mountains, so he mans a single guard tower over the northern passes."

General Kim snorted. "Shin is a fool." The officers muttered their agreement.

"During the initial battle, Captain Pak will lead his men to the northern gates from the mountains for a surprise attack. When Kwan and his men hear the captain's war cry, they will open the gates."

What would happen if they were not there to open the gates was left unsaid.

Taejo approached Kwan. "I am going with you," he said.

"Absolutely not!" Kwan retorted, pushing Taejo away. "It's too dangerous for you."

"My mother is in there!" Taejo shouted. "You can't keep me from helping her!"

Kira stepped between them before her brother said something he would regret.

"This is a dangerous mission. Only the strongest and fastest swimmers have a chance of making it through," she said.

"I can do it," Taejo said. "I may not be as strong as you, but I'm fast."

"It's not safe for you; you can't go," she said.

His face turned mulish. "You promised to take care of me! You're supposed to always be by my side! You swore an oath to my father!"

Kira's lips tightened. "Fine, then I won't go," she said.

"No, we are all going and we are going to save my mother!"

Kwan heaved a frustrated sigh. "Listen, this is not a rescue mission for your mother. This is a mission solely to open up the gates for the army. You are too young to—"

"I am not too young, and I am still your prince. I

order you to take me!" Taejo said.

Kwan threw up his hands and sought King Eojin, who had stayed quiet throughout the argument. "Your Majesty, I defer to you on this matter," Kwan said with a bow.

Eojin studied Taejo. If she hadn't been so angry, Kira would have enjoyed watching her young cousin thrust out his chin and glare at the king.

"I will not stop him," Eojin said with a weary smile. "I tried before, and all of you sneaked away. I won't risk that again. Go with the gods, young prince."

They left early the next morning. Their group consisted of Kwan, Kira, Taejo, and three soldiers who Captain Pak personally selected. Jaewon and Seung would ride with Captain Pak, although Jaewon had tried to convince Kwan to take him. Her brother, already fed up with Taejo's stubbornness, refused to respond to Jaewon's request.

Kira once again entrusted her bow and arrows to Jaewon. She also left him with her travel bag, which contained all that remained of her home and family. Lastly, she handed over her favorite nambawi. She didn't want to risk ruining it in the underwater swim. He accepted her bow and bag with gravity, but his hands gripped hers hard over her nambawi.

"Why can't I go with you?" he asked.

"It's not your responsibility," she said. "It's ours."

"But I want to help."

Kira shook her head. "It would be better for you to help the king."

"I'm not here for the king, I'm here for you," he said.

Kira pulled her hands away. "You know I've never had a friend before," she said. "And now I think, so this is what it feels like—to have someone care for you and want to help you. It's a good feeling." She smiled. "Thank you for being my friend."

She gave a small bow and went to Taejo's side. Her cousin was having a difficult time leaving Jindo behind with Seung. Kira almost believed he'd change his mind, so wrenching was the parting. But Taejo collected himself and left without a backward glance. The big dog's yelps of distress followed their departure.

They rode west of Hansong before crossing over and riding back upriver for nearly half a day to get to the mountainous border of the kingdom. Full of cliffs and dense woods, there was no entranceway into the city from this approach.

Dusk had fallen when they arrived at the rocky cliffs of the western wall. They took off all their outerwear and left it with their horses before climbing down the rocky cliff to the river below. Now that they were right outside the palace, they had to avoid detection by the sentries that patrolled the top of the wall.

"Remember, before we go under, take a big, steady breath. Do not breathe rapidly or you will black out!" Kwan said.

Kwan passed a glowing rock to each of the team members. Following his lead, they entered the water one after the other. Kira braced herself against the frigid water, trying to ignore the numbness of her extremities. She could see the city walls soaring above her through the overhanging branches of the trees, which shielded their group from the sentries above. Kwan kept them close to the wall, submerged up to their eyes and lifting their heads occasionally for a breath of air. Taejo's teeth chattered. Kira wished she could move about and warm herself, but fear of the enemy kept her motionless. She watched as Kwan dived under for a long moment before reappearing. Her brother pointed in the direction they were to take. Using his fingers, he counted off from three to one.

She took a deep breath and submerged into the murky water. Ahead, she saw her brother and the other soldiers kicking powerfully toward a large opening. Another form passed her. Thinking it was Taejo, she followed after him. She swam quickly through an underwater entranceway. It was completely dark, but it took only a moment for her vision to adjust. She couldn't see where the others had gone. Right above her was hard rock. She pushed against the rock, propelling herself forward.

Her lungs constricted as she kicked forward, trying to swim faster. Suddenly, another light cut through the murkiness. She broke into the dank air of the underground chamber, next to an ancient pier. She saw Kwan and the soldiers, but no Taejo.

Kira dived back under. She saw a figure struggling in the distance. She swam as fast as she could and grabbed Taejo's arm. But he continued to flail, fighting her so that she couldn't get ahold of him. Kira knew they were in danger of both drowning. Instinct drove her to reach into her leather pouch and grab the tidal stone. As she focused all her attention on the ruby, it turned red hot in her hand. A huge pulse of water propelled them through and up out of the river.

Several hands pulled the prince to safety before helping her. On the cold stone floor, Taejo lay gasping.

"Are you all right?" Kira asked, kneeling by his side.

Taejo looked dazed and woozy but he was able to nod at her.

"What happened?" Kwan asked.

"I . . . I panicked," he said. "I forgot to use my glowing rock."

Kwan ruffled his hair.

"I'm just glad you made it," he said. "Come on, we need to get moving."

Kira took in her surroundings. It was quite dark, except for the glowing rocks that they carried. Kwan headed toward two diverging tunnels.

"This way," he said, pointing to the right.

The tunnel led them farther into the depths of the palace underground. A streak of bright light shone down upon a wall from between the cracks of a locked door. Kwan inspected the wood, slowly running his fingers over the surface while pressing against portions of the door. Pushing against a spot on the lower right-hand corner, he worked a long dagger slowly into the wood. The dagger sank in.

"Rotted wood," he said triumphantly.

Standing up, he lashed out with a strong front kick against the dagger handle, making an opening for them to pass through. Once clear, the group found themselves in another tunnel, lit with weak lamps. They passed storage rooms filled with crates containing cured meats and root vegetables, and earthen ceramic jars, large enough to hide a man, used for storing rice, beans, and millet.

They heard a man's singing voice.

Kwan and the other soldiers raised their swords and waited on either side of the entranceway.

36

A white-garbed servant trudged in carrying a basket on his shoulder. He froze at the sight of them, his broad face changing from horror to delight.

"Your Highness, is that really you?" he asked. Dropping the basket, he fell to his knees and bowed several times. "It *is* you! Thank the gods!"

Kwan pointed his dagger at the man and placed a finger to his mouth.

"Be quiet," he whispered. "Is there anyone else with you?"

The servant shook his head but lowered his voice in response. "There is no one in this area but me. The

Yamatos don't come down this way because they can't stand the smell of the soy bean paste. I came to bring some up for the cooks."

Kira peered down at the man now smiling up at them. He had drooping eyelids and a flattened nose that looked vaguely familiar.

"I know you," Taejo said. "You're Chang. You used to bring me my morning meals."

Chang's round face beamed with delight. "We thought we'd never see you here again. The queen will be so happy to hear you're safe."

"My mother," Taejo said, moving forward. He pulled the servant up onto his feet, as the man continued to bob his head in respect.

"Tell me, where is my mother? Is she still imprisoned?"

Chang frowned and nodded. "She is in a bad way. King Shin has lost his patience with her and locked her up without food or water. She is very weak."

Taejo's whole body jerked, his face enraged. He ran for the door but was caught by Kwan.

"We have a mission!"

Taejo raised anguished eyes to Kwan and then Kira. "I know you're right. But I only came because I thought I'd have a chance to save my mother."

"You're going to jeopardize everything!" Kwan said.

"I'm sorry," Taejo said. "But please, you must help me. I need to see her before it is too late."

It pained Kira to see him beg for help. Before Kwan could respond, she stepped between them.

"I'll go with him," she said. "We owe it to our aunt to try and save her. You waste time arguing when you need to be gone. We'll meet up with you at our rendezvous point."

Kwan released Taejo and embraced Kira hard.

"Be safe, little sister. Keep the prince alive. Keep yourself alive." His eyes were alight with worry.

"We'll be fine, Oppa. I will see you soon."

Kira nodded and bowed, watching as Kwan and his men disappeared down the tunnels. She turned to Chang, noticing his wide-eyed expression.

"Can you show us the safest way to the dungeons?" she asked.

Chang nodded, but his narrow eyes twitched nervously. Taejo gripped Kira's hand hard in silent thanks. They followed Chang down many tunnels to reach the dungeons on the other side of the palace.

At the dungeon entrance, Kira signaled Chang forward. She stood to the side and crouched low as Chang knocked on the door.

It opened to a large guard, holding a bowl with chopsticks. "Who are you, and what are you doing here?" he asked.

While Chang stuttered a response, Kira peeked between their legs and noticed only one other guard in the room, sitting at a small table slurping noisily from a bowl of noodles. The guard stepped aside and let Chang enter.

Kira jumped forward. Bending low, she threw a reverse lunge punch hard into the guard's groin and then back-kicked him in the chest. He crashed to the ground as the other guard came charging forward with his sword drawn. Kira crouched and executed a reverse roundhouse kick and took out the guard's legs. She cut off his shout with a bash to his head.

Babbling about his need to return to his duties, Chang murmured an apology and fled.

Taejo ran down the dungeon hall, peering through the barred windows, searching for his mother. Kira checked on the guards, making sure they wouldn't rise anytime soon. Closing the door behind her, she picked up the guard's sword and hurried down the hallway. In the last cell, they found the queen asleep on a dirty straw pallet. Her long hair hung in a tangled mess about her beautiful face. Taejo ran in and knelt by her side.

"Mother, I'm here," he said, his voice breaking. "I'm here."

For a long moment, she didn't move, and Kira wondered if they were too late. Then they heard a soft moan, and the queen opened her eyes.

"My son! My son!" she cried. She grabbed hold of Taejo and hugged him tight.

With her free arm, the queen reached over to hug Kira as she wept. "Thank you, thank you."

Kira's flesh tingled all over as she caught a whiff of demon. Pushing herself up off the floor, she tiptoed to the door and peeked down the corridor.

"We need to go now," Kira said.

"Mother, have they have been starving you?" Taejo asked.

The queen nodded, trying to control her tears. "But it's fine now that I have seen both of you again." She caressed Kira's face. "How I miss my poor sister!"

Kira was in a panic. She had no way of knowing how much time they had left, but she knew danger was imminent.

"We have to get out of here," she urged. She slid an arm around her aunt's body and lifted her to her feet, leading her to the door. She was unsteady but could walk. At the guard's table, Taejo poured a cup of water for his mother. The queen gulped the water down.

"We have to go," Kira hissed at them.

Taejo jumped and nodded. Kira half carried her aunt toward the door. They were moving too slowly. How were they ever going to escape with the queen in her weakened condition?

"I feared I would never see you again," Queen Ja-young said. "Now I can die happy."

"No, Mother, we are going to get you out of here," Taejo said.

The dungeon door flew open with a crash. The queen tried to push Taejo behind her, but he resisted. Kira stepped in front of them with her sword raised.

"Well, well, well. I see the son has returned to his mother's loving embrace," Shin gloated. "What a pleasure to see you again, Prince Taejo. But who is this grubby urchin in front of you? Let me guess. Can this be Kang Kira?" He laughed mockingly. "What a fine lady you make—or is this a new court trend you wish to begin: the dirty, smelly, lady soldier look?"

Shin entered the guardroom with a dozen Yamato soldiers behind him.

"I fear it will not be very popular with the other ladies," he said.

Stupid, stupid fool! She could taste the acid burning in her throat as her gut knotted up. It was her fault. She'd known that they were in danger. She should have forced them to leave immediately. There was no chance of escape now.

"But you've never been popular at court, have you, my dear?" he continued. "What with your ugly yellow eyes and your masculine predilections, you are a disgrace to your name."

Lord Shin moved closer, his black eyes glittering with malice. "You must have been so shocked when I agreed to your betrothal to my nephew. For what man would want to marry a freak like you? But the queen was so desperate to see you married. So happy to throw you away at the first eligible man willing to sacrifice himself. My queen was very grateful to me."

"You dog!" the queen spit at him.

"The truth is hard to hear," he chuckled. "The betrothal was merely a ruse to gain everyone's trust, particularly General Kang's." He pointed at Kira. "I fear your father never liked me. But once his only daughter was promised to my nephew, he would have to respect me."

"My father never trusted you," Kira muttered.

"Yes, that's true. But he had to stop speaking badly of me to the king, and that was all I needed."

"If it was all a trick, then why send your nephew after me?" Kira asked.

"Correction, I only sent him after the prince. I told him to kill you. But it appears that my nephew actually finds you attractive. Which makes me question his wisdom."

"Well, you don't have to worry about it anymore, since he's dead," Kira said.

Shin's face tightened as his eyes narrowed into gleaming slits. "Then I have no reason to keep you alive. Lower your gaze or I'll cut your eyes out!"

Kira looked down, unwilling to antagonize him further.

"I must thank you both, for your timing is impeccable. I've grown weary of the queen's refusals, and my threats have had no effect," Shin said. "But now that I have you, I predict a sudden change of heart. Guards, seize the prince."

Four Yamato soldiers moved forward. Kira shoved her

aunt and Taejo farther behind her. Taking a deep breath, she centered herself before attacking. She raised her arms high and twisted her right side toward the first soldier, executing a lethal head strike. Kira let the weight of the heavy sword swing her arms around for an underbody thrust at the second soldier. The third soldier wasted a precious moment pushing away his comrade and met Kira's sword across his neck. Her aunt's scream stopped her from finishing off the fourth.

Taejo was dragged over and forced to kneel before Shin. With a swift movement, Shin pulled a dagger from beneath his cloak and placed the sharp point against Taejo's throat.

"Put down your sword or the prince will die," Shin said.

Kira caught her cousin's eye as she let the sword slip from her hand. She gave a tiny shake of her head. *Don't do anything stupid.*

Showing her empty hands to the guards, she reached down to help her aunt up from where she'd fallen to the ground.

"What say you, my queen? What is your answer now?" Shin tightened his grip on Taejo.

"Don't hurt my son!" the queen cried.

"You know the only answer that will save him."

"No, Mother! Don't do it! Don't disgrace my father's memory by marrying his murderer!" Taejo shouted.

Shin smashed the hilt of the dagger on the top of

Taejo's head. He fell unconscious onto the dirty floor. With an anguished cry, Queen Ja-young clung onto Kira.

"You're naught but a pretender!" she spit. "A lowlife. Worse than a peasant. I've been the consort of a real king, one you could never hope to replace."

Kira wished her aunt had remained silent as Shin's face flushed. He grabbed a whip from the belt of a prison guard and lashed it at Kira's face. A strangled cry broke from her lips, too painful to swallow. She put a hand to her left eye and felt blood course through her fingers.

"Stop it!" the queen raged. "I'll do what you ask of me, only don't hurt them!"

"Too late!" Shin snarled. "Let's put out those ugly yellow eyes forever!"

He lashed the whip again. This time, the queen covered Kira with her body, taking the blow on her back. Kira embraced her aunt, who trembled in pain.

"Don't protect me," Kira whispered. Her left eye was rapidly swelling shut.

Shin had lowered the whip, listening as a stocky Yamato officer spoke to him.

"Yes, you are right, Lord Ito. They would make an excellent example for the people!" Shin said. He tossed down the whip. "Before the sun rises, we will bring them to the cliff! Just think how glorious it will be! The rising sun in the background for our falling royals."

With a final glare at Kira, Lord Shin left with several of his soldiers, leaving Lord Ito and a few guards behind.

Kira found Ito's menacing face more frightening than all of Shin's histrionics. She stared into his narrow, black eyes and saw a flicker of madness—and something else. The foul, charred smell of demon magic filled her nostrils. It wasn't strong enough to be an actual demon. But she recognized it. She knew exactly what it meant.

"You're a shaman!" Kira's voice was hoarse.

His lips curved into a travesty of a smile.

"I've been looking forward to meeting the great Demon Slayer. But how strange, you look nothing like your mother," he said. "Although she was brave, like you. She didn't make a sound when I killed her."

With a scream of rage, Kira pushed away from her aunt and launched herself at the shaman. He punched her injured eye and grabbed her by the throat, strangling her.

"Some of our soldiers have been babbling about a water dragon," he said, his tongue flicking between his lips like a snake's. "Only one thing in the world is powerful enough to control the waters in this manner." He leaned forward, bringing his mad eyes level with hers. "The tidal stone."

He released her throat and ripped the pouch from her neck.

"No!" Kira choked.

Ito pulled out the tidal stone and the little haetae statue. He laughed maniacally as he held the large ruby up to his face.

"Lord Shin is an idiot. He had the greatest treasure in the world before him and walked away. But then again, my master, Daimyo Tomodoshi, never told him about the treasures."

He placed the tidal stone back in its little bag and tied it around his neck. He flung the haetae to the ground. Before she could retrieve it, a guard kicked it beyond her reach.

"How ironic that you brought the most powerful treasure directly to us! Who needs the other treasures now that my master, Daimyo Tomodoshi, can rule the seas," Ito said. "You are no longer a threat."

He was heading to the door when Kira shouted.

"Why did you curse my mother? Why send her and all the other women to the shadow realm?"

Ito stopped at the door and faced her. "It's so simple, really," he said. "Their souls for my powers. Quite an excellent bargain for me, wouldn't you say?"

The door slammed behind him, leaving Kira in despair over the loss of the tidal stone and her haetae.

The remaining soldiers roused Taejo by roughly slapping his face. They pushed the royal family down the hallway, back into the queen's cell.

Queen Ja-young helped Kira down onto the straw pallet. She ripped off a strip of white cloth from her underskirt and patted it against Kira's wound while a dazed Taejo stared in horror at the bloody mess that was her face.

"I'm sorry, Mother! I'm sorry, Noona," he said. "I made a terrible mistake! I have failed again."

"No, my son, you are a blessing to me," the queen said. "I longed to see you once more. It's all I wished for, and here you are. You and Kira. It's as if the gods have answered my prayers."

The pain was intense, but Kira was devastated by the realization of what she'd done. She'd destroyed them all by losing the tidal stone. And the loss of her father's haetae felt as if a part of her had been cut off. She gulped air to stop from crying, but the tears began to fall.

"He has the tidal stone," she said to Taejo. "It was in my pouch—he's wearing it around his neck."

She leaned against the wall. It was hopeless. What could any of them do now?

Her aunt took Kira's hand and placed something in her palm. It was her precious haetae. She sobbed in relief and closed her hand tight, pressing it to her chest. She thought of her brother's mission and Eojin's army so close to the city walls. Kwan was a great warrior. She knew he would succeed.

They still had a chance. She tucked her little haetae within the bindings of her bust wrap. Her sobs died down. Tears wouldn't help her now. What she needed was her strength. She heard Lady Mina's voice again: *Don't give up on the world, trust in the heavens that you are on the right path.*

The queen sat between Kira and her son, holding their hands.

"Your clothes are all wet," she said.

She wrapped the only blankets in the cell around Kira and Taejo and then hugged them close.

Placing a hand tight over her haetae, Kira plotted.

37

At dawn, the guards woke the tired trio. They were dragged from the dungeons, their wrists tied in front with a long chain linking them together.

Queen Ja-young peered into Kira's face and gasped in surprise.

"Your eye, it looks so much better. How can that be?"

Kira raised cautious fingers to her face. The swelling had subsided and the blinding pain was gone. All that was left was a dull ache. Her left eye was not entirely healed, but she could open it and see. She gave silent thanks to her tiger spirit, who must have come, even for a short time during the night, to help her.

"It's my tiger spirit," she replied. "That's why I've always been a fast healer."

"Thank the heavens," the queen said. "I am so proud of you both."

Queen Ja-young leaned her forehead against Taejo's, caressing his face with her fingertips. She then stroked Kira gently on her uninjured cheek.

"Taejo, Kira, always remember that you are descended from the Ko clan of Guru. The blood of a hundred warrior kings runs through both of your veins. Do not doubt yourselves, and you will never truly fail," she said.

The guards yanked the queen away, forcing the other two to fall in line behind her. They passed through drafty tunnels and into the palace compound. White-garbed servants stopped in shock at their approach, only hurrying back to work at the threats of the Yamato soldiers.

The guards forced the trio into the dark city streets. The frigid winter winds of the first month of the year assailed them with painful intensity. Kira's clothes were still damp, and the cold soaked through to her bones.

As their procession passed through the streets, it seemed as if all the citizens of Hansong were assembled. They bowed and wept at the sight of their queen and crown prince in chains. For the entire walk to the southern cliffs, growing numbers of men and women, young and old, followed behind.

The royals climbed the rough-hewn steps of the

mountain. At the very top, Kira could see the pointed roof of the pagoda structure. Many a night she'd sat there, exploring the stars and the heavens with Taejo and Brother Woojin. Many a day she'd picnicked with her mother on the mountain plateau. But the happy memories were marred by the vision of the court ladies and her mother jumping to their deaths.

Shin was waiting for them, seated in an elaborate open sedan chair. He hid his shock at the sight of all the people with a cruel smile.

"It appears we have a huge audience for the demise of the last of the late King Yuri's line," Shin said to the citizens.

Kira found Ito's stocky form standing at the farthest corner of the cliff, right above the southern walls. His fiendish eyes and broad smile enraged her. It was all she could do not to hurl herself at him.

"Bring the prisoners forward," Shin said.

The queen walked proudly to the edge of the cliff, Taejo and Kira close behind her. The guards unchained them but left their wrists bound. Behind them, the skies were lightening with the first rays of the rising sun.

Kira pressed her hands to her chest, feeling the outline of her haetae.

"We must give our audience a worthy performance," Shin said.

With a wave of his hand, six Yamato archers marched into place. They pointed their bows at the three prisoners and waited. Kira's gut wrenched with the realization that she had failed to keep the prince safe. She would die having broken her vow to her father. She glared at Lord Ito. The Yamato was five horse lengths away to her right. He wore her pouch around his neck. Suddenly, Kira knew what to do. She would sacrifice herself to save Taejo and her aunt, but she would not die alone.

Shin sauntered over to the queen. He leaned close to her and traced one long fingernail down the side of her face.

"What a pity to waste such beauty on the river gods," he said. "You could have been my queen." He continued to caress the side of her face. "But once again, you will have the pleasure of watching as those you love are killed."

"No!" Queen Ja-young screamed as Shin jerked her away from the others.

Taejo tried to throw himself at Shin, but the guards shoved him, sending him precariously near the edge of the cliff. Kira grabbed hold of his sleeve and took advantage of the distraction to slide them both away from the cliff.

She noticed something strange—the crowd of citizens had moved closer, so that they were in arm's reach of the Yamato soldiers. And their mood was ugly.

Queen Ja-young fell to her knees, beating her bound fists against Shin's abdomen. Kira saw her aunt glance desperately at her and Taejo before raising her hands in a pleading gesture.

"Please don't make me live without them. Don't leave

me alone," she begged. She grasped at Shin's shimmering black silk robes. "Don't do this to me! Please, I will do anything!"

Kira looked away from the naked lust on Lord Shin's face as he pulled the weeping queen to her feet. The queen staggered, bringing them both closer to the cliff's edge.

"This is what I've been waiting for," he said. "You will do anything I want now."

"I'll do anything! Please, please, please," the queen sobbed, shaking and twisting in his grasp. They now stood only steps away from the precipice.

"Yes, of course," he said. "You will be mine."

She nodded. "I will be yours."

Shin smiled as he pressed her body to his. "I have wanted you from the moment I saw you. How I loathed Yuri. He didn't deserve you. I would make you the most powerful queen in the entire world. As long as you're mine, you will have everything you've ever wanted."

"Your Majesty, there is only one request I would make of you," the queen whispered. She leaned closer to him, as if to kiss him.

"What would you ask of me, my queen?" Shin ran his hands through her hair. His attention was solely on her.

"I wish you to die screaming!" The queen threw her tied hands over Shin's neck. She chanced only one last backward glance at her son before flinging her entire body against Shin and sending them both sideways over the cliff.

"Mother!" Taejo cried out.

Shin's screams ceased abruptly.

Taejo broke free of the stunned guards and ran to the edge. Racing after him, Kira hooked her fingers into his belt, holding him back. She caught sight of the fluttering robes waving in the water below before she dragged him away from the edge. She felt the pain of her aunt's sacrifice even as she sought to use it for an opportunity to escape.

Suddenly an angry mob charged the archers that stood before them. The crowd rushed forward and pushed the Yamato guards over the cliff. Kira glanced at Ito for a split second, wishing she could kill him, but her aunt had sacrificed herself to save Taejo. The prince was her first priority. Without hesitation, she gripped Taejo by the sleeve and ran for the stairs.

Kira saw Ito pointing at them and shouting at the guards just as a rock flew through the air and struck the Yamato lord in the face. The force of the blow threw him off-balance, causing him to fall from the mountain onto the southern wall below, where he lay dazed.

She kept ahold of Taejo as she ran. The crowds made a pathway, hiding them from the guards.

At the bottom, she led Taejo into a narrow alley. Kira kicked over a ceramic urn, knocking it down with a loud crash. She used a fragment from the urn and cut their bindings.

Taejo collapsed onto the ground in a daze. She pulled him up and shook him.

"Taejo, we have to go now to help Kwan," she said.

He nodded, his young face unnaturally grim. "Let's go."

They moved swiftly, following the back streets of the city. As they reached the end of another alleyway, a thundering approach sent them crouching against the walls. In the opening ahead, Yamato soldiers marched in attack formation, along with mounted officers shouting their orders.

Kira looked at Taejo and whispered, "They're here."

The soldiers rushed past her, their numbers never ending. The Iron Army was laying siege to the city. Kira bit at her nails, waiting for the last of the soldiers to pass. If the northern gates were not opened in time, then Captain Pak and everyone else would ride headlong into certain death. Jaewon's face flashed in front of her eyes. Kira took in a harsh breath and tensed. She would not let that happen.

38

They cut through the side streets, taking shortcuts that would keep them well ahead of the Yamato battalion. Kira urged Taejo to run faster, even as he began to wheeze from the effort. Soon they reached a main thoroughfare from which the tall sentry towers of the northern gate were clearly visible.

Yamato voices brought Taejo and Kira to a grinding halt as they faced four guards with their swords drawn. Neither Taejo nor Kira were armed. Kira swiftly canvassed the area, seeking anything that could be used as a weapon.

An old man ambled out of a nearby doorway, leaning on

a thick walking stick. He looked around with great interest.

Kira bowed to him. "I'm truly sorry, grandfather, but I need to borrow your cane for a moment."

Before he could protest, Kira snatched it away and smashed the heavy knob end into the closest soldier's face, knocking him out. She kicked his sword toward Taejo. Two soldiers rushed at Kira. In a flurry of movement, Kira pounded at the knees, crotches, and necks of both men before crashing her stick into one soldier's chin and whipping it back into the face of the other, rendering them both unconscious with one move.

She picked up a sword and whirled to face the last soldier just as he charged Taejo. The enemy was much larger. But Taejo was faster and unencumbered by heavy armor.

"Use your taekkyon training!" Kira shouted.

Taejo crouched down and aimed a low roundhouse kick at the soldier's knees, causing him to fall backward.

Kira jumped forward, knocking the sword from the man's hands and clouting his head with the pommel of her sword.

"Nice job! Let's go!" Kira said. She threw the cane back to the old man, thanking him as she ran. The old man caught his stick and waved it high in the air after them.

The heavy gates were directly before them. A crowd of Yamato soldiers stood shouting up at the towers.

"Oh no! Kwan!" Taejo gasped, pointing to the gate tower.

Kwan fought with several swordsmen on the narrow walkway above the gated wall. The men on the archery tower above could not get a view of the action on the gate, as the elaborate pagoda roof blocked their sight. It was the bowmen below who were the real threat. Kira charged forward, slashing her sword across the hamstrings of five archers and creating immediate chaos. She moved into the offensive, skewering one bowman while back-kicking another into three others. But the soldiers gaped in astonishment at something coming from behind her.

Hundreds of Hansong citizens, armed with swords, spears, axes, pitchforks, shovels, sticks, and lit torches, advanced upon the gates. She ran to them when she saw Taejo speaking to the crowd.

"Thank you, my people!" he said. "We must open these gates so my uncle, the Guru king, can enter and drive out our enemies!"

The citizens roared in agreement, shaking their makeshift weapons in the air. Taejo faced the Yamato soldiers, his face grim and determined.

"For Hansong!" he cried. Holding his sword up, he raced forward. Kira stayed close to him. Within seconds, the horde was on top of the soldiers, fighting with a lack of skill that they compensated for with their fury and greater numbers.

From above, she heard Kwan's voice calling to them. He pointed to the gate just as she parried a vicious blow from another swordsman.

"Noona, cover me!" Taejo raced for the unmanned gate crank, Kira at his heels.

The people overtook the soldiers on the ground and were trying to reach the sentries in their towers. Bowmen flanking the gate above turned their bows to the crowd and began to shoot. Kira desperately wished she had her bow. Grabbing a shield, she held it over Taejo's head as they ran.

The entranceway was blocked—first by wooden doors, and then by a heavy iron gate. A group of urchins stood off to the side, pelting the bowmen with rocks. Kira seized a boy and pointed at the gateway. "Go and get those doors open!" she yelled.

The boys were running toward the first set of doors when a new sound caught her attention. A mounted Yamato company was approaching the main thoroughfare.

With no time to waste, Kira and Taejo ran to the massive iron crank. Several arrows flew in their direction, one hitting and bouncing off the spoke near Taejo's hands.

From outside the city walls, Kira heard battle cries.

"They're here!" Kira yelled. Throwing down her shield and sword, she heaved at the wheel of the crank with all her might, helping Taejo pull open the gate. Behind them, the Yamato battalion had reached the square and began wreaking carnage on the poorly armed citizens. She concentrated all her energy on the wheel, but the movement was slow. The massive gate would normally take four men to maneuver. As strong as Kira was, she couldn't turn it quickly enough, and the Yamatos were drawing nearer.

"Push harder!" Taejo screamed.

She took in a deep breath and called out to her tiger spirit. *Help me now,* she asked. *Give me a little more of your strength.* She felt a fresh burst of energy and the familiar warmth of her tiger spirit. Pushing hard, the wheel suddenly caught momentum and began to move faster, until it came to a grinding halt and Kira locked it in place.

Kwan appeared at her side. "Good work," he said. "Let's go." He threw Kira a sword and they charged forward, brother and sister, shoulder to shoulder.

"Wait for me!" Taejo shouted.

A deafening noise erupted as Captain Pak and his army burst through the open gateway. The few surviving citizens ran for their lives, desperately trying to avoid the hooves of the incoming army and the swords of their oppressors. Pak's forces charged the Yamato battalion, attacking with multitipped long spears and axes, making short work of the enemy and heading into the city.

Kira and Taejo both gave a huge sigh of relief. But Kwan raced after Captain Pak's forces.

The streets were littered with the dead. They weren't just soldiers. They were ordinary people who had sacrificed themselves for their prince.

For Hansong.

Innocent lives taken.

Like her mother.

Her head shot up. Her mother's soul was still trapped in the shadow realm.

You must destroy the one who cursed her. Lady Mina's voice echoed through her mind. She needed to find the shaman and kill him.

Pak's men were now in control of the gate and patrolling the perimeter. Dragging Taejo over to a nearby building, she pulled him inside, where several families were hunched over in the rear of the room.

The men rose to their feet at their entrance and bowed, loud excited chatter breaking out.

"This is your prince, keep him safe," Kira ordered. Turning to Taejo she said, "Stay here!"

"Where are you going?" Taejo asked.

Kira didn't answer. She ran toward the cliff, where she'd last seen Ito.

She heard footsteps coming from behind her. Halting, she caught sight of Taejo, his small face determined.

"You're not supposed to leave me behind! You promised to always protect me!" he yelled as he caught up.

"I'm trying to protect you! I have unfinished business to take care of and I want to keep you safe," she said.

He shook his head stubbornly. "My place is by your side. I fight with you."

She smiled down at her young cousin. He was growing up. One day he would be a great king. "Always," she said. They gripped arms in solidarity and continued running.

As they neared the cliff, Kira faltered. Her nose was overloaded with the stench of demons. Suddenly, the streets were filled with soldiers and people running madly. Kira shoved Taejo aside, pressing him flat against the walls. A swarm of sharp-clawed imps were attacking the faces of their victims. An imp shrieked at Kira. She sliced its head off with one swipe of her sword.

"Stay close behind me. If an imp gets too close, cut off its head," she said to Taejo before plunging into the midst of the melee. Immediately several imps flew at her, claws extended. She stabbed one out of the air and flung it away while punching another imp in the face. Taejo was close behind her, holding tight to the bottom of her jacket. Demon-possessed Yamato soldiers were massacring Guru soldiers and Hansong citizens alike. Panic engulfed her. She should never have brought her cousin here.

When they finally reached the stairway to the cliff, the ground shook beneath them. Cracks appeared in the pavement, the dirt between the stones crumbling away. In the middle of the street, something was bursting through the stones. Kira looked up, unsurprised to see Ito at the top of the cliff. His arms were raised before him and his lips moved in a rapid chant. He faced away from the staircase, staring intently at the break in the road.

Kira bolted up the stairs, her sword held low. A piercing shriek ripped through the air, causing her to stumble. Down below, a monster broke through, its massive eel-like head surging through the hole in the street. Its utter blackness was relieved by the red of its wide-open mouth and the sheen of sharp fangs. The monster slithered straight up into the sky, a mass of undulating muscle, before it doubled over to scoop up a dozen soldiers in its gaping jaws. Archers let loose their arrows, piercing the monster's hide, but still it attacked.

"Imoogi," Kira breathed.

Taejo's trembling hand gripped her arm. Memories of the monster in the lake flooded her mind. Once again, she was seven years old, trying to save her cousin.

They kept climbing, away from the monster and the screams of the terrified people. As she neared the top, she ordered Taejo to stay back. She raised her sword for a killing blow, all her attention focused on the chanting figure at the top of the steps. Kira rushed at Ito, aiming her sword at his neck. But when she thrust her weapon, it encountered nothing but air, her forward momentum sending her crashing to her knees. She twisted up to see Ito's body shimmer and dissolve. It was a mirage.

Stunned, she whirled around to find the shaman right behind her. He smashed a rock into her face, hitting her injured eye. Kira dropped to the ground with an agonized scream, fighting to retain consciousness but unable to rise.

"Now I have you," Ito rasped as he bent down and pressed his fingers into her temples. "You'll see your mother soon enough, and I'll throw your empty shell of a body over the cliff, just like I did to her."

Kira writhed in agony. It felt as if her insides were being ripped out of her. How could she have been so stupid? She'd rushed in without relying on her senses and had fallen right into his trap.

The pain vanished when Ito released her suddenly. She could barely raise her head to see, her vision blurred by her injury. From the corner of her eye she saw Taejo darting away, wielding his sword with two hands. Blood coursed down from Ito's right arm where he'd been stabbed. Ito raised his sword and attacked. The force of the blow dropped Taejo to his knees.

The young prince rolled on the ground and kicked out with his feet, unbalancing the other man and sending Ito flat on his back. The older man attacked again, pushing Taejo toward the cliff's edge.

Kira raised herself up, but her head spun with sickening force, nearly causing her to black out. She'd lost a lot of blood. Swallowing, she got up on her knees. Bile rose in her throat. Yet her eyes remained locked on the battle before her.

Taejo quickly skirted to the right and leveled a blow before tripping over a rock and losing hold of his weapon.

Kira staggered to her feet and swung her weapon down on Ito's sword arm, slicing his hand off. He screamed and clutched his arm, staring at the blood pouring from the stump.

Kira thrust her sword at Ito's chest. He knocked her blade aside and grabbed its hilt, pulling her close and swinging the blade back toward her. She struggled for control, but she was dizzy and weak. He chanted what sounded like gibberish, and yet it sent slivers of dread down Kira's spine.

Taejo darted forward in a surprise move and ripped Kira's pouch from Ito's neck. Before Kira could stab the shaman again, he was gone, leaving only an eerie glimmer in the air. Kira couldn't believe it. She'd never seen this kind of magic before. How could a human have demon-like abilities? There was only one answer—he wasn't human.

Ito was stalking Taejo. As he chanted, they heard the answering shriek from the imoogi below.

"Noona!" Taejo yelled. He threw the bag to Kira.

She caught it and quickly pulled the ruby out. Ito refocused on her, his chanting louder as the dreadful cries of the imoogi came closer.

Kira raised her hands up and saw the ruby flare to life with a scorching heat. This time, when the tidal stone asked what she wanted, she didn't hesitate. She let her mind meld with that of the ruby. Together they plunged into the depths of the Han River. She called the water to her and it began to swirl around her in a great column. She was one with the water. She was the water dragon.

The ruby hummed with power. You are my master, it said. And Kira knew it was true.

Kira exploded from the river like an enormous geyser, plunging down on Ito. Her dragon let loose a tidal wave, knocking the Yamato down.

The shaman struggled to his feet and continued to chant. An answering roar was heard from below and in the next moment, the imoogi soared up into the air and crashed against the water dragon. The impact caused Kira to lose contact with her creation as it began to disintegrate, water spraying everywhere. She fought to control the water dragon, to retain her consciousness with it. The ruby pulsing in her hands matched the drumming in her blood as she pulled the great creature into being again. But she knew she needed something stronger.

The ruby suddenly shifted from scorching hot to a freezing cold that spread up her arms and chest, chilling her heart and pumping icy blood through her veins. She opened her clear dragon eyes and stared at Ito. Kira bellowed, sending an icy blast through the air. Her watery scales solidified into sheets of blue ice. She extended her claws, letting the chill from her heart freeze into long, hooked talons. As the imoogi rushed forward, Kira struck with all eight of her ice talons, slashing and puncturing the creature's skin.

The imoogi roared in rage and pain. Black blood coursed down its leathery skin, dripping onto the ground in steaming puddles. It attacked again, clamping its jaws around her dragon neck, cracking her scales of ice. She felt a searing pain as the imoogi's fangs punctured her frozen skin and water began to leak from the wound. She clawed at the creature, plucking out its eye. The imoogi released her, flailing in the air before falling down the stairs.

"No! I command you to kill her!" Kira heard Ito rage at his creature.

The imoogi slithered up the stairs, its eel-like head shifting left to compensate for its lost eye. Kira flew straight up into the air and spiraled down, landing on the imoogi's back, her talons piercing clear through its heart and out the other end.

The imoogi collapsed, its body shuddering. Kira withdrew her talons, watching as the monster crashed down to the bottom of the stairs.

A scream pierced the air. She whirled around to see the Yamato holding a dagger to Taejo's neck.

"Throw me the stone or the prince will die," Ito snarled.

The power of the tidal stone still pulsed in her blood, urging her to kill him, to slash him through the heart with one frozen talon. She stared at the mad eyes of the shaman and thought of her mother doomed in the shadow realm. She would never be free if she didn't destroy him.

Taejo whimpered as the blade bit into his throat, blood seeping from the cut.

She could feel the ice melting away even as her blood pounded for vengeance. Lady Mina's voice rang within her mind. Revenge for the dead should never occur at a price to the living.

"Taejo!" Once more she felt the crippling pain of her

head wound as water crashed to the ground, soaking them all.

"I said throw it to me!" Ito stood at the edge of the stairs, above the massive body of the slain imoogi.

As she looked into the eyes of absolute evil, the world around her seemed to come to a standstill. She was frozen in terror. Had she come so far, only to fail?

What am I to do? Father, what do I do?

Kira heard only her own breathing and the beating of her heart. Then suddenly, there was a stirring in the air, and her tiger spirit appeared beside her. She gazed at it in wonder. Twice it had come to her in the same day.

She heard the tiger speak in her mind.

Do not doubt yourself any longer. You are the Dragon Musado.

The tiger spirit faded into the air.

For the first time in her life, her sight and her mind were completely clear.

I am the Dragon Musado.

Even the tidal stone had called her master.

I am the Dragon Musado.

Calm filled her. She had no doubt about what she was to do.

Kira threw the stone high into the air, forcing the Yamato to push Taejo away and drop his dagger in order to catch it. As Kira launched herself at Ito, her hands grasped for the stone from the air and her foot slammed down with a force that sent him hurtling down the stairs.

He landed on the stone sidewalk next to the dead imoogi, his neck twisted in an unnatural angle.

Kira crashed to the ground, the pain excruciating. But then she heard her mother's gentle voice and sweet laughter.

Thank you, my little tiger.

"Mother," Kira whispered.

Water splashed on her face as Taejo dropped to the ground next to her.

"Noona!"

Kira opened her eyes a crack and saw Taejo. Tears flowed down his face.

"Noona, you are the Dragon Musado," he cried out in a choked voice. "You saved Hansong! You saved everyone! Noona! Did you hear me? I'm glad you're the One. I'm proud you are my cousin. Please be all right. Noona! Please stay with me. Please . . ."

Her eyes were too heavy. She couldn't keep them open. The pain in her head caused a ringing in her ears. Then blackness enveloped her, and she slipped into oblivion.

39

It was early spring and she was at a picnic with her family. Her mother had traveled by carriage while she rode on horseback with her father and brothers. It was their annual pilgrimage to a nearby mountainside lake, surrounded by hundreds of cherry blossoms in full bloom.

Thin, soft rush mats were spread under the shade of the trees as servants laid out a feast of various rice rolls, dumplings, meat, and seasoned vegetables. Everyone sat eating and laughing, enjoying the warm spring weather as gentle winds blew pink blossom showers, which adorned their hair with tiny petals.

Her father and mother sat nearby, watching Kwan

tease her by snatching food from her fingers. Kira berated him for being such a pig, while Kyoung administered punishment by catching Kwan by the scruff of his neck and wrestling him in a mock match.

She was so happy to be with them all once again. She had missed them with a fierce intensity that was a physical pain.

Her father stood up and helped her mother to her feet.

"It's time to go," he said.

"So soon?" Kira complained.

Kira's mother smiled radiantly. "You saved us. I can now join our ancestors in heaven. My little tiger! We will always watch over you."

Alarmed, Kira rushed to them, but her brothers held her back as they watched her parents pulling away.

"Please, let me go with you," Kira begged.

Someone was calling her name, but she didn't want to answer. Already the picnic was fading. She could see her mother and father waving good-bye.

Kira opened her eyes and saw Taejo, Kwan, Brother Woojin, and Jaewon's faces. Seung stood behind them, peering anxiously at her. Turning her head, she noted that she was lying on a large table covered with furs inside a guardhouse. She put a hand to her forehead and found it bound with a tight bandage. She fingered the long gash that puckered across her cheek.

Jaewon pulled her hand away, clasping it between his strong ones. "Leave it alone. It must heal," he said.

His eyes filled with concern and affection that left Kira feeling warm.

"How long have I been asleep?" she asked.

"Several hours," he replied.

That explained why she was still in pain; she needed an entire night with her tiger spirit to be completely healed.

Taejo pressed closer, jostling Jaewon in his eagerness to speak to her. "I'm so glad you're all right," Taejo said. "I couldn't bear it if something happened to you too!" His voice caught, and he quieted. Leaning over, he gave her a quick hug.

"I should be mad at you!" Kwan said. "Here I am risking my neck to save Hansong, and who does everyone talk about? My baby sister! The big hero! The imoogi slayer! What about me? Doesn't anybody want to know about me? Huh?" He gazed at her with bright eyes. "You've done well, little sister. I'm proud of you."

Leaning closer, he whispered, "What of Mother?"

"She is finally at peace," Kira said.

Her brother closed his eyes in relief. "Thank the heavens!" He carefully caressed her face, cautious of her injury. "And I have some more good news for you. There's someone here to see you."

Kira tried to sit up with Jaewon's help, when another pair of hands grabbed hers. It was her oldest brother, Kyoung. She shouted in glee and immediately regretted it as her head throbbed in pain. He laughed down at her and hugged her.

"Where have you been?" she asked.

"I arrived in Hansong several weeks ago. I've been hiding, working with the resistance," he said. "The citizens of Hansong all opposed the Yamatos and Lord Shin."

"The people saved us on the cliff and at the gate," she said. "Was that because of you?"

He nodded. "I'm sorry I wasn't there too, but I had my hands full trying to coordinate efforts with the other Guru infiltrators in preparation for the attack," Kyoung said. He ran a finger softly across her scarred cheek. "Forgive me."

"Never mind that," Kira said. "I'm just so happy you are here!"

"So many good people died today," Kyoung said. "But they have not died in vain, for they have given us victory."

Kira said a silent prayer for the gods to welcome all who'd lost their lives in the battle.

A loud noise at the door sounded the arrival of Captain Pak, who headed straight for Taejo.

"Congratulations, Your Highness! We are victorious," Pak said with a broad smile. "General Kim's division is chasing the Yamatos into the Kudara borders, but King Eojin has led his army into the city! The people are already cheering him and calling him the One!"

Everyone in the room broke out in cheers except for Kira. She looked up to find Jaewon watching her. He winked at her before placing a warm hand on her shoulder.

"The king and your people would like to see the prince. And you too, Kang Kira." Pak bowed to Kira and gave her a big smile. "It would be an honor to escort you both."

Kira grimaced. She had no intention of standing before another crowd.

"Why do you look like that?" Kwan asked. "Don't you realize who you are? You're the legendary Dragon Musado who saved Hansong from the evil imoogi. They claim that with you and King Eojin together, the prophecy has been fulfilled and the Yamatos will be defeated!"

She put a hand to her cheek and fingered the bandage. She eyed Taejo with a troubled expression.

"It's all right, Noona. I'm glad you are the Dragon Musado."

"Yes, but I don't understand one thing. The Heavenly Maiden told me that Taejo is Dang's heir, not Eojin."

Brother Woojin came forward and sat by her side. "Young mistress, I have been pondering this puzzle ever since you discovered the tidal stone and have come up with a theory. Only the Dragon Musado can find and wield the Dragon King treasures. Yet the Heavenly Maidens have ordered you to protect the prince."

Kira nodded.

"You accepted the stone from the giant turtle, and you used the power of the tidal stone to defeat the Yamatos. That means you are the warrior, the Dragon Musado. All this time, the monks have believed that the warrior is the One. We followed Master Ahn's theories. But we were wrong. You are the Dragon Musado, the protector of the One, and the prince is the future king. The two of you are the prophecy."

Kira wasn't surprised by the monk's words. Ever since she'd unleashed the power of the tidal stone, she'd felt the rightness of her actions. The stone belonged to her. She was the Dragon Musado. What Brother Woojin said made sense. She'd sworn over and over to protect Taejo. It was her fate. Yet, she was still troubled.

"I don't understand," Taejo said. "The prophecy says 'one will save us all.' But there are two of us. How can that be?"

Brother Woojin clasped his hands and laughed. "Remember, the warrior was never part of the original prophecy. It was part of Master Ahn's interpretation. We monks have put the two together for centuries. But we were wrong."

"So, I'm no longer the yellow-eyed kumiho?" Kira asked with a grin.

Kyoung stepped forward and grabbed her hand, pressing it firmly. "No one will ever call you that again."

Kira saw Taejo smiling at her.

"Do you feel up to coming?" he asked, his face hopeful. "I'd rather you were with me."

She nodded, watching the relief sweep over his face. With a bow, Taejo walked out, the captain and Jindo at his side.

Ignoring the pain, Kira stood up and followed them. When Kyoung tried to put his arm around her, she glared at him. "I'm fine, Oppa," she said. "Don't hover."

Kyoung laughed. "All right, little sister. I'm here if you need me." He moved ahead to catch up with Taejo.

Jaewon stood close by on her other side. Catching Jaewon's eye, she was relieved to see he was still carrying her bow and arrow case. He placed her nambawi in her hands. Kira was happy to have it back. It was like an old friend. But instead of wearing it, she shoved it into her arrow case.

She smiled up at him.

"Thank you."

The warmth and steadiness of his gaze made her nervous. She put an uncertain hand up to her face. The bandages covered the damage over her eye, but her cheek was badly scarred.

He leaned close to her ear and whispered, "It makes you look very dashing. Like a lady bandit. You can be the most dangerous criminal in all the Seven Kingdoms!"

She laughed. "Then you can be my bumbling sidekick who must do everything I say."

"But of course, my lady!" He bowed. "I will even gladly wash your stinky feet."

"Ya! My feet aren't stinky!"

"Whatever you say, my lady."

They bickered back and forth as they walked to where a group of soldiers and horses stood waiting for them.

Taejo mounted his horse and gazed anxiously down at her. "Are you sure you're all right?" he asked.

"Of course," she replied.

With a nervous smile, Taejo rode ahead with Kwan and the captain. Kira pulled herself slowly onto her saddle, her head aching and dizzy from the small effort. She was relieved to have Kyoung lead her horse. They followed Taejo's group to the palace grounds, with Jaewon and Seung taking up the rear.

The sun was setting, casting the streets and buildings into half shadows, hiding the fallen bodies that littered the street in semidarkness. She heard cheering, getting louder. Thousands of people filled the main plaza before the palace. As the crowd became aware of the soldiers waiting to pass, they opened up a pathway. The cheering exploded as cries of "Prince Taejo!" erupted throughout the city.

Kira watched her young cousin greet the citizens of Hansong. She felt happiness and pride mixed with sadness and regret. At that moment, she couldn't have been prouder of Taejo, who rode with great dignity for one so young.

On the steps of the palace, King Eojin awaited him.

Kira, Kyoung, Jaewon, and Seung joined Kwan and the captain, watching the young prince riding through the masses. Around them, they heard a new chant: "Dragon Musado." Wary and uneasy with the attention, Kira started to shrink down into her saddle, and then she stopped herself.

No more hiding, Kang Kira, she told herself.

She straightened and waved to the people bowing to her.

Kyoung laughed. "You're a hero!"

Kira shrugged. For the first time ever, the crowds were cheering her. It was all a bit too much. It was such a change, and she wondered if she could trust it. The word *trust* hung in her mind, a whisper of a memory. *They saved us at the cliffs.*

She marveled at how different it was to be accepted. Something she'd always wished for but thought would never happen. And yet how strange it was that it didn't matter anymore.

Tuning out the chants, she focused on her cousin, who had now reached the king.

Eojin looked splendid in his black armor. He stood above the heads of the crowd of Hansong citizens. Beside him were several of his generals, all battle worn and grimy, their faces proud and stoic.

At the foot of the palace stairs, Taejo dismounted and hesitated. This was where his father and hers had been executed. In her mind, she urged him forward. He straightened his shoulders and climbed up to Eojin's side.

The crowd became silent, sensing something momentous. The king embraced him. Eojin kept his arm on Taejo's shoulders as he announced, "My good people, I bring to you your prince!"

The crowd roared with wild enthusiasm.

Eojin raised a hand for quiet.

"Today, Hansong has become part of the Guru Kingdom. As your new king, I will provide you with the full protection of the Iron Army. We will fight on, and drive these Yamato devils back across the seas!"

Eojin waited for the crowds to quiet down before continuing.

"On this momentous day, I declare Prince Taejo of Hansong, my nephew and clansman, to be my heir and successor."

This time the response was deafening. Taejo looked up at Eojin in bewilderment.

"Look to your people, young prince!" Eojin said with an indulgent smile.

Taejo faced his audience and seemed to search for someone. His eyes caught and held Kira's. She released the breath she'd unconsciously been holding.

His smile, tinged with sadness, made her ache with sympathy. She knew his grief at losing his parents. She smiled in encouragement, forgetting the pain in her head.

Kira raised her arms in victory. He responded in kind, whooping a great loud cheer.

They weren't done yet. There was still too much to do. The Yamatos had retreated south. Kudara needed to be dealt with. Kaya and Jinhan had to be rescued. And she still needed to find the last two Dragon King treasures. But for now, nothing else mattered.

They were home.

Glossary

Baduk—Korean term for the ancient Chinese board game Weiqi and the Japanese game Go

Daegam—Your Eminence or Your Excellency; term of respect used for high ranking officials

Daimyo—powerful Japanese feudal lord

Dongji—winter solstice; usually falls on December 22 of the solar calendar

Haetae—mythical fire-eating dog

Hanbok—traditional Korean dress

Hanja—Korean name for Chinese characters used to write the Korean language

Imoogi—half-dragon, half-snake mythical creature

Jangseung—totem poles made of wood or stone traditionally used to ward off evil spirits; also used as village boundary markers

Jesa—memorial service

Ki—life-force energy

Kumiho—nine-tailed fox demon

Li—Korean measurement unit; 1 li is equivalent to 500 meters, 0.5 kilometers, or 0.31 miles.

Makkoli—milky rice wine drink

Musado—warrior

Nambawi—traditional winter hat

Noona—boy's honorific term for an older sister

Ondol—a floor heating system unique to Korea

Oppa—girl's honorific term for an older brother

Sang gum hyung—double-sword form

Saulabi—soldier

Suchae—untouchables, the lowest members of the caste system, including actors, butchers, hunters, and prostitutes

Sunim—honorific term used for monks

Taekkyon—the original martial-art form of ancient Korea that has evolved into what is referred to as tae kwon do

Ya—hey; can also mean "you"

Acknowledgments

While writing a novel is largely solitary, getting it ready to be published is a team effort. I have been so fortunate to have a wonderful team at HarperCollins help bring *Prophecy* into the world. The very first thank-you is to my brilliant editor, Phoebe Yeh, who believed in my book from the first moment she read it. I believe she is a genius. Big thanks also to the incredible Jessica MacLeish, who is so awesome to work with. To my fabulous HarperCollins team made up of the following amazing people: Emilie Polster, Olivia deLeon, Jenna Lisanti, Stefanie Hoffman, and Molly Thomas. My brilliant art directors, Amy Ryan and Joel Tippie, and Sarah Hoy, who created my beautiful cover. To my copy editor, Kathryn Hinds, and production editor, Kathryn Silsand. And of course to Kate Jackson, editor-in-chief, and Susan Katz, publisher extraordinaire.

This book would never have happened if it weren't for my awesome agent, Joe Monti, who said those four very important words: "I love your book." Joe, you rock! And I'm so fortunate to be part of the Barry Goldblatt agency and have the fabulous Barry Goldblatt and Tricia Ready, who make all their authors feel special.

My infinite gratitude to:

My ninja writer buddies, Mike Jung and Martha Flynn. What would I do without you guys?

My wonderful writer friends who supported me in all their various ways, including Cindy Pon, Juliet Grames, Caroline Richmond, Marie Lu, Robin LaFevers, Jenn Reese,

Elsie Chapman, Carrie Harris, Kiki Hamilton, Laura Riken, Christy Farley, Lisa Liebow, Michone Johnson, Joy Wiznauski, Renee Ahdieh, Aerin Rose, Richard Levangie, and Charles Gramlich. You guys saw me through the hard years.

The incredibly talented Virginia Allyn, whose kindness and generosity I'll never forget.

Verla Kay and all my blueboarder friends, especially the No Newsers. My Inkies over at the Enchanted Inkpot and my Friday the Thirteener buddies, especially Erin Bowman, who started it all with me.

The supersmart and amazing Stacy Whitman.

Professor Wontack Hong of Seoul University, who so generously shared his time and work with me during my research process.

The best friends a girl could have: Sylvia Lara, who always knew what to say and when to say it, and Anna Hong Kim and Jennifer Choi Um, who were my very own cheering squad.

My dad, who has always been so amazing and supportive; my sister, Janet Poirot, who is an incredible writer herself; my brother-in-law, Laurent Poirot, whose genius tech brain kept me sane; and to my mom, who told me not to be a plain old chicken but to soar like an eagle.

My three daughters, Summer, Skye, and Gracie, who would sit at my feet and listen to my stories, laughing and crying and cheering. Everything I do, I do for you girls.

And my everlasting appreciation to my husband, Sonny, who told me "to just write that book already and buy me a boat!" You are Da Man.

PROPHECY

The Facts Behind the Fantasy

Ellen Oh on Asian Mythology

**Excerpt from *Warrior*,
the second book in the Prophecy trilogy**

The Facts Behind the Fantasy

When I first became interested in writing a fantasy novel set in ancient Korea, I contacted a professor of Korean history at Harvard University. I asked him what I could do about historical accuracy, given my many challenges in finding sources of research for my subject. He stated that it was a good thing I was writing fiction because not a whole lot is known about this period! And he was right. This is a difficult period of time to research, but what is known about it is fascinating.

I decided to base *Prophecy* on the time period between 360 and 300 CE in ancient Korea, when there were many walled city-states and warring kingdoms. Some of these city-states became famous kingdoms of ancient Korea. They were Koguryo, Paekche, and Shilla—known as the Three Kingdoms (Eckert, 32). These were violent and turbulent times as the armies of all these kingdoms were always fighting against one another.

On top of all the infighting, over the course of its history, Korea was invaded numerous times—by several Chinese dynasties, the Mongols, and Japan. Because of its violent history, Korea is filled with legends and tales of nationalistic pride. I was fascinated by so much of my research that I was determined to use many of these stories in my trilogy. For instance, the Rock of Falling Flowers, Nakhwa-am, is a real place where legend has it that during the Shilla and Tang invasion of Paekche in 638 CE, 3,000 court ladies leaped to their deaths into the Baengma River (Nelson, 222). If you've seen the *Prophecy* trailer, you will recognize this scene.

The Yamato invasion in *Prophecy* is based, in part, on the Japanese invasion of 1592–1598. It was led by Daimyo Toyotomi Hideyoshi, who is also the basis of the evil shaman daimyo Tomodoshi in *Prophecy*. The real daimyo was born a peasant and rose to become more powerful than the Emperor of Japan. Extremely ambitious, he invaded Korea for the sole purpose of conquering China. During a stretch of seven years, the Koreans fought valiantly and beat back the samurais, but at a great cost to Korea. Ancient palaces were burned down and priceless historical artifacts were destroyed because of this terrible invasion.

It was during this war that another famous historical anecdote arose. Legend has it that Nongae, a beautiful *gisaeng* (female entertainer) lost her lover during the siege of Chinju fortress. She formed part of a group of gisaeng who were to entertain the samurai leaders at a party on the top of a cliff. During the entertainment, Nongae embraced the victorious Japanese general and hurled them both into the river (Pratt, 133). I blame all of this cliff-jumping on the fact that Korea is extremely mountainous.

Speaking of gisaeng, I've got some dangerous assassin gisaeng showing up in Book 2 of the Prophecy series who kick some serious butt and were awesome to write about.

Prophecy is a fantasy novel that incorporates the myths and legends of Korea with real historical places. Complete factual accuracy was not what I was going for. I doubt anyone can truly do that given the loss of so much of Korea's historical documentation, especially as a result of the Mongolian and Japanese invasions. But what I hoped to achieve was a flavor of ancient Korea coupled with Korean mythology and legends. I hope you will enjoy it.

Works Cited:

Eckert, Carter J. *Korea Old and New: A History.* Cambridge: Published for the Korea Institute, Harvard University by Ilchokak, 1990. Print.

Nelson, Sarah M. *The Archeology of Korea.* Cambridge: Cambridge University Press, 1993. Print.

Pratt, Keith. *Everlasting Flower: A History of Korea.* London: Reaktion Books, 2006. Print.

Asian Mythology

One of my strongest memories of being young is reading all about the Greek, Roman, and Norse mythologies, along with practically every fairy tale book every printed. I have a special fondness for the Andrew Lang's Fairy Books of Many Colors. I remember rereading the blue, red, yellow, and pink books over and over again. I never got tired of them. It wasn't until I was older that I realized that these books I loved were not very diverse. In fact, it began to dawn on me just how underrepresented my culture was in children's literature. This became an issue for me when I had my three girls. Trying to find multicultural books became my mission. It was easier in picture books, but as my girls got older, I began to notice that something was missing. Right around when my first daughter was born, I'd begun what has now become a lifelong love affair with Asian history. I read everything I could about Asia, specifically Korea, and I was fascinated by everything I'd learned. Asian myths and legends are just as fascinating as European ones, but not as well known. For example, there's the Korean myth of the *kumiho*—a nine-tailed fox demon who takes the form of a beautiful woman and lures men into marriage in the hopes that they can become human. But just as the kumiho sees her goal within her grasp, the man becomes aware of her demon nature, and she is forced to kill him and eat his heart and liver. Or what about the Japanese kami? A kami is a water sprite monster that has a crater on the top of its head that is filled with water. Kamis are famous for lurking in pools of water and trying to drown people. But they are known for being so polite that if you bow to them, they will immediately bow back, which spills out the water from their crater heads and renders them immobile. There are still signs in front of some ponds in Japan that say BEWARE OF THE KAMI! Many myths and legends of Asia are completely unknown in the West. Even my children had no idea of what Asian mythology was like. And this is why I wrote *Prophecy*. I wrote it for my daughters, who loved to sit by my side and hear all those long-ago stories. I wrote it so they could be exposed to a side of their heritage they don't get to read a lot about. And I wanted them to be able to point to a strong Asian girl hero instead of the smart, quiet, nerdy, Asian sidekick. I wanted to destroy the Asian woman stereotype once and for all and give my daughters their own Katniss or Katsa to root for. I say this now, but I actually wrote *Prophecy* way before *Graceling* and *The Hunger Games* ever came out. And it is interesting to me that the year my first agent began submitting the manuscript for *Prophecy* to publishers was the year that *Graceling* and *The Hunger Games* were both published. I've always thought of it as a wonderful coincidence—women authors who were simultaneously writing about strong female heroes. We even all gave them names starting with K for kickass! I admit that I worried about how people would react to the Asian mythology in my book. When I first tried to get published, I came across so many people who told me that "no one wants to read about ancient Korea" and "these names are too strange and too hard to pronounce; nobody wants to deal with it" and "it's just too foreign." I have to admit that it hurt a lot. Because it felt like they were telling me no one cared about my culture. But here's the thing, like all things in life, these naysayers are not everyone. For every person who might hate reading a book about another culture, there's at least one other person who does want to. And that's who I focused on, my true audience—kids. Because diversity

7

is such an important issue for me, it was a natural decision to write a book for teens and give them exposure to another culture. And the reaction has been all that I could have hoped for and more. I've been overwhelmed at the amazing response I've gotten from them. It made me realize that teens are eager for exposure to new and different things. They aren't close-minded or hyper-critical. What they want is to be entertained, and if in the process they are exposed to diversity, so much the better! And the more diversity we are exposed to, the more we can hope that one day diversity isn't something we have to go hunting for. That diversity in literature will become the norm.

Read an excerpt from

WARRIOR

the second book in the Prophecy trilogy
by Ellen Oh!

1

Kira was on the hunt. Her boots crunched softly on snow-covered ground. Icicles hung like shimmering crystal blades from the bare tree branches above her. Yet the delight Kira initially had for the wild, breathtaking landscape and the beauty of the ancient forest was short-lived. She had no idea where she was and she no longer felt the deep isolation of the eerie woods. There was a trail of human footprints before her.

She was not alone.

Welcome to the Sea of Trees, a voice whispered in her head. Stay here with us forever. Stay. Stay.

Suppressing a shiver, she studied the tracks. One person. Heavy gaited, large in size, and most likely male. The footprints led her to the entrance of a cavern that gaped open in the forest floor—a fierce black maw, as if a gigantic imoogi, a cursed half-dragon, half-snake—like creature, had tunneled its large serpent body and erupted from the ground. Unrelenting darkness layered with cool fog met Kira's gaze.

She blinked and her yellow tiger's eyes adjusted to give her night vision, but it was still difficult to see.

She descended with caution down the rough stone staircase, slick and treacherous from the snow. The interior walls of the cavern were made from ancient lava flows and were draped with sheets of ice. The long narrow corridor twisted and turned before entering a large cave. Huge ice formations hung from the black ceiling and lava shelves decorated the walls. Toward the end of the cave was a narrower passage that led down into a chamber filled with red light and pulsing heat. As Kira approached the beckoning light, the floor became wet with melting ice. Although she'd hardly felt the winter cold outside, down here in the caves, she could feel the heat emanating from underground.

Bending low, she entered the narrow passage and walked through. It opened into a wide cave dominated by a pool of molten lava that boiled in the center, shooting up large flames. The lava began to churn and bubble over explosively. From the depths of the fire rose a dark gray column that erupted into the blazing figure of a demonic visage. Once again Kira was faced with the Demon Lord.

"You have failed me!" The voice sounded like the grumbling of earthquakes.

A figure lay prostrate before the Demon Lord. He wore a

heavy silk brocaded coat, and his hair was oiled and slicked into a fan-shaped queue topknot that was folded forward. When he raised his head, Kira focused on the long jagged scar etched into his cheek and jaw. Even with his bearded face contorted with fear, he was a cruel-looking man. He displayed a large, jewel-crusted gold medallion on his chest, and the richness of his clothing established his high ranking.

Small winged imps flew out of the Demon Lord's gaping mouth, launching themselves at the nobleman's face with sharp talons that scratched, pierced, and pinched his exposed flesh.

"No, my lord!" The nobleman tried to protect his eyes, fighting off the imps that were attacking him. "I have done all that you've asked. Please! Spare me! Let me prove myself to you!"

The imps subsided with one last painful gouge. They hovered in the air above him, their claws outstretched in readiness. The nobleman lowered his trembling hands from his bloodied face and prostrated himself again before the Demon Lord, begging for mercy.

"Why should I bother? You will only fail me again."

At his words, a larger group of imps assaulted the man, shredding his fine robes and ripping chunks of hair. His once immaculate appearance was now a tattered mess. They left him shaking violently on the ground.

"Please, master, please give me another chance," he cried.

Kira felt a sick kind of pity for the nobleman. He was nothing more than a puppet for the Demon Lord, and yet she felt sorry for him.

The nobleman pulled himself slowly to his feet, keeping

himself in a bowing position before his master. "The Guru king and the Hansong prince will die soon. I promise this my lord. I shall not fail you again."

Kira gasped. This was Daimyo Tomodoshi, the human medium of the Demon Lord. He was the reason for the Yamato invasion of the Seven Kingdoms. He was the reason for the loss of her parents. Her pity disappeared as fury ignited within her.

Now she knew the face of her enemy.

Now she knew who she had to kill.

Another flock of imps flew at the daimyo. They ripped the clothes off his body and slashed his naked flesh with their razor-sharp claws, until he was a bleeding mass from head to toe.

The great demon head laughed. "No, you will not fail me again. I have something for you." Another imp flew from the gaping mouth holding a long rectangular box in its claws. The daimyo cringed as the imp screeched and flung the heavy metal box at his feet before returning to the flames.

The daimyo opened the box with shaking hands. Inside were seven daggers with long, thin, sharp black blades that came to a wicked tip. Each blade was inscribed with unreadable characters etched along the middle. Smoke seemed to rise from the lethal weapons as they glistened. They whispered of a dark death.

"Don't touch them with your bare hands if you value your life," the Demon Lord said. "They carry something very special on them—a part of my essence. Choose your assassins wisely!"

Tomodoshi snatched his hand away and snapped the box shut. "It will be as you command."

"And what of the girl?" The flames shot higher.

"She will not see another birthday," Tomodoshi said with an ingratiating bow.

"No," breathed the voice as the figure in the fire began to fade. "Bring her to me alive. I have other plans for her." The imps raced into the fire as the demon face disappeared with one last mocking laugh that sent shivers down Kira's spine.

One imp spun around and came flying at her face, its claws extended. Kira ducked and ran, feeling the claws snatching at her hair as she fled from the overpowering heat.

Hansong Palace

Ten days had passed since Kira had defeated the evil shaman and his imoogi. Ten days since the Iron Army had beaten the Yamato army and freed Hansong. She was finally home. And yet in those ten days, Kira had not returned to her family house. She'd been avoiding it. Her brothers had asked her to look for her mother's treasure box, which was hidden in her mother's rooms. They'd refused to let the servants into the area, wanting Kira to have her private moments alone with her memories. But Kira hadn't been ready.

She'd been present when her father was killed. It was his heroic sacrifice that had allowed her to save her cousin, Prince Taejo, from Lord Shin Mulchin and the Yamato army. But she'd been forced to leave Hansong without seeing her mother, only to hear that Shaman Ito had murdered her mother and trapped her spirit in the shadow world with his dark shaman magic. When Kira had killed Ito, she'd freed her mother's spirit so she could alight to heaven. But Kira had never forgiven herself for leaving her behind, even knowing she had no choice. Every day, she was filled with a desperate longing for her parents. She missed their love and wisdom. Being in Hansong again, Kira ached for them with a fierceness that was almost crippling at times. But her guilt had kept her from her family home. Until now.

After a few days of finally feeling safe, the frightening visions had started again. Shaken, Kira sought out the one place that she'd always felt the safest—her mother's rooms.

Kira stood in the women's quarters of her family home. Here her mother had sat on the cushioned warmth of the heated floor, embroidering on luxurious folds of colored silk. Now the large lacquered chests that held the silks and threads were destroyed, their delicate contents befouled by the muck of enemy boots.

Kira walked through the doorway that separated her mother's inner sanctum from the outer chambers. She shivered as the cold winter winds swept through the broken walls.

Entering the room, she was catapulted back into the

past, remembering the comfort of a childhood spent hiding in her mother's sanctuary. Instead of the broken pieces of furniture and slashed embroidery, she saw it the way it once was. At the far wall stood an eight-paneled folding screen of a plum tree painted through the four seasons. Several small and large chests inlaid with mother-of-pearl designs of peacocks and flowering branches framed the room. She could see her mother, sitting beside a low table covered with threads, bits of fabrics, and small embroidery scissors. Her blue *hanbok* billowed around her as her long slender fingers worked the needle through the delicate silk. Smoothing down the dark, shiny fabric on her lap, she smiled and beckoned to Kira.

Kira stepped forward and the vision faded, leaving her standing in the dusty ruins. The loss of her mother was like a knife through her heart, causing her wrenching pain when she thought of her. Kira wondered if she would ever be able to think of her mother without agonizing grief.

She picked through the debris, hoping to find unbroken mementos to treasure. The Yamato had done a thorough job, but they didn't know about the secret panels hidden beneath the floorboards and behind the walls.

Kira pushed away the memories and pawed through the torn cushions, damaged hanboks, and wrecked furniture. She paused as she collected fragments of her mother's belongings. Beads from a broken headpiece, the tooth of a jade comb, a small pair of jeweled embroidery scissors—Kira's fingers caressed all of them. Each item was a distinct memory of a time shared with her mother. Lessons learned, laughter shared, meals eaten together in private, hidden from prying eyes. She could no longer keep the tears from falling as she sorted through her mother's things. Wiping her eyes with her sleeve, Kira continued to pick through the remains. Anything salvageable went into a large bag slung over her shoulder, but there was very little left unbroken.

She pulled aside the woven carpet in the far left corner of the room. Underneath, the floor was layered with sheets of thick, oiled paper over large flat stones that covered the network of flues carrying the heat. But this corner contained no flues.

She'd always complained about how cold this one spot had been. It wasn't until she was thirteen that she'd discovered the reason why, for this was where her mother kept hidden the Kang family treasures. When Kira had asked her mother why she kept them in the floor and not in a locked chest, she'd been told that some things needed to be hidden. She respected her mother's decision. The locked chest, which had held some coins and valuable silk hanboks, had been completely destroyed, but the floor had been untouched.

Kira ripped the yellowed, oiled paper and lifted up the farthest corner stone. Within the deep cavity lay a large bundled box. Grabbing it by the knot, she lifted it up from its hiding place, coughing as clouds of dust flew all around her. She waved the worst of it off and untied the wrapping cloth, revealing a large rectangular box covered with an ornate design of two dancing dragons.

Opening the lid, she was dazzled by the treasures within the box: jewelry she'd never seen her mother wear, gold coins, and other items worth a small fortune. In the corner, there was a small silk-wrapped parcel with her name written on the cloth. She was glad the Yamatos had not gotten their hands on her family treasure, but she would have traded it all to see her parents one last time.

She leaned against a wooden beam and opened the little parcel. Inside it, there was a small scroll and a black embroidered bag. She unrolled the scroll and found her father's bold calligraphy of the flowing pictorial characters of *hanja*. A bolt of emotion shot through her at the sight. Her father's presence shone through his words, reminding Kira of all she'd lost.

Unlike other noble fathers, who barely spent any time with their daughters, her father had trained her to be a fighter since she was a little girl. He'd always said, "Kira, if you'd been born a boy, you could become the greatest general in all the Seven Kingdoms." She'd laughed and said, "Just like you, Father!"

Even when the king would make his dislike and contempt of her clear to all, her father had always stood by her side. When the entire court and citizenry had followed the king's lead and shunned Kira, her father had always protected her.

As a young child, she'd once asked him why everyone hated her.

"*They don't see the real you,*" her father had said. "*They see only the outside and are frightened by your differences, and in their blindness they can't see how truly wonderful you are.*"

"*And my uncle? Why does he hate me?*" she'd asked him.

"*He doesn't hate you, he is afraid of you—a small child who can see demon possessions and who was able to save the prince's life. Instead of recognizing your worth, he fears your strength because they are powers he doesn't have and can't understand. But I will help you fulfill your destiny and train you to be the greatest warrior of the Seven Kingdoms, and one day you will be respected and loved by all.*"

Her father trained her to be the best soldier and the prince's bodyguard, which saved her from the king's enmity. In her heart, she knew that if she had not become useful to her uncle, he would have found a reason to be rid of her long ago. Even the love of her aunt, the queen, wouldn't have been enough to protect her.

She missed her aunt. Bright and beautiful, she was a larger-than-life figure. The queen had always kept Kira's mother by her side. They were sisters, but more important, they were the best of friends. Even though Kira had been more likely to clash with the queen, she'd loved her very much. The queen had supported General Kang's decision to train Kira as a *saulabi*, a member of the king's elite army. She was the one who insisted Kira would be the prince's bodyguard.

For the queen's sake, Kira had agreed to dedicate her life to protecting her cousin, Prince Taejo. She was seven years old the first time she saved him from a demon who tried to sacrifice him to an imoogi. Despite her uncle, Kira and Taejo had always been close. To Taejo, Kira was not only his bodyguard but also his big sister. And now he was the one, the future king of the prophecy, destined to unite the Seven Kingdoms. Protecting him was the most important priority for Kira. As the Dragon Musado, it was her destiny. It was her father who had first said she could be the Dragon Musado, the one to fulfill the Dragon King's prophecy—the warrior who would unite the kingdoms and save their world from the Demon Lord. Even when the Dragon Springs Temple monks, who'd studied the prophecy for centuries, had proclaimed that her cousin, Prince Taejo, was the one, her father had believed in her. She didn't know how he'd known, but he'd been right. Unfortunately, he hadn't lived to see Kira fulfill her destiny.

"I believe that one person can change the world. Whether he is the Musado or a girl with a tiger spirit. The monks teach that we mere mortals cannot question fate. But I say that we control destiny by our every action. Our power lies in the choices we make."

If the loss of her mother was a knife through her heart, the loss of her father was the hammer that pounded on it. She missed them fiercely.

In the upper corner of the scroll was an ink brush

painting of a tiger. Underneath it, a caption read "Golden Tiger." Quickly scanning the writing, she realized the scroll was the court shaman's prediction of her fortune, written at her birth. The characters for death and betrayal leaped from the paper before she rolled up the scroll, unwilling to read any more. She didn't need to know what was in store. It was bad enough that she was plagued with prophetic visions that nearly always came true. There was a danger in knowing too much of what the future held.

Setting it aside, she opened the little bag and removed a thick gold chain with a small tiger medallion. She'd never seen it before, but it was clearly a gift for her. No one else in the family had been born in the year of the tiger. She wondered why her mother had never given it to her. What had she been waiting for? What would she have said when presenting it to her? Kira's heart hurt to think of another missed opportunity.

She remembered a long-ago conversation with her mother when she'd been only five years old. They'd been sitting in this very room, her mother embroidering a tiger on a pillow for Kira. It was the first time that her mother had told her about the tiger dream.

"See this tiger?" her mother asked. "It is your animal symbol, your protector."

"Like me. I am the year of the tiger," Kira said.

Her mother nodded. "But it is also something more. It represents you as I first saw you, before you were ever born."

"How is that possible?" Kira asked.

Lady Yuwa caressed the silk before passing it over to her daughter.

"It was in my dream. I was in a meadow bordered by a thick bamboo grove, sitting on a large rock before a beautiful persimmon tree filled with ripe fruit. Chills ran down my spine when I sensed something behind me, stalking me. From within the bamboo grove, I spied two golden-amber eyes ringed thickly with deepest black. Only then did I realize that it was a large tiger, sleek and sinewy, its immense head held low to the ground while its golden eyes stared fixedly at me. Suddenly, it leaped toward me. I was so frightened I fell off the rock and landed on my back. The tiger was right on top of me and I flung my arms over my head, thinking I would be devoured. When nothing happened, I opened my eyes and found the large beast lying on its stomach before me. It yawned and shook its massive head as if it was nothing more than a house cat, batting a paw at a passing insect.

"Slowly I sat up, and the tiger rose onto its front legs. It raised its right paw and placed it gently upon my thigh. Within its razor-sharp claws was a perfect pink peony. It uttered a low purring growl and nudged me with its head, knocking me over and out of my dream."

Lady Yuwa had a faraway expression on her face, as if she was reliving the vision in her head. Kira waited for her mother to continue.

"It was definitely a good omen, but of what? I called the local village shaman who entered into a trance to commune with the spirits. When she revived, she told me I would bear a child in the year of the golden tiger, who would be the greatest warrior of all the seven kingdoms."

"That was me?" Kira asked.

Yuwa nodded. "After you were born, your father laughed to hear that the great warrior was an infant girl. But I knew my dream was an omen, for when you opened your eyes at me, they were the same golden amber as my tiger's eyes."

Kira was quiet, surprised by the story. Was this an explanation of why she was so different?

"Is that why Father makes me do my taekkyon training?" she asked. "So I can be a warrior?"

She'd been so proud to think she was special.

"Never doubt that you were born to do great things, my child," her mother said.

Her parents had been right: she did have a tiger spirit. Ever since she was a little girl, whenever she'd been sick or injured, she'd dreamed of a tiger that would comfort her. Now she knew it wasn't a dream but the spirit of a large gentle tiger that would curl up beside her and emit a golden light surrounding them both. Its *ki*, pure tiger energy, would transfer into her body and heal and rejuvenate her. Kira and her tiger spirit were deeply connected. Without it, she would have died a long time ago.

The bright golden medallion gleamed in the dim light. Kira heaved a deep sigh. She still grieved for her parents, missing them terribly.

She replaced the medallion in its small bag and closed the box, her hands trembling as she retied the wrapping cloth around it. With a heavy heart, she hoisted the treasure box onto her shoulder, leaving behind the ghosts of her past.

FIRST SHE RAN.
THEN SHE FOUND NEW POWER.
NOW HER FIGHT RAGES ON.

"What an adventure! When I finished my journey with Kira, all I wanted was more. Spectacular!"—Marie Lu, author of the Legend trilogy

WARRIOR
· A PROPHECY NOVEL ·
ELLEN OH

Don't miss the exciting sequel to
PROPHECY.

HARPER TEEN
An Imprint of HarperCollins Publishers

www.epicreads.com

JOIN
THE COMMUNITY AT

Epic Reads
Your World. Your Books.

DISCUSS
what's on
your reading
wish list

FIND
the latest
books

CREATE
your own book
news and
activities to share
with friends

ACCESS
exclusive
contests and
videos

**Don't miss out on any upcoming
EPIC READS!**

**Visit the site and browse the
categories to find out more.**

www.epicreads.com

HARPER TEEN
An Imprint of HarperCollinsPublishers